"I never meant for that to happen."

It was the truth. Sam would never have anticipated the emotions he was feeling now, and he damn well didn't want them! "I don't expect you to believe this, but I seldom maul women I've just met when I'm working on a case."

"*I* don't expect *you* to believe *this*, but I seldom neck in the front seat of a car with FBI agents I've just met, either!"

"Then we're even, aren't we?" He traced a fingertip down the curve of her cheek. The light touch was like a brand on Jessie's skin. "Are you okay?"

"Yes."

"Good." He started the car. "I want to get you home so we can start working out the details of this case."

"It's funny to think that I'm a case for the FBI."

Sam said nothing, but his mouth tightened. She was more than that. A whole lot more.

Dear Reader,

When two people fall in love, the world is suddenly new and exciting, and it's that same excitement we bring to you in Silhouette Intimate Moments. These are stories with scope and grandeur. The characters lead lives we all dream of, and everything they do reflects the wonder of being in love.

Longer and more sensuous than most romances, Silhouette Intimate Moments novels take you away from everyday life and let you share the magic of love. Adventure, glamour, drama, even suspense— these are the passwords that let you into a world where love has a power beyond the ordinary, where the best authors in the field today create stories of love and commitment that will stay with you always.

In coming months look for novels by your favorite authors: Kathleen Eagle, Heather Graham Pozzessere, Nora Roberts and Marilyn Pappano, to name just a few. And whenever you buy books, look for all the Silhouette Intimate Moments, love stories *for* today's woman *by* today's woman.

Leslie J. Wainger
Senior Editor
Silhouette Books

Lucy Hamilton

The Real Thing

Silhouette Intimate Moments

Published by Silhouette Books New York

America's Publisher of Contemporary Romance

SILHOUETTE BOOKS
300 East 42nd St., New York, N.Y. 10017

ISBN: 0-373-07278-3

First Silhouette Books printing March 1989

Printed in the U.S.A.

Books by Lucy Hamilton

Silhouette Special Edition

A Woman's Place #18
All's Fair #92
Shooting Star #172
The Bitter with the Sweet #206
An Unexpected Pleasure #337

Silhouette Intimate Moments

Agent Provocateur #126
*Under Suspicion #229
*After Midnight #237
*Heartbeats #245
The Real Thing #278

*Dodd Memorial Hospital series

LUCY HAMILTON

traces her love of books to her childhood, and her love of writing to her college days. Her training and the years she spent as a medical librarian translated readily into a career as a writer. "I didn't realize it until I began to write, but a writer is what I was meant to be." An articulate public speaker, the mother of an active grade-school-age daughter, and the wife of a physician, Lucy brings diversity and an extensive knowledge of the medical community to her writing. A native of Indiana, she has resided both in the Midwest and on the West Coast, and has returned to her home state with her family and two friendly felines.

Chapter 1

Fear was a bitter taste in the back of Jessamyn's throat as she entered the large shopping mall, her heels tapping out a sharp tattoo on the glossy floor. She was scared, and she hated it. Still, being afraid made her angry, and it was anger that was helping her keep the fear from showing.

She'd been on the edge of panic all afternoon, but she wouldn't succumb to it, because she knew what she had to do. She'd mentioned to some co-workers that she was coming here to look for shoes, so she would behave as though she were actually shopping. It made as good a cover for her real purpose as any.

She fought the urge to look over her shoulder and kept walking as casually as she could. *Act natural,* she told herself. Someone might be watching, even now. She stopped at a display of stiletto-heeled pumps in neon-bright colors. After studying a vivid purple shoe for a few seconds, she shook her head and put it back on the display rack. With her fingers still resting lightly on the gaudy shoe, she looked casually around her.

She saw nothing unusual, but then she really hadn't expected to. Anyone sent to follow her would be good at the job.

The store was quiet, with clerks straightening the colorfully stocked counters and chatting during the dinnertime lull. Everything looked blandly ordinary, but that very normalcy was oddly threatening. The events of this day had turned Jessie's quiet, carefully ordered life upside down, and she could no longer believe in surface calm.

She walked on, moving quickly but, she hoped, without appearing to hurry. Her hands were trembling a little, and she pushed them into her pockets. Her collected manner was difficult to maintain, and beneath it she was seething.

She'd known something like this was a possibility, but she'd never really expected it to happen. Now that she was face-to-face with the unbelievable reality, she could hardly wait to dump this preposterous problem in someone else's lap.

The public telephone was beside a cluster of benches and tubbed trees at the north end of the mall. Jessie walked naturally, fishing in her purse for change. She could feel a prickling between her shoulder blades, and she knew that someone was watching her.

Who? she wondered. Who was tailing her? The stout woman who had asked her opinion of a truly awful purse? The swarthy man who had hovered near as she'd selected a *faux* pearl brooch? Again and again she had to warn herself to look at the merchandise, not at the people. Fighting the urge to look over her shoulder, she fed coins into the slot and punched out the number she'd memorized.

The office wasn't small, but it had a claustrophobic feel to it. A square room that should have been spacious and airy, it was overflowing with too many battered metal desks and dented file cabinets, too many messy piles of papers and too many men and women laughing and talking with boisterous Friday-afternoon, end-of-the-work-week high spirits.

Most of them were clustered at one end of the room, embroiled in a heated discussion of the Rams' prospects for the current season. One man sat alone at his desk near the bank of windows that looked out over downtown Los Angeles. Tall and burly, with a hard but handsome face and thick salt-and-pepper hair, he was sorting methodically through a pile of reports, listening with half his attention to the argument about quarterbacks.

Sam King seldom participated in these discussions. In fact, though he was highly respected for his professional abilities, few of the men and women he worked with would have said they really knew him. None of them had ever visited his house, none of them knew what his hobbies were—or even if he had any—and none of them had ever gone to a ball game or a bar with him.

The phone rang in the middle of a burst of laughter. As he lifted the receiver, Sam automatically put his hand over his other ear to block out the noise.

"Special Agent King. How can I help you?"

There was silence on the line.

"Can I help you?" Sam repeated.

"I...uh, are you the person I need to speak to?" The voice was female, and it was soft and controlled, but Sam could hear the strained tone and the unnaturally high pitch that revealed fear or tension.

"I'm special Agent Samuel King, miss." He kept his voice low and reassuring. "How can I help you?"

"I don't really know how to put this...."

"I'm the foreign intelligence specialist. If your inquiry concerns something else, I can transfer you." Espionage within the United States was Sam's specialty. If the switch-board had given her his line by mistake, he would dump this right into somebody else's lap. It was Friday, and his plans for the evening didn't include working late.

"No," she whispered. "No, it concerns spying—uh, foreign intelligence."

"I see."

Sam bid a silent, regretful farewell to the steak that was marinating in his refrigerator and the football game that would be waiting on television. Not an exciting time by most standards, but the kind Sam favored. He liked simple pleasures and no complications, and he'd been looking forward to a quiet evening.

He wasn't pleased at the thought of having a case interfere with his plans. With luck, though, he could handle this over the phone, and quickly enough to have his steak and catch the kickoff.

"I see," he repeated. "And do you want to report an incident?"

"An incident?" Her voice wobbled on what was nearly a laugh. "Y-yes, I guess I *do* want to report an incident. It happened—"

"Wait!" His interruption was curt and effective. The woman immediately fell silent. Sam was glad she could take orders, but if this was for real he was going to need willing cooperation, not resentful obedience. He gentled his tone. "Before you say any more, miss, tell me where you're calling from."

"Woodland Hills."

"Are you at home? Are you calling on your own phone?"

"No, I'm at a pay phone. In a mall."

"That's good." Sam tried to make his voice reassuring. He yanked a blank report form from the drawer. "That's smart. It's safer to talk on a pay phone. Tell me your name, please."

"Ames. Jessamyn Ames."

"Ames." He wrote it down. "Jessica?"

"Jessamyn." She spelled it for him, as if she'd had to do it often. "It's a variation of Jasmine."

An unusual name, Sam thought absently. Pretty, if you cared about things like that. "And what prompted you to call the FBI, Miss Ames?"

"It's Mrs. Ames," she told him. "I'm widowed."

"I beg your pardon, Mrs. Ames. You called because . . ."

"Well, I—" She hesitated, and Sam heard her take a deep breath. "Today I was asked to sell air force secrets to the Soviets."

He straightened sharply in his chair, his attention abruptly removed from steak and football and fully focused on Mrs. Jessamyn Ames. His elbow struck a stack of papers and sent them slithering to the floor. He ignored the mess.

"You were approached about selling defense information?"

"Yes." Her voice was steady. "Air force."

"And do you, in fact, possess information that would be of interest to another government?"

"Yes, I do," she replied without hesitation. "I work for Anchor Software in Woodland Hills. We have several defense contracts. They want a program I wrote for the air force."

"If your firm is a defense contractor, then you should have someone in the company as a security officer. Why didn't you go to him or her with this?"

"I couldn't, Mr.—?"

"King."

"Mr. King. I couldn't go to him, because he's the one who introduced me to the spy!"

Her voice rose slightly as she spoke, and Sam ran his hand roughly through his hair. A company security officer introduced her to the agent? He had to investigate this himself. Tonight.

"I see. You say you're in a shopping mall?"

"Yes. Topanga Plaza."

"I know where that is." He paused for a moment, thinking hard. "You're widowed?"

"Yes." Her tone made it clear that she didn't see what difference that made.

"And are you dating right now? Involved with anyone?"

"No, she said tersely.

"Then I'll meet you for dinner tonight, at that mall."

"You'll *what*?"

"Meet you for dinner. For the sake of a cover."

"For a cover?" she repeated obviously skeptical.

"We have to have a reason for meeting," Sam explained. "You might be under observation. And in case someone's watching you right now, will you smile as if I just said something funny?"

There was a moment's silence. Then: "All right."

"You're smiling?"

"I'm smiling."

She didn't sound as if she were, but he had to take her word for it.

"Good. I need to speak to you in person, Mrs. Ames, tonight, but our meeting has to look innocent. If they think it's a date, they're less likely to be suspicious."

She caught her breath audibly. "Then you believe me?"

"I believe something has happened that warrants further investigation," Sam said carefully. "Can you name a convenient restaurant there at the mall? Something suitable for a date. You know, dark and cozy?"

"Well, there's a deli at the north end of the mall, and an Italian restaurant at the south end. The restaurant's darker."

"That sounds good," Sam said as his stomach bid a regretful farewell to his waiting steak. "It'll take me about an hour to get there. Can you occupy the time?"

"I have some shopping to do."

"Okay. Behave as you normally would. I'll meet you outside the restaurant."

"O-okay." He heard her hesitation, though he could tell she tried to suppress it.

"Now, could you tell me what you look like?"

"I beg your pardon?"

"I have to be able to pick you out of the crowd. Just tell me the basics. You know...how old you are, how tall? What's your hair color; what are you wearing?"

"Oh," she said after a moment. "I see. Well, I'm twenty-nine. I'm five-four and I have brown hair, and I'm wearing a gray suit with a red blouse. I'll wait on one of the benches outside the restaurant, Mr. King."

"Sam. Call me Sam."

"As you wish." She paused. "Uh, could you tell me what you look like?"

"Sure. I'm thirty-four, six-three, and my hair is gray. I'm wearing navy slacks and a gray jacket." He looked down at himself, checking. "And my tie's red. I'm leaving now, and I'll meet you in about an hour, all right?"

"All right."

He could hear tension in her voice, and he wished she would calm down. People usually did once they knew he was on his way. "Could you say, 'I'll meet you in an hour, darling?' And say it loud?"

There was a long moment of silence. Sam was beginning to wonder if she'd left the phone when he heard a soft giggle.

"You people really are thorough, aren't you?" she asked, amusement warming her voice.

"We're known for it," he replied.

"Well, far be it from me to interfere with procedure. I'll meet you in an hour, darling," she said in a clear, carrying voice. "And don't be late." There was a teasing note to the last words.

"I won't be," Sam told her. "We're known for our promptness, too. And try not to worry, Mrs. Ames. We'll get this straightened out."

"God, I hope so." Her whisper was fervent.

Sam slowed his pace as he neared the wide archway leading into the mall. He paused by a display of china and picked up a fragile teacup, balancing it in his palm and looking past it at the small brown-haired woman sitting on a bench out in the mall, leafing through a paperback.

His first thought was that Mrs. Ames didn't look twenty-nine. Small and slender, she could have passed for twenty. Her gray suit was tailored and conservative, with a slim skirt and jacket that fitted closely over a red blouse of some silky fabric. Her outfit went nicely with her glossy brown hair, which was cut in a chin-length bob, but the overall effect was almost plain. The only thing that didn't match was the pair of spike-heeled red pumps on her elegantly narrow feet.

Sam wasn't sure what he'd expected a computer expert to look like, but he supposed she might fit the bill. She looked quiet, serious, intelligent . . . sheltered. Hardly the popular image of a spy, yet she'd been approached to sell secrets.

"Can I help you, sir?"

He glanced at the salesclerk and put the teacup in her hands. "No, thanks. Just browsing."

Jessie looked up, for about the hundredth time, from the novel she was unsuccessfully trying to read, and froze at the sight of the tall figure striding toward her. The book dropped from her suddenly nerveless hands.

"Charlie?" Her whisper was barely audible, even to herself. She pushed herself to her feet, her heart pounding in heavy, painful thumps. She stared at the silvery hair, the erect carriage, the powerful physique. They were so familiar, so loved.

A smile of pure wonder spreading across her face, she started toward him, stumbling over her shopping bag. She took three steps and he was there.

Jessie reached for him, gazing up with eyes soft with love and longing—but it wasn't Charlie standing there, it was a stranger. A stranger with the gray hair she remembered so well, a stranger whose face was cruelly familiar. Yet this wasn't the face she loved. These weren't the eyes she longed to see.

She blanched, and the glowing happiness drained away, to be replaced by bottomless pain. She had grabbed his hands; when she pulled back, he caught her.

"Hold on there, sweetheart!"

He held her upper arms, supporting her and keeping her close when she would have pulled away. He drew her toward him in a lover's motion, while his eyes, eyes the clear blue of a cloudless sky, searched her ashen face.

"Are you all right?" He bent his head close to hers and spoke softly. "You *are* Jessamyn Ames, aren't you?"

Jessie closed her eyes, willing away the memories and the wrenching sense of loss. "Yes." She blinked hard and forced herself to look at him. "Yes, I am. And I'm—I'm all right."

"Are you sure?" He studied her with concern. "You looked like you just saw a ghost."

A shiver slid down Jessie's spine. How could he know? "I did," she said after a moment.

It was Sam's turn to look puzzled, but there wasn't time to worry about it just then. "I apologize for this," he murmured, and before Jessie could protest he drew her into his arms to kiss her.

The touch of his lips, the feel of his strong body, sent a shock of pure pleasure through her. An instinctive softening started in her own body, resurrecting memories of a passion she'd almost managed to forget. But even as the sweet warmth of it blossomed in her veins he lifted his lips and loosened his arms.

Sam set her back on her feet, watching her face closely. His heart was pounding, his breathing was rough, and it cost him all the control he could muster to conceal his reactions. With a hand under her arm, he led her back to her spilled shopping.

"I hope I didn't keep you waiting too long."

He squeezed her arm, and Jessie caught the warning. She blinked and drew a steadying breath.

"I've only been here a few minutes."

Her voice was breathless, but steady enough. Sam released her arm and stooped to gather her packages. "It looks like you kept busy."

"What is it they say?" She retrieved a blue calfskin pump, as elegant as the red shoes she was wearing. "When the going gets tough, the tough go shopping?"

Sam grinned in spite of himself. "I don't know if that's what they say, but I know some people it describes perfectly." He dropped the last package into the shopping bag and rose, catching Jessie's hand and lifting her to her feet, as well. "Are you hungry?"

"Uh, yes, I am. I didn't eat much lunch." Jessie didn't know how she managed to form a sensible reply, because the only thing she could seem to think of was his hand, big, warm and hard, enclosing hers. She tried to assemble her scattered wits. "The restaurant's over there...."

"I see." Still holding her hand securely, he hefted the shopping bag and led her toward the door. The hostess gave them the "private" table he requested, which was in a dimly lit corner of the dining room.

Jessie stiffened when he slid onto the upholstered bench beside her, so close that their bodies touched. She started to edge away, but he draped an arm across her shoulders. She knew it looked like a gesture of casual intimacy, but his fingers clamped down on her shoulder, warning her not to move.

"What are you doing?" she demanded in a whisper.

"I'm acting like your date!" he retorted sotto voce, then smiled at the approaching waitress.

No, they weren't ready to order yet, and yes, they'd like something to drink. Some red wine, perhaps? The waitress bustled away, and as soon as her back was turned Jessie tried to ease away from Sam King. He removed his arm from her shoulders but stayed where he was, so close beside her that she could feel the warmth of his body and smell the faint, lingering scent of a spicy after-shave.

"What's good here?" He opened the laminated-plastic menu.

Jessie edged slightly away from him. "I've only been here twice. The spaghetti's okay."

"Stay put." He slid along the seat, closing the small distance between them again. "We're supposed to be on a date. How about the veal?"

Jessie had had the veal. She shook her head, and he sighed regretfully. "Spaghetti for two, then."

He closed his menu as the waitress approached with a carafe and two glasses. When she left them alone again, he lifted his glass.

"Cheers."

"Cheers." Jessie knew what to expect, and she sipped cautiously, watching the man with her take a deep swallow.

He coughed as the wine went down. "What *is* this stuff, anyway?"

Jessie smiled in spite of herself. "The menu says it's imported from Italy."

"Yeah." Sam took a swallow of water. "From an Italian Laundromat."

He smiled at her, and she felt that eerie sense of déjà vu again. Though he was a stranger to her, he was uncomfortably familiar.

He looked even taller than the six-three he'd told her he was. He was built like a linebacker, with heavily muscled shoulders and a broad, deep chest. His face was square boned, angular and tanned, softened only by those unearthly clear blue eyes. The eyes were the most striking difference, for Charlie's eyes had been brown.

She looked away, but his image stayed clearly in her mind. Everything else, including the prematurely gray hair could have been Charlie's. But they weren't, and she was gradually getting used to that unsettling sense of familiarity. This was Special Agent Samuel King, not the late Major Charlie Ames.

And he had kissed her, shatteringly. She toyed with her glass, keeping her eyes lowered until their spaghetti arrived, then picked at her food while he ate. When he laid down his fork and caught her fidgeting hand, she tensed and looked up warily.

Sam smiled in her direction, but he was looking past her, toward the restaurant entrance. "Is there anyone behind me?" he murmured.

Jessie mimicked his casual examination of the other patrons. "Nobody near enough to hear us."

"Good. We can talk." His tone was quiet and business-like, though he was still smiling at her like a lover. "What should I call you, by the way? Jessamyn?"

"Jessie. My friends call me Jessie."

"Okay, and please call me Sam."

She nodded.

"I'm afraid you'll have to repeat all this for a formal statement, Jessie, but I need some idea of what's going on."

"All right."

"Then tell me again why you called the FBI. What happened to you today?"

Jessie's stomach tightened with tension, and she took a deep breath.

"I called you because they asked me to sell secrets. I don't really know why they picked on me." She paused. "Except that I wrote the program."

"The program they want to buy?"

Jessie nodded.

"And they contacted you today?"

"Yes and no. I've been thinking about it, and I realized that it actually started three weeks ago, at a party the security officer gave. Security officer at Anchor isn't a full-time job, you know. It's something you do in addition to your regular work. Somebody serves for a year, and then they pass the job on to someone else. This year it's Bernie Martin."

"What's his regular job?"

"Marketing. I always kind of liked him," she added on a note of puzzled dismay. "He's one of those people who are friendly to everyone, you know? He gives a lot of parties and invites the people from Anchor. Three weeks ago he introduced me to a friend of his, a Russian defector."

"What's this defector's name? Or, I should say, what name is he using?"

"Antonov. Leonid Antonov. You don't think that's his real one?"

"Not a chance. What happened at the party?"

"Bernie made a point of introducing me to Leonid. He told me Leonid had been in the U.S. for about a year. I didn't like the man much. He was kind of sullen, and he was way too pushy."

"Pushy? How do you mean?"

"He kept trying to get me into dark corners." Her voice was tart with distaste.

"I see." Sam kept his voice bland. "What then?"

"I tried to get away, but every time I escaped, Bernie would track me down and sic his friend on me again. After that, Bernie kept harping on what a great guy Leonid is, and how did I like him. I didn't want to hurt Bernie's feelings, so I didn't tell him what I really thought. Bernie is still trying to push us together, but I've managed to escape so far."

"Did you suspect his reasons for throwing you at Leonid?"

She shook her head, disgusted with herself. "It never even occurred to me. I just thought Bernie was matchmaking. It seemed kind of sweet, even if he did pick the wrong guy."

"So his matchmaking efforts didn't work. What happened today?"

"Today." The word was a shaky sigh. "Today Bernie invited me to lunch to celebrate the completion of the White Eagle program. It took me six months to write it. I finished it last week, and the test runs on the computer were completed yesterday."

"White Eagle?" he repeated, and she nodded. "What is it?"

"It's an advanced autopilot program for fighter planes."

"Which means?"

"It's close to artificial intelligence. If the pilot is incapacitated, a computer in the plane and another one on the ground will work together to land the plane."

"Without the pilot?" She nodded, and he whistled. It was a long, low note. "That's pretty spectacular. How many other people at Anchor have seen this program?"

"The vice president who handles air force accounts, the company president and the air force people. With a defense project, only the person or persons working on it ever deal with it. For security reasons," she added.

"So Bernie Martin hasn't seen this program?"

"No. He wouldn't understand what he was looking at, anyway. He's not a systems designer or a programmer or an analyst. He sells commercial programs."

"Yet he knew it was finished."

"Lots of people know it's finished. They still don't know what it is."

"But Bernie took you to lunch today."

"Uh-huh. And Leonid met us at the restaurant."

"Did that surprise you?"

"Not really. I thought Bernie was matchmaking again. After lunch I was going to tell him I wasn't interested and would he please stop throwing Leonid at me. Anyway, we started eating, and Bernie got a phone call right in the middle of his pastrami sandwich. He had to get back to the office, so he left us to finish lunch."

"And Leonid had more on his mind than pastrami."

She grimaced and leaned her chin on her hand. It was a small hand, Sam saw, slender, lightly tanned and ringless, with nails filed to neat ovals and painted a light pink. A soft hand, fragile, like her.

"He sure did," she said dryly. "He congratulated me on the program, and after he talked for a while he made a joke, something like there always seems to be too much month left at the end of your money. It sounded like something Bernie told him." She sighed. "That's when he told me there were people who would give me fifty thousand dollars for just a part of the White Eagle program. He said they'd pay me a hundred and fifty thousand for the whole thing."

"What did you do?" Sam was smiling easily, but Jessie could feel the tension in him. "It's important, so try to remember *exactly* what you said when he made the offer."

"I just sat there with my mouth open. I started to ask what the hell he was talking about, and he interrupted me. Don't answer right away, he said. He told me to think it over and he'd get in touch with me."

"But you didn't say anything like 'How dare you ask me to sell secrets, you swine!'?"

Jessie bit back on a shaky giggle. "No, but I like that line. It would have given me a lot of satisfaction to have used it."

"It probably would have, but an important opportunity would have been lost."

Her eyes flicked to his face. She sat silently for several seconds. When she spoke, her voice was a whisper. "What opportunity is that, Sam?"

It was the first time she'd used his given name. Sam found he liked the way it sounded in her low, slightly husky voice.

"If you'd rejected the offer outright," he told her, "or if you'd reacted with shock and horror to the idea, Leonid Antonov would no doubt have ceased to exist by now."

"What?"

"Oh, yeah." Sam nodded. "He'd have a new name, a new passport, and we'd have a damn tough time trying to find him. As it is, he'll probably lay low for several days, just in case you report this and the authorities start looking for him."

"And the opportunity?" Jessie was afraid she already knew what she was about to hear.

"Antonov isn't the head of this operation. He's low man on the totem pole, the man they put at risk in order to approach you. We could probably catch him, but with your cooperation we might be able to catch him *and* the people he's working for."

"The spy ring."

"If you like."

She thought about that for a moment. "With my cooperation, you said. What does that mean?"

"It means you convince Leonid Antonov you're ready to sell out your country for a hundred and fifty thousand dollars."

Chapter 2

No!''

Jessie's protest was louder than she'd meant it to be. Sam caught her hand, the pressure of his fingers not quite painful, but hard enough to serve as a warning.

"Don't turn me down so quickly," he said, his gently amused voice pitched to carry to the tables around them. "I know you don't usually like science fiction, but this movie's different." Jessie's eyes widened, but she had the presence of mind not to ask what on earth he was talking about. "Just give this one a chance, all right, sweetheart?"

"Okay." Her bright smile was as false as his. "I'll go." She paused, and her forced smile widened into an honest grin. "As long as there aren't any giant bugs in it."

"No giant bugs. I promise." He leaned over to brush her cheek lightly with his lips. Jessie stiffened, more in surprise than rejection, but the caress was over almost before it had begun. His face close to hers, he murmured, "Thanks. That was quick thinking."

"I almost blew it."

"No harm done." He sat back, taking his warmth and his scent with him, and Jessie was uncomfortably aware that she missed both. He glanced at her plate, which was still half-full. "Are you finished?"

"Yes."

"Would you like dessert? You didn't eat much."

Jessie shook her head. "No, thanks. I'm not hungry."

"All right." He rose and took her hand. "I think it's time we went for a little drive."

"I'm assuming that you don't intend me to *really* give my program to the Russians."

Jessie watched the taillights ahead of them as they merged with the traffic on the freeway. They had stopped for a few minutes while Sam had called the FBI office from a public telephone, and then they'd returned to the freeway. His car was a nondescript, not-quite-new, brown four-door sedan, but its engine throbbed with a powerful note that didn't match its sedate exterior.

"You assume right. What you give Antonov will *look* like the real thing, but that's all."

"You want me to pretend to go along with this deal of his, and dummy up a program to give him?"

"Exactly."

He glanced in the rearview mirror and frowned as he changed lanes. Without signaling, he abruptly swung hard to the right. A horn blared angrily behind them as he cut in front of a shabby van and shot up an off-ramp with the tires squealing in protest.

Jessie had to grab for the door handle to keep herself from falling into his lap. She checked her seat belt, braced herself more securely and sat back again.

"Do you always drive this way?" she asked. She'd seen the van driver's face—and his gesture.

Sam stopped for the light at the top of the ramp and glanced at her, grinning. "I just thought it was time for us to do a little necking."

"I'm going to assume you have a particularly good reason for saying that."

"I do." The light changed, and he drove on, then glanced at her, making a quick survey of the slim lines and curves of her body beneath the conservative gray suit. It was as impersonal a look as she could have wished, and it brought the blood rushing to her cheeks.

"I see." Jessie's voice was cool, but she turned the dashboard vent to direct the flow of air toward her hot face.

"We need to talk." He took a corner too fast, moving onto a road that rose rapidly toward the crest of the coastal mountains. "In private. I'm not positive someone's been following us, but if they have, they didn't make that exit."

"So that's why you—"

"Risked a reckless-driving ticket back there? Yeah. They'll probably find us again, but they'll have to get off the freeway at the next exit and double back. That'll give us time for some unobserved conversation."

"And if they are following us? If they double back and find us, what do we do?"

"We let them see us acting like sweethearts on a date, since that's what we're supposed to be."

Sweethearts. The old-fashioned word came easily to him, and Jessie liked the gentle sound of it, but it didn't seem to fit with his all-business manner.

"And that's why we're on Mulholland Drive?" The mountaintop road was famous as a lover's lane.

He nodded grimly. "We're going to park in a spot where we'll see them coming, and while we're waiting I can tell you what the FBI would like you to do."

"I have an idea what they want, and I can tell you why I don't want to do it." Jessie looked at him. Lit from below by the dashboard lights, the angles of his face looked hard, even dangerous. She turned away, gazing out at the night. "I meant it when I said no, Mr. King."

"Sam."

"Sam. I've worked for the government most of my career, so I knew I had to report this. I want you to catch Leonid and stop him from spying, but I can't get any more involved myself."

"Why can't you?"

"Because it could be dangerous," Jessie said quietly. She could feel his gaze on her, but she didn't look at him.

"The FBI will do everything in our power to protect you, Mrs. Ames. The risk will be as minimal as we can make it."

"Any risk is too great." She twisted suddenly in her seat. "It's not myself I'm worried about, Mr. King—" He glanced at her, and she corrected herself. "Sam."

"Then who is it?"

"My daughter. For myself, I'd do whatever you asked. I want to see these people caught as badly as you do. I could risk my own life, but I can't take risks with my daughter's mother. She's only six, and she's already lost a father she never knew. I'm all she has left."

Sam said nothing for several minutes. They were following the crest of the Santa Monica Mountains through the rugged near-wilderness area that divides downtown Los Angeles from the San Fernando Valley. After a couple of miles, Sam pulled off the road into a narrow overlook. The lights of the valley sparkled below. He put the car in park and killed the engine. In the echoing silence that followed, he turned in his seat to look at her, his expression unreadable.

"You didn't say you had a child."

Jessie shrugged. "It didn't come up."

"I think I can understand your feelings."

"So you see why I can't do this."

He shook his head. "I can see why you feel protective. I think we can work around that." She parted her lips to protest, but he spoke quickly, cutting her off. "Wait, please. Before you decide, let me tell you why this is so important."

"I don't think I'll change my mind," she said.

"I know." He turned toward her and laid his arm along the back of the seat. His fingertips brushed her shoulder lightly, then withdrew as he moved his hand away to a more discreet distance. "Are you comfortable? Warm enough?"

"I'm fine." Curiously enough, she was comfortable, and in more than just a physical sense. She might not agree with him, but she had confidence in Sam King. He and the FBI would deal with this dreadful mess.

"Good." He paused, and when he continued his voice was cool and determined. "Leonid Antonov will contact you again, probably in less than a week. You have a couple of choices. If you tell him you won't cooperate, we can still probably arrest him or get him expelled."

"That's what you want, isn't it? To catch him?"

"I want to catch the people he's working for," Sam corrected her. "You've seen his face, you can identify him if you see him again. The people behind this have put him on the line, but you can be sure that there are more valuable operatives behind him, people they haven't risked."

"And it's those people you want to catch."

"With your help."

"I don't know." She shifted on the seat, pulling her feet up to tuck them beneath her and facing him directly. "I don't know if I can do that." She bent her head, studying her hands as her silky curtain of hair swung forward to brush her cheeks and hide her eyes from him.

"Mrs. Ames." Sam reached out and lifted her chin in his fingers so that he could see her face. "Jessie. Let me tell you what this would involve before you make a decision. I—*we* don't want to endanger you or your daughter. This shouldn't be a complicated operation, but it could greatly benefit our government. Will you let me explain it to you?''

Jessie gazed into the clear depths of his eyes. His fingers were warm and gentle on her throat, heating her skin and the blood beneath it. Slowly she nodded.

"Thank you."

Sam spent almost half an hour explaining what her cooperation would entail. When he'd finished, she sat back, gazing out the windshield. The lights glittered below them in a stunning vista and the cry of a bird was carried in the open window on a breath of cool, sea-scented air, but the beauty of the night was wasted on Jessie. She was silent and motionless for a full minute. Then she turned to Sam.

"I'll do it."

"You don't have to decide right now," he told her quickly. "I don't want you to feel I've put any pressure on you."

"You haven't put pressure on me. *They* have!" Suddenly angry, she grabbed his arm, emphasizing her words with little shakes as she spoke. "Don't you see? These people think I can be bought! They think that fifty thousand dollars can persuade me to betray my country." She released his arm and struck the dashboard in frustration. "I'm scared, sure, and I'm worried about Kerry. But I'm more angry than I am scared. I can't be bought, dammit! And I *won't* betray my country! I want to help you catch them, Mr. King."

"I'm glad you feel that way." He smiled as he held out his hand to seal the bargain. "I'll do my best to see that you don't regret it."

As Jessie grasped his hand, she heard the distant thrum of an engine coming along the road. Headlights raked over a heap of massive boulders at the edge of the overlook, sending weird shadows leaping across the gravel.

Before the beams touched the car, Sam caught her by the shoulder, pulling her roughly to him and wrapping her in a hard embrace. She gave a little squeak of surprise and indignation as he shoved her back and down, pressing her into the seat, his body hard and tense above hers, his face against hers, his day's growth of beard rasping against her skin.

"Sorry," he muttered in her ear, "but this has to look good. They may have binoculars on us."

Jolted by the realization of what was happening, Jessie stopped fighting him. She placed her arms lightly around his neck.

Sam's voice was a deep rumble against her throat. "I'll apologize later for liberties taken in the line—" He pulled her farther beneath him, his lips brushing the tender skin below her ear.

Jessie moved her hands tentatively over his shoulders and hair, scared and self-conscious. She'd never been asked to feign passion for an audience before, and she wasn't even sure which gestures would look right.

With a smooth motion that belied the rigid tension in his muscles, Sam ran his fingers through her hair, ruffling it, then lifted his body aside slightly and began to unbutton her blouse.

Jessie grabbed at his hand. "What are you—?"

"Shh!" Sam brushed her fingers out of the way.

She swallowed hard, put her hand on his shoulder again and tried to make herself relax. This was strictly for the benefit of whoever was spying on them. It wasn't real, but unfortunately it felt real. She stroked Sam King's silvery hair lightly, finding it soft and thick and springy beneath her fingers. She caressed his shoulders, which were strong and muscled. She held him in her arms as her mouth went dry and her heart started to race.

"Unbutton my shirt," he ordered in a whisper. "They're getting out of the car. We've got to be messed up."

Jessie replied with a little mutter of assent. She fumbled to pull his tie off, then began to unfasten his crisp white shirt.

He pushed her silk blouse off one shoulder and down her arm, and she slid her hands inside his shirt. His skin was warm, his chest hard beneath a mat of soft hair. As Jessie's palms brushed delicately over his skin, she thought she heard him catch his breath, but she couldn't manage to concentrate on anything besides the feel of his hand moving from her shoulder to her collarbone, then lower.

Her heart skipped a beat, and her breast tightened in anticipation of his touch, but his fingers only skimmed down to tug her blouse free of her skirt. He left his hand resting lightly on the slender curve of her waist. In the silence that followed, Jessie could hear footsteps crunching on the gravel outside the car, and she went cold all over.

Sam skimmed his lips over hers as the footsteps stopped. Then knuckles rapped sharply on the windshield.

Sam jerked his head up, for all the world like a startled lover interrupted in his necking. With one part of her mind, Jessie was aware that he pulled her blouse closed again before he cupped her nape in his hand and pressed her face into his chest to shield her from curious eyes.

"Whaddaya want?" he demanded roughly through the open window.

"Could you tell me where is Cold Creek Road?" The voice was a man's, deep and rather hoarse. The phrasing was not that of an English speaker, and the accent was Slavic—Polish or Russian. Jessie listened intently, her face against Sam's chest, barely breathing. She wanted to be able to recognize the voice if she heard it again.

"It's west of here, for God's sake!" Sam snarled. "Miles west of here!"

"Thank you, sir. You are very kind. Thank you, sir. Excuse me. Excuse me, please." Jessie could tell the man was backing away from the car.

"Get a map!" Sam yelled after him. Then he bent his head to Jessie again.

He didn't kiss her, but she could feel his breath stirring her hair. He was looking at the other car, his body taut, though his breathing was regular and unhurried. She didn't think he even realized that his hand was now covering her breast, which was barely shielded by the thin silk and lace of her teddy. His thumb moved in an unconscious caress across her taut nipple.

Jessie bit her lip to suppress a gasp of pleasure. The sensation shot through her like liquid fire, with half-forgotten, melting longings welling up in its wake. She had to make him stop, and yet she never wanted him to stop, and if he didn't stop soon . . .

"He's gone," Sam said quietly. Jessie hadn't even heard the other car drive away. "We can leave now. They wouldn't expect us to stay here and be intruded on again."

He lifted his hand from her breast, and levered himself slightly away from her to pull her blouse together. He carefully fastened a couple of the small buttons and brushed the tumbled hair away from her face.

"I don't know about you," he said, smiling ruefully into her eyes, "but it's been a long time since I did this kind of thing in the front seat of a car." He chuckled softly. "And now I know why!" He shifted his legs, and his knee struck the steering wheel. The horn gave a piercing blast. He swore under his breath, and Jessie stifled a laugh.

"Maybe you were shorter the last time." She tried to wriggle into a more comfortable position and winced.

"What's the matter?"

"The door handle. It's digging into my neck." She moved beneath him again, then froze when she realized what she'd done.

Sam gazed at her, his gray eyes darkening to charcoal as laughter faded into desire. With tender care he slid his hand beneath her neck, cradling her head in his palm. His fingers moved through her hair, caressing, and his body lowered to hers again. She could feel the tension in his muscles, the desire he was struggling to keep in check, and she knew he could feel the softness, the surrender, in her lax and supple limbs.

He seemed to be waiting for her to refuse him, but she was helpless to stop what she wanted so much. Slowly, so very slowly, he touched his lips to hers. He kissed her gently at first, teasing and tasting and tempting, until her lips parted, inviting more.

Jessie didn't know what Sam was thinking as he deepened the kiss and she responded with an upsurge of desire that blotted everything else from her mind. Perhaps, like her, he wasn't thinking, had moved beyond thinking to feeling. She was mindless, sinking into the taste and feel and warmth and strength of him.

It was only a kiss, yet it promised so much more. Sam was the one who broke it. Dragging his mouth away with a shuddering sigh, he tensed his muscles, fighting down his longing for what they both so patently wanted. Jessie whispered a wordless protest as his weight and warmth left her and the night air chilled her skin and cleared her brain.

The sweet madness evaporated like a burst bubble, leaving sanity and shame in its place. Mortified, she let Sam help her sit up, but when he started to pull her clothes into place again, she shoved his hands away.

"Jessie," he said to her averted face. "Look at me, please."

"I can't," she muttered, her head downcast.

"You can." He waited until she lifted her head. "I never meant for that to happen." It was the truth. He would never have anticipated the emotions he was feeling now, and he damn well didn't want them! "I don't expect you to believe this, but I seldom maul women I've just met when I'm working on a case."

Jessie gave a spurt of dry laughter. "I don't expect you to believe this, but I seldom neck in the front seat of a car with FBI agents I've just met, either!"

"Then we're even, aren't we?" He traced a fingertip down the curve of her cheek. The light touch was like a brand on Jessie's skin. "Are you okay?"

"Yes." Her voice was breathless but steady.

"Good." He started the car. "I want to get you home so we can start working out the details of this case."

Her clothes in order once more, Jessie fastened her seat belt as he pulled onto the road. "It's funny to think that I'm a case for the FBI."

Sam said nothing, but his mouth tightened. She was more than that. A great deal more.

"Do you think he was working with Leonid?" Jessie asked a few minutes later. She was more comfortable with business than with tense silence.

"The guy who came to the car?"

"Yes."

"I think he was there for a reason. If I hadn't thought so, I wouldn't have put on such a performance for him," he added. "He's not American. Maybe Russian, Polish, East German."

"Not German," Jessie told him. "His accent was Slavic."

Sam shot her a quick, assessing glance. "It was, huh?"

"Mm-hmm." There was a moment of silence. "My undergraduate major was Slavic languages. I speak Russian pretty well, and a little Polish."

He gave a low whistle. "That's a lucky break. It might come in very handy."

"I think I could recognize his voice if I hear it again."

"Good. I wish I could have taped him, but I didn't have time to get the recorder out."

"I'll remember," Jessie assured him. "When do you think they'll contact me?"

"In a week or so. They'll give you time to decide, and then they'll give you a little extra time, let you sweat."

"Sweat over what?"

"All that money. The Soviets are convinced that Americans will do anything for a few bucks. They want you to dream about that hundred and fifty thousand, to spend it in your mind. The more you want the money, the more you'll do for them."

"That makes me furious! How can they think I would be that way? I make a good salary. Why are they picking on me?"

"Because you have what they want. You wrote the program, so presumably you're the one who can provide it for them. If you were susceptible to drugs or blackmail, they might have tried that on you. It's cheaper. Evidently you lead a blameless life," he said with a cynical smile, "so they tried money. All too often that's a very effective tactic."

"Blackmail?" Jessie was incredulous. "Drugs?"

"If you were vulnerable. They'll have checked you out, looking for your weak spots."

Jessie was silent for a moment, then blew her breath out in an angry hiss. "This makes me glad I've agreed to help you. I still don't feel good about putting Kerry in jeopardy, but I can't just lie down and take this! My privacy's been invaded by these people, and they've picked me to turn traitor." She shook her head, her expression grim. "I want to get them for this. For what they've done to me, as well as to the U.S."

"You keep that attitude." He looked at the road ahead of them for a moment. "I have a suggestion to make, but I don't know whether you'll like it."

"Try me."

"I don't blame you for worrying about your daughter's security. There would be something wrong with you if you didn't feel that way."

That all seemed obvious to Jessie. She said nothing, just waited for the other shoe to drop.

"If you have no current romantic involvement," he went on carefully, "the best way I can think of to protect you both is by pretending to be your new lover."

If Sam was waiting for an outraged explosion, he was bracing himself for nothing. Jessie wondered what he would say if he knew he wouldn't be a new romantic interest, he'd be the *only* romantic interest in her life since Charlie had died in that fiery crash. Despite the obvious problems it would cause, the idea made sense.

She couldn't have explained it, even to herself, but she felt safe with Sam King. It wasn't just that he was an FBI agent and knew how guns worked, though that didn't hurt. She felt protected with him. She knew without being told that he would use his skills and strength and training to keep Kerry and herself secure. With his help, she could satisfy both her patriotic impulses and her need to protect her daughter.

Safety and security. Those had been her touchstones in the years since Charlie had died. Life with him had been filled with risk and adventure, and when he'd died her taste for both had died with him. If Sam King thought he could keep her and her daughter out of danger, then she'd let him try. Cautiously.

"What would we have to do to 'pretend'?"

He didn't smile. "Just that. Give the appearance of a close involvement to onlookers. Of course, when we're alone, this will be strictly a professional operation."

It hadn't been entirely professional up there on the mountain, and Jessie knew that he was trying to reassure her. She knew he meant what he said, too, and she was glad. She had just learned that she was shockingly vulnerable to this man's embrace, and if she had to brace herself every time he was near her, this would never work.

"Thank you," she said quietly. "I just hope we can put these people out of business quickly so everything can get back to normal."

Normal. Jessie looked at Sam King, thought of that kiss and wondered if anything would ever be normal again.

Chapter 3

Jessie unclipped her seat belt as Sam turned into the driveway of her house in Woodland Hills. The area south of Ventura Boulevard on the edge of the San Fernando Valley was considered prestigious, but her house, though comfortable, was modest. Sam parked in front of the garage, and she opened her door as he killed the engine.

"Wait a minute!" He caught her hand before she could slip out of the car. "Where are you going?"

"To get Kerry. It's late, and she should be in her own bed."

"Where is she now?"

"Next door." Jessie nodded toward the stucco two-story on the other side of the hedge. "My neighbor does family day care. Kerry stays with her after school."

"Okay." He released her wrist and stepped out of the car. "I'll come with you. I've still got to check your house."

"No!" Jessie's voice was sharper than she had meant it

to be. "Don't bother, please. Marcie will have a million questions."

"Questions?"

"Yes, questions. And I just don't feel like answering them tonight. Will you wait here for me?"

"Wouldn't this be a good time to start spreading our cover story?"

Jessie's head was beginning to ache. "Maybe it would, but I just don't think I can deal with it now. Will you wait here for me? Please?"

Sam must have heard the plea in her voice. After a moment, he nodded.

"Thank you." She turned on her heel to stride away across the lawn.

When she returned, she was carrying her daughter in her arms. Sam could see little more than a blanket-swathed bundle with a dark head at one end and fuzzy slippers at the other. Jessie was walking slowly, carefully, picking her way across the dark lawn.

Sam went to meet her. "Here. Let me carry her."

"No!" Her whisper was emphatic. "I'm fine." As she spoke, she stumbled on a tuft of grass.

Sam caught her arm to steady her, then eased the little girl from her grasp. "She's too heavy for you. I'll take her to her room, that's all."

He strode off toward the house with Kerry in his arms, leaving Jessie to follow. She watched him walk ahead of her, a tall, broad-shouldered man, holding her daughter with tender care. He could have been a father taking his child home to bed.

Suddenly uneasy, Jessie hurried after him. He was a stranger, and the child he had in his arms was Kerry. Despite the pretense they would play out over the next few weeks, he was still a stranger, and when the pretense was no longer necessary he would be gone.

She unlocked the back door and let him into the kitchen.

"I'll take her now." She reached up to take Kerry from him, but he shook his head.

"That's okay. Where's her room?"

He was already walking past her through the house. Jessie's lips tightened in irritation, but she pointed to the left. "That way."

Sam preceded her into Kerry's room, which was decorated in bright colors and filled with toys, books and games. He walked through the door and stopped.

Jessie brushed past him, turning down the covers and setting the dolls aside. "Just lay her on the bed."

Sam bent down to lay Kerry gently on the bed, hesitated a moment when she stirred and muttered in her sleep, and then eased his hands from beneath her. Wavy auburn wisps were escaping from the two pigtails on either side of her face, and he brushed them back gently before he straightened and moved away.

His hand was large and strong and blunt-fingered, dusted with dark hair. It was a hand Jessie could easily imagine holding a gun or making a fist, but he'd touched Kerry's cheek with exquisite tenderness.

He would touch a woman tenderly. *He touched me tenderly.* Jessie stiffened, resisting the unbidden thought. She didn't want to remember, but the hand on Kerry's face was as gentle as the hand on her breast had been. She had caressed his shoulders, and she knew the power under the thin shirt. His legs, strong-muscled, had tangled with hers. She pulled her gaze away from his flannel slacks, which molded the muscles of his thighs, and looked at his face. She was startled by the bleakness she saw there.

She'd watched the emotions flicker through his eyes that night—anger, laughter, determination—desire. Underlying them all had been an innate hardness and reserve, as if he kept his feelings at a distance. When he looked at Kerry, there was no reserve, only a seemingly bottomless sorrow.

He stepped back, jamming his hand into his pocket, and when he turned to Jessie his expression was controlled, all emotions concealed.

"Do you need anything else?"

Jessie shook her head. "I'll tuck her in. There's coffee in the kitchen."

He nodded as he left the room. Jessie waited until she heard running water and the clinking of the coffeepot before she went to Kerry. It was only a matter of a minute to arrange the sleeping child comfortably beneath the covers and turn on the night-light, but she lingered. She stroked her daughter's cheek lightly, and Kerry turned toward the caress, smiling in her sleep.

Jessie was reluctant to rejoin Sam King, to be alone with him. She didn't want to remember the things she'd felt when he had held her in his arms. She'd pushed those feelings aside after Charlie's death, sure that the need would fade in time. And it had—or at least it had seemed to, until a silver-haired stranger with a hard face and a heart filled with unnamed sorrow had kissed her and reawakened them all.

Several minutes passed before she quietly closed Kerry's door and went to join Sam. The kitchen was redolent of coffee but otherwise empty, and the lights were on in the living room. Jessie poured herself a cup and, holding it to her nose to savor the aroma, followed him.

She stopped short when she saw him. He was standing by the fireplace mantel, which was lined with framed photographs. He held one of them in his hands, a silver-framed photograph of Major C. Ames, USAF, standing beside his jet fighter, dressed in a flight suit, his prematurely gray hair ruffled by the wind.

She must have made some sound, because he looked up suddenly, his eyes meeting hers across the width of the room. She thought she saw his fingers tighten on the picture frame.

"Now I see why I startled you so badly." He set the picture carefully back on the mantel. "The resemblance is surprising, isn't it?"

"It certainly surprised me," Jessie answered. Her dry smile startled Sam with its quick flash of humor. "I really *did* think I was seeing a ghost." She brushed past him without looking at the pictures and curled up in a chintz wing chair beside the fireplace.

"I'm sorry." He took his own coffee to the sofa. "I didn't mean to scare you that way. I would have—"

"You couldn't know," she told him, closing the subject. "Don't worry about it."

Sam let it drop. He tasted his coffee while he studied the small woman in the chair opposite him. Light from a table lamp slanted over her face.

She wasn't pretty, not really. Her face was too thin, almost elfin, and her eyes were too large, and her mouth just a touch too wide. No, not pretty, but intriguing. She sipped her coffee again, then turned to him. "It's late, Mr.—" She caught herself. "Sam."

"I know it's late. I'll leave in a few minute, okay?"

"But why—"

He silenced her with a finger to his lips. "I have to do a couple of things."

Jessie watched in amusement, then disbelief, as he set his cup aside, rose and prowled the living room, looking underneath the furniture, peering inside lampshades and dismantling the telephone. She followed him through the house and kept her peace until he finished up in the kitchen.

"What on earth," she demanded, "was all that about?"

He was busily taking apart her kitchen phone. "Looking for bugs."

"Bugs?" Jessie repeated. "As in roaches, or electronic eavesdropping?"

"Electronics."

"Did you find any?"

Sam looked at her with raised eyebrows. He'd taken the receiver apart, and he was carefully lifting something small and shiny from inside it. "Well, hello," he murmured.

Jessie glanced from the buttonlike object between his fingertips to his face and caught her breath. His emotional guard was down now, and the handsome face was more than hard, it was dangerous. His eyes were cold as chips of ice and very, very determined.

It was warm in the house, but Jessie rubbed her upper arms as if to ward off a chill. She wouldn't like to have that implacable hostility directed at her.

He placed the tiny bug back inside the phone and screwed the pieces together again, his large, blunt-fingered hands quick and deft.

Jessie waited until he had replaced the receiver on its rest. "Why did you put it back?"

"Hmm?" He had unhooked the telephone from the wall and was probing behind it.

"Why did you put that back? I don't want it there!"

"Would you rather they know you're on to them?" He hung the phone on the wall again. "Because that's what'll happen if you take it out."

"Oh." This time her glance at the phone was wary, almost fearful. "What do I do?"

"Nothing." He looked amused, but in a detached way, with that wall around his emotions again.

"Nothing?" she repeated, and wrapped her arms around herself. "How can I call people?"

"The same way you always do." He noticed her frightened posture and walked over to take her shoulders. "You aren't scared, are you?"

"Scared?" Her tone was brittle, sarcastic. "Someone broke into my house and tapped my phone. Why should I be scared?"

"You don't need to be."

"How do you know I don't?" She flung his hands off and stalked agitatedly across the kitchen. "They already broke into my house! What makes you think they won't do more?"

"They didn't break in here to steal anything. They just want to make sure you don't report to the authorities."

"Like I already did, you mean?"

He nodded, half smiling, but she didn't respond.

"What would they do to me if they found out?" she asked, her voice tight with tension.

The silence seemed unbearable. She didn't hear him cross the room. When he spoke, he was right behind her.

"They won't hurt you." He laid his warm, comforting hands on her shoulders and gently turned her around. "I won't let them hurt you. Everything will be okay."

Jessie looked up at this stranger who she'd so quickly let into her life. Okay? Yes, maybe it would be okay, but would it ever be the same?

It was well after midnight when Sam let himself into his house. A bungalow built in the 1920s, it sat on a bluff in Santa Monica, surrounded by bougainvillea and hibiscus, with a palm tree in the front yard and an olive tree in the back. A stone wall marking the edge of his backyard ran along the clifftop, with the Pacific Coast Highway and the ocean beyond. Sam had paid a not-so-small fortune for that ocean view.

His drive and garage were a few feet from the side door, and as he crossed the graveled strip a blob detached itself from the shadows and came out to meet him.

"Hi, Cat." He opened the screen door, and the blob disappeared inside. Sam reached in to switch off the burglar alarm and followed. When he turned on the light, a large gray tomcat was sitting beside a dish labeled Beast, waiting for his dinner. He yowled.

"Okay, okay." Sam rummaged in a cupboard and took out a can. "You'll get fed. You don't need to get huffy about it."

The cat's only reply was another yowl as Sam set his dish on the floor.

Cat had appeared in Sam's backyard a year ago, scrawny, half starved and wary. It had taken weeks of patient coaxing to persuade him to come close enough to be petted, and even longer to persuade him to enter the house. He still wasn't a cuddly cat. He'd sit near Sam's chair, close enough to have his ears rubbed, but he only sat on laps when he chose.

That was fine with Sam. He and Cat understood each other, and they both kept their independence. Sam wouldn't have wanted the kind of slavish devotion a dog gave. Cat's studied indifference was more his style.

Sam left Cat eating and went to collect his mail from the floor just inside the front door. He took the stack to a deep leather armchair beside the fireplace to sort through it, but only half his mind was on his task. He looked up from his monthly electric bill, studied his living room and smiled wryly.

It was a comfortable space. He'd used the character of the house itself, with its built-in bookshelves, leaded-glass windows and hardwood floors, as a starting point for a look that resembled that of an exclusive men's club. Antiques, leather chairs, an Oriental rug on the floor in front of the brass fireplace screen. It was a man's room, a bachelor's room; no one would ever have mistaken it for anything else.

There were no photographs on his mantel, no child's crayons on the kitchen table, no woman's makeup in the bathroom. He lived alone, and that was just the way he wanted it. He avoided personal attachments, even friendships with the agents he worked with. He'd seen the damage love could do, seen how it could destroy a man, how it could strip him of his pride, his self-respect and the respect of others. Sam wanted no part of it.

Jessamyn's house was clearly a woman's home, with needlework cushions on the sofa beside a child's doll and coloring book. There was something there that went deeper than lace curtains in the kitchen and crayoned pictures taped to the refrigerator door.

Love. He frowned and let the electricity bill fall on the pile with the rest. Their home was a showcase for the love she and her daughter shared. It was no wonder the house made him feel uncomfortable.

Jessamyn Ames made him uncomfortable, too. Though she wasn't classically beautiful in the way of the women he was usually attracted to, there had been something almost irresistibly seductive about the way she'd felt in his arms, all silk and lace and warm, soft skin. He frowned again and shifted in the chair. Who would have thought there was silk and lace beneath that plain little suit? Who would have thought she would respond as she had to his feigned love-making?

At least he'd *meant* the lovemaking to be feigned, but for a few minutes there in the car it hadn't felt like pretense. He remembered the way her small, round breast had felt beneath his hand, the way her nipple had tightened under his touch. He hadn't meant to caress her that way, hadn't meant to become familiar.

Familiar! He laughed under his breath at his choice of words. You couldn't get much more familiar than lying on top of a woman in a car seat, unfastening her clothes.

They'd made it look so authentic that the pretense had damn nearly gotten out of hand.

Sam knew that would have been nothing less than disastrous. A woman like that would give not just her body but her heart. And she would expect love in return.

He pushed himself impatiently out of the chair and walked into the kitchen with quick, irritated strides. His steak was still in the refrigerator, and Cat watched with rapt interest as he turned it in the marinade.

He glanced at the animal. "Yeah, we'll have some lunch tomorrow, won't we?" He covered the pan again and closed the refrigerator. "Just us guys."

Her office looked the same as it always did on Monday morning. For some reason, she felt it should be different, since so much had happened. Her weeping fig still dominated the corner where the windows met, a picture Kerry had drawn at school still hung on her bulletin board along with some flow charts and memos, and her desk was still a mess. Nothing had changed. She'd lost her Empty Desk— Empty Mind sign last year, but as far as Jessie was concerned the sentiment still rang true.

She moved a stack of printouts out of the way, put her briefcase on the desktop and dropped her purse into the lower drawer. She usually didn't bother, but this particular morning she locked the drawer and pocketed the key.

And promptly unlocked the drawer again, searched through her purse and put a small card in her pocket along with the key. Sam had given her three different numbers to call if she needed him, saying he could be reached at any time. She didn't know if she'd have to contact him, but she felt better with the numbers handy.

She felt better when she settled down to work, too. She was searching through the White Eagle program for bugs, working with only a tiny bit at a time. For a defense project, no one, not even the author of the software, could have access to more than a small segment at once, and all disks, tapes and papers had to be returned to the company vault each night.

If she had really meant to sell the program to Leonid, the security precautions would have made her task slow and difficult. Instead, Sam planned to have her use those precautions to delay delivering anything to Leonid until the FBI was ready. She flipped a page and ran her pencil down the columns of digits, searching for anything that didn't belong.

At midmorning, her intercom buzzed. She reached across to punch the flashing button and lift the telephone receiver.

"Yes, Sally?"

"Mr. Howell would like to see you," her secretary informed her.

"Did he say when?"

"Now, if you can."

"I can." Jessie was folding the printout and her notes together as she spoke. "Thanks, Sally." She didn't leave her office until everything concerning White Eagle was locked in a concealed file cabinet, and then she locked the office door as well.

"Here you are, Sally." Jessie handed her secretary the office key and kept the file key, as required by procedure. "Did Mr. Howell say what he needed to talk about?"

"Nope." Sally looked up from the printer and grinned. "Just that he wanted to see you right away."

"Okay." Jessie shrugged. "I'll go and find out, then."

Sally tucked the office key away in her drawer. "Are you expecting anyone?"

"No."

"I'll take my coffee break when this finishes printing, then."

"Fine. I'll see you in a little while." Jessie left her with a smile and a wave.

Mr. Howell's secretary looked up when Jessie entered her office. "He's waiting for you, Mrs. Ames. Just go on in."

"Thank you." Jessie tapped on the door, heard a quiet "Come in" from inside and walked in.

Marshall Howell rose and came around the desk as she entered the office, his smile of greeting thin and tired.

"Hello, Jessie." He crossed the deep carpet to meet her and closed the heavy door firmly. "Thank you for coming so quickly."

"It was no problem." Jessie returned his firm hand-shake. "Is something wrong?"

Mr. Howell hesitated for a moment. "I just spoke to a Mr. King from the FBI."

"Oh." Her eyes widened. "Then you know—"

"About what happened on Friday?" He nodded grimly. "Yes."

"I'm sorry I didn't come and tell you then," she said quickly, "but I didn't know what was the best thing to do. I just knew I had to call the FBI, and—"

"You did the right thing," he said, interrupting her. "Mr. King explained that. He also explained that he was talking to me because my security clearance checked out—just like yours did."

Jessie relaxed a little. "And you want to help?"

"Yes." His distinguished face settled into angry lines, and he raked a hand through his thinning hair. "Yes, I damn well do!" He stepped back, ushering her toward a chair. "Come and sit down, please. We don't have much time, and we have to settle some things."

Sam had plainly explained everything to Mr. Howell in detail, and when Jessie left the office half an hour later her head was buzzing with plans and cautions and warnings. The first step was to begin preparing the dummy program.

The second step was the most important, she thought wryly, but it was pushed to the back burner by everything else. It was simply to finish debugging the real program so that the air force could begin testing. Funny how priorities could be rearranged by events.

Sally wasn't there when Jessie returned to her fourth-floor office. She took the key from Sally's desk, unlocked her office door, pushed it open and gasped.

The intruder jerked away from the file cabinet he'd been trying to open. He relaxed a little when he saw who it was and smoothed a hand over what was left of his hair.

"Uh...hi, Jessie."

It was Bernie Martin.

Chapter 4

Bernie! What are you doing here?"

Jessie closed the door quickly, before anyone could see who was in her office. She'd never been afraid of Bernie Martin, but now something in his posture and his face made her apprehensive.

"Waiting for you, of course." His smile was made up of equal parts threat and nerves.

She walked calmly around behind the protective bulwark of her desk and seated herself. She wasn't about to be intimidated by the likes of Bernie Martin. "You took the key out of my secretary's drawer and broke in here."

"Sally was away." Bernie's suit strained at the seams as he leaned his plump body against the desk.

"Don't do it again, Bernie."

He shrugged dismissively. "I wanted to talk to you. I thought you might have something to tell me."

"I don't." She took out a legal pad and dated the top

page. As she began to write, Bernie grabbed her wrist, dragging the tail of a *y* across the paper.

Holding her tightly, he waited until she looked up. "How soon are you gonna give Leonid what he wants, Jessie? When will you deliver?"

She pulled against his grip, but he didn't release her wrist. "I don't have anything to say to you, Bernie." Her voice was low and cold. "Anything I have to say, I'll say to Leonid."

"You can tell me!" He leaned over the desk and tightened his grip until it hurt, but Jessie refused to react. "What are you going to give him, and when will you deliver?"

She rose slowly from her chair so that she was facing him across the desktop. "Take your hands off me, Bernie. Now."

Her voice was quiet, but something made him do as she commanded. With a little flip of his hand, he let go, swinging his arm to one side to show that she was free.

Her wrist ached, but she didn't rub it. "You tell Leonid that if he wants to talk, he can talk to me directly. And if you don't want to blow your little scam right out of the water, you'll stay out of my office." She glanced at the closed door. "You don't have any reason to be here, Bernie. I don't know why you'd say you were in here alone if Sally came back, but I'm sure not going to stick my neck out for you."

Bernie followed her glance at the door. When he looked back at her, his forehead was dabbed with sweat. "Is she out there?"

Jessie shrugged, indifferent to his problem. "I don't know. You want to go now, or wait for her?"

He tensed visibly, but then he apparently thought better of whatever it was he'd been about to say. His smile, when it came, was cold and threatening.

He crossed to the door. "I'll go this time. But remember, Jessie, you're in this, too. You scratch my back, I scratch yours."

He slipped out, and Jessie heard rapid footsteps move down the hall before the door opened again and Sally looked in.

"What was Bernie Martin doing up here? Did he want something?"

Jessie shook her head tiredly. "Nothing important. He was just being Bernie."

"Oh." Sally shrugged. "I've got those printouts done. Would you like them now?"

"Yes, Sally. Thank you."

Jessie waited until her secretary left, then sagged into her chair and let out a long, ragged breath. Bernie Martin hadn't broken into her files, but only because she'd interrupted him. He hadn't found anything this time, but she'd been warned. She'd dealt with him this time, but she'd tell Sam about it when she saw him. She would have to be very, very careful.

The day was taut with tension for Jessie. When she left the building just after five, her head was splitting, and Kerry's after-school surfeit of energy was too much for her to deal with. In self-defense, she fixed a supper of sandwiches and apples and took it out to the patio.

Kerry bolted her supper and ran to the swing set, while Jessie ate more slowly, then carried her glass of iced tea to the hammock strung across the corner of the pergola. It was heaven to lie there, swinging gently, listening to the rustling leaves of the orange tree a few yards away and the twitter of birds in the evening hush. Bit by bit she relaxed, and the band of pain around her temples loosened.

"Mommy!" Kerry yelled from the swing set. "Look at me!"

Jessie looked, and saw her daughter dangling from one of the crosspieces by her knees. Her face was red, and she was waving furiously, grinning a gap-toothed, upside-down grin.

"That's great, sweetie! I didn't know you could do that!" Jessie called back.

Not for the first time, she was extremely glad she'd had a sand pit dug underneath that swing set. If Kerry fell, at least she'd have a soft landing. Jessie watched her daughter climb down from the crosspiece in a complicated maneuver that was all angular knees and elbows. Kerry plopped into the soft sand, dusted herself off and clambered up again.

"Watch me, Mommy! Watch me!"

Jessie waved and gave a push with her toe, setting the hammock into lazy motion while she watched.

From the gate at the corner of the yard, Sam watched, too. When there had been no answer to the doorbell, he'd walked around the house, following the sound of a child's laughter.

He took it all in at a glance, the large yard and the big, comfortable patio, which was furnished with a table and chairs, a lounge and a hammock. He glanced at the little girl playing on the swing, and then at her mother, a very different Jessamyn Ames from the primly dressed, frightened angry woman he'd encountered on Friday.

She wore a roomy polo shirt and pleated shorts that bared her long and shapely and evenly tanned legs. Her hair was ruffled by the evening breeze, and for the first time he saw her relaxed, smiling an easy, natural smile.

It transformed her, making her face beautiful, enjoyment and amusement and affection lighting it from within. Sam could see love in her eyes, in the glow that illuminated her when she glanced at her daughter. A mother should look at her child that way. A mother should care for her child, but Sam knew from bitter experience that not all mothers did.

His lips tightened unconsciously, and he pushed the gate open with a bang. He didn't have time to stand here daydreaming.

Jessie saw movement out of the corner of her eye, and as Sam King walked into the yard she swung out of the hammock and went to meet him. She saw his gaze flick over her bare legs, and her breath seemed to catch in her chest. When he looked at her that way, it was far too easy to remember how it had felt to be held in his arms.

"Hello, Mr. King. What are you doing here?" Despite her surprise, she was pleased to see him.

"Checking in to see what happened today. And call me Sam."

"What makes you think anything hap—"

"Hi!" Kerry sprinted across the grass and tackled Jessie from behind, clinging to her legs as she gazed up at Sam. "Who are you?"

"Hi, there." He squatted to put himself on her level. "I'm Sam. Who are you?"

"I'm Kerry." She studied him for a moment. "Are you going to marry my mom? If you did, you'd be my daddy," she added with the air of someone imparting important and startling information.

"Yes, I would." Sam straightened slowly, meeting Jessie's embarrassed gaze with a cynical smile. "Wouldn't I?"

"Sweetheart." Jessie bent and brushed Kerry's hair back off her forehead. "Mr. King and I aren't going to get married. We just have to talk about work for a while."

"But Alice says—"

"Sweetie, I know what Alice says, but Alice is five years old. She doesn't know everything yet. And anyway—" she looked at her watch "—it's time for you to have your bath and get ready for bed."

"Aww, Mommy..."

"Go on. Bath and pajamas and teeth, and come tell me when you're ready, okay?"

Kerry went reluctantly. When Jessie heard the back door close, she smiled ruefully at Sam. "I'm sorry about that.

Lately she seems to have decided that she wants a father like the other kids. I hope she didn't embarrass you.''

"I don't embarrass easily." He glanced toward the house. "Did you coach her?"

"Coach her?" Jessie didn't understand.

"Oh, I'm sure a lot of people would find it touching. 'Will you be my daddy?' It's adorable." He put a slight but definite tinge of sarcasm on the last word.

Jessie felt something go very cold inside her. "I did not," she said carefully, "nor would I, coach my daughter to ask *anyone* to be her daddy. She had a daddy, and he was a wonderful man. I'm not looking for a substitute, and, frankly, I can't imagine anyone—" she coolly looked Sam up and down "—filling his shoes."

She turned on her heel and walked to the door. "I'm going to put Kerry to bed. There's iced tea in the pitcher, if you really do have anything to discuss. If not, you can go." She went inside, closing the door sharply behind her.

Sam swore heavily under his breath before pouring himself a glass of tea and sitting down to wait. He was still sitting at the table, looking out at the rapidly darkening sky, when Jessie came out again. She sat down opposite him, added a little tea to her glass and sipped. She didn't look at him, nor he at her.

"I apologize," he said abruptly. "I don't know much about kids and what they say, but that's no excuse. I was out of line. I'm sorry."

"You were," she agreed. After a moment, she added, "But I'll accept your apology."

She didn't sound as if she wanted to, but Sam would take her acceptance any way he could get it. He didn't like the cold disdain he'd seen in her eyes when he'd accused her of coaching her daughter.

"Thank you."

Jessie sipped her tea. "*Did* you come for a reason?"

"Yeah." Sam was half turned away from her, his face shadowed by the deepening dusk. "I wanted to know if Leonid tried to make contact with you today."

"No, but Bernie did."

"Martin?" He looked around. "What did *he* want?"

Jessie frowned uncertainly. "I'm not entirely sure. He got into my office while I was gone, and when I showed up he was trying to open one of the file cabinets."

"Did he succeed?"

"No. And he was trying to open the wrong one, anyway. I keep ordinary stuff in the one he was trying. The classified information goes in a file built into the wall. It's concealed in the paneling, and I don't think Bernie even knows it's there."

"Good. Did he want anything else?"

"Yes." She rubbed her temple, where the remembered headache was starting again. "It was weird. I'd never imagined being afraid of Bernie, but today—"

"What did he do to you?" Sam demanded. He didn't touch her, but his hand moved toward her on the tabletop.

"He didn't *do* anything to me, really. Well, he did grab my wrist, but he let me go when I told him to. It's just that—"

"This wrist?" Sam caught her hand and pulled it toward the light slanting out through the windows. He turned her arm until he could see a row of finger marks, bluish against her pale skin. His thumb slid over the ugly bruises in a light caress. "He did this to you?" His voice was too quiet.

Jessie pulled her hand away. "I have thin skin." She put her hands in her lap, covering her wrist with her fingers. "But that wasn't what scared me. It was the way he talked."

"How did he talk?"

Jessie paused, trying to put it into words. "He was tense, edgy, angry and scared, all at the same time. He wanted to know what I was going to tell Leonid, when I would have something for him, and how much. He was really insistent."

"What did you say?"

"That I didn't want him taking the key out of my secretary's desk and breaking into my office, and that anything I had to say I'd say to Leonid, not to him."

"And he accepted that?"

"Not at first, but I think I convinced him. I pointed out that he'd have a tough time explaining what he was doing in my office. Then I told him to get out, and he went."

"Do you think he'll leave you alone?"

"Who can say?" She shrugged. "I thought I knew Bernie, but everything that's happened since Friday has shown me I don't have any answers, only questions."

"Yeah." He studied the tabletop for a few minutes. "Do you know how to use a gun?"

Sam didn't look up, but he sensed that she had turned to glance at him. Several seconds passed before she spoke.

"Yes, I do. Will I need to?"

"I don't know," he said heavily. "I hope not. I did some checking today on your Bernie Martin."

"Don't say that!" she snapped, and Sam looked at her in surprise. "He's not mine."

"You're right." Sam leaned back in his chair, crossing his ankle over his knee. "He's not yours, but he does belong to some other people. Some very nasty other people."

"The Russians?"

He shook his head. "Loan sharks."

"Loan sharks?"

He chuckled, but there was no humor in the sound. "You'd expect it to be something more dramatic, wouldn't you?"

"For him to be doing what he's doing, I'd think there would have to be some important reason."

He shook his head ruefully. "Life's not like the movies, Jessie. People seldom turn traitor for dramatic philosophical beliefs, more likely for little, cheap reasons. In Martin's case, they're pretty common ones."

"What are they?"

"He gambles, and the last couple of years he's gotten in over his head. He started telling loan sharks that he was going to get a big raise, or a commission or something, and they raised his, 'line of credit,' shall we say. He backed a bunch of losers at the track, and there was no commission to pay back the loans with. They gave him enough rope to hang himself, and then they pulled it up short."

"And then?"

"The KGB stepped in. He needed a lot of money in a hurry. He was ripe for the picking, and they used that."

After a moment, Jessie nodded. "That all makes sense, but why was it Bernie they went after? He's just an office manager, really, not even a salesman. He doesn't have access to information anyone would want."

"Oh, but he does." Sam smiled. "He has the most important information of all."

She frowned. "What?"

"Names. Your name, and the names of any other people in the company who have security clearance, who work on defense projects, who have access to secrets. You yourself have valuable knowledge, but Martin's may be the most important. He's the one who's giving them the names."

"And that's what they're paying him for?"

"That's my guess."

She nodded, accepting his assessment. Then she frowned. "If he already gave them my name, why was he trying to frighten me this morning, telling me to give the program to Leonid as soon as I could? He acted like he had a personal stake in what I did, and how soon I did it." The darkness was growing, and Jessie could no longer see Sam's face clearly, though she could hear mingled resignation and disgust in his voice.

"He probably does. They wouldn't make things too easy for him, you know. He won't get all the money he's been promised until the goods are delivered. He has a vested interest in having you produce quickly." He grinned, and she saw his teeth flash white in the darkness. "I almost feel sorry for him, you know, caught between the KGB and the downtown guys with the brass knuckles."

Jessie didn't return his grin, but frowned, turning her empty glass restlessly in her hands. "I don't know what to feel. I might have felt sorry for him, but he tried to bully me this morning, to scare me."

"Hey." Sam reached out to capture her fidgeting hands with his own. "You didn't let me get away with pushing you around. He tried to intimidate you, it didn't work, and I don't think he'll try that again."

Unconsciously she gripped his hands. "Do you think he'll leave me alone?"

Sam shook his head at that. "He won't ignore you. You're too important to him for that. I don't think he'll try to push you around anymore, though."

"Well, thank goodness for small favors." Jessie sighed. She closed her eyes tiredly for a moment, and Sam sat quietly, her hands clasped in his. They were small and soft and warm, and he stroked his thumbs lightly over her smooth skin.

She suddenly noticed that they were sitting there holding hands, and she straightened sharply in her chair and pulled away. "Is that—" She cleared her throat. "Is that all you had to tell me?"

Sam sat back, watching her. "Pretty much."

"What else, then?"

"My cover story." He grinned. "I'm going to be a writer working on a screenplay. That way I can be free to see you any time of day."

"Writing a screenplay?" Jessie smiled in spite of herself. "Isn't that too much of a cliché?"

"Not in L.A. I live in Santa Monica, and two of my neighbors are screenwriters. It fits."

"Whatever you say. Am I supposed to know what your script is about?"

"I hadn't thought about it." He gave it a moment's consideration. "A crime drama?"

"Okay. You're a writer and the movie is a crime drama. How did we meet?"

"Through mutual acquaintances?"

"Anybody in particular?"

He shook his head. "Be vague. Once we've been seen together a few times, people will be more interested in what's going on now than in how we met."

"I know they'll be interested." She sighed. "I just don't know how I'm going to explain it."

"What's there to explain?" He tried to read her expression in the dimness. "We met, we like each other, we're seeing each other. That's no big deal."

Her soft lips tightened. "It's going to be awkward."

"Why? I know I'm no matinee idol, but am I that bad?"

Jessie gave him a wry glance. "It's got nothing to do with what you look like."

"What is it, then? Tell me, and maybe I can help. Is it my cover? I could change that if—"

"It's not that...."

"Then what on earth is it?"

She hesitated, searching for the right words. "It's not you, it's me. I don't know how I'll explain being involved with a man."

Sam blinked in surprise, watching her profile in the dim light. "Why should that be so odd?" he asked lightly. "A woman like you must have lots of men asking you out."

She shook her head, laughing under her breath. "I've been asked out, but I didn't go."

"You didn't?"

She shook her head again. "At first I was still grieving. Then, later, it seemed like all they wanted to do was console the lonely widow."

"So you don't go out much?"

"I don't—" She broke off, wishing she didn't have to say it. It was his fault. If she'd never met Sam King she wouldn't have had to get into any of these embarrassing explanations. "Look, Mr. King, I don't—"

"Sam."

"Sam. I really don't want to get into this, but I guess you have to know so you can understand. I don't... I don't date."

There was a moment of silence. "At all?"

"At all."

Sam hid his surprise. He understood the need to be alone, he was most comfortable that way, but even *he* went out occasionally. There were no strings, no commitments, but there were women now and then.

But this woman hadn't been out with a man since her husband's death. He remembered the feel of her in his arms, the taste of her lips, the quick passion that had rushed through her, inflaming them both.

He leaned back, and the patio chair creaked beneath his weight. They sat for a few minutes, listening to the night sounds—birds and distant traffic and the breeze. There was no need to talk. It was as if they were sharing something deeper and truer than words.

Suddenly Jessie shoved her chair back briskly and stood. "It's late. Is there anything else you need to tell me?" she asked. "Anything I have to do?"

"Just be patient." Sam rose. "And try to forget about Martin."

"Right." She nodded, then caught her lower lip in her teeth.

Sam walked around the table and caught her hand in his. It was cold. "Jessie, if I thought there was the remotest chance of Martin causing you any more trouble I'd have him arrested tonight, and to hell with the investigation."

She frowned. "But you want so badly to catch them. You don't want to ruin your whole case because of me."

His mouth firmed to a hard line. "I said I wouldn't put you at risk, and I won't," he said, sounding almost angry.

After a moment, she nodded. "All right."

His grip on her hands tightened fractionally. "Howell has a cellular phone. It's much more difficult to tap, so if anything happens when you're at work, use it to call me, *immediately*." He pulled her closer, and she had to tilt her head back to look into his face. "You have the numbers I gave you?"

She nodded. "I memorized them."

"If anything happens, you call me. *Call me!*"

"I will." She returned the pressure of his hand.

"I'm not kidding about this," he said harshly. "It isn't a game. Don't take chances with these people, Jessamyn. You do *nothing* without proper backup. That means you contact me if they approach you, or send you a message, or want a meeting. Anything."

She nodded again. "I will."

"Make sure you do." Still holding her hand, he touched her cheek with a fingertip, looking down into her eyes. "Make very sure you do, Jessamyn."

He bent and kissed her quickly, then strode away into the darkness. Jessie heard the creak of the gate, followed by the sound of rapid footsteps on the driveway and the roar of a powerful car engine.

Long after the sound of his car had faded into the night murmurs, she still stood there, her fingers pressed to her tingling lips.

Chapter 5

The waiting was the worst.

On edge ever since Leonid had approached her, Jessie rapidly grew tired of wondering when the other shoe would drop. By Wednesday the suspense had given her a chronic headache and a case of irritability that had Sally treating her with kid gloves.

"So come on, already!" It was five-thirty, and she was jamming papers into her briefcase and muttering to herself. "I'm sick and tired—" she tossed in a stack of green-striped printout paper "—of waiting around! Oh, *phooey*!" She slammed the lid closed and spun the combination dials.

She knew perfectly well she was being childish, but that didn't help much. It was easy enough for Sam King to tell her to wait and be patient. He wasn't the one spending entire days on pins and needles!

Sally looked up warily when Jessie appeared.

"Sally." Jessie closed and locked her office door, then smiled apologetically. "I'm sorry."

"Is there anything I can do?"

"It's not you, Sally. It's me. But thanks for the offer." She walked to the outer door, then looked back. "And thanks for not bopping me over the head today. I know I deserve it!" Sally just laughed.

Outside, it was a typical September afternoon in the San Fernando Valley, the temperature hovering in the nineties and a dirty curtain of smog hiding the mountains from view. The hot air was painfully dry, chapping lips and fraying tempers. Jessie's no-longer-new Mercedes was parked in the baking sun, and when she reached to put the key in the lock a spark of static electricity snapped from her hand to the car.

"Ow!" She shook her shocked fingertip, tapped the car with her hand to dispel any remaining static and tried again.

"Hello, Mrs. Ames."

The familiar voice came from inches behind her. She gasped, jumped and dropped her keys. Bending to retrieve them from the scorching pavement gave her a moment to collect herself, and when she straightened she looked at Leonid with cool distaste.

"Good afternoon, Mr. Antonov."

He'd meant to frighten her—that was obvious from his expression. He would have enjoyed seeing her scared, so Jessie made sure nothing showed in her face. She had to pretend to be a venal amoral traitor, but she didn't have to cower. She wouldn't give Leonid the satisfaction.

"Have you been waiting to hear from me?"

She shrugged. "I figured you'd be in touch. What do you want?"

Put off his stride by her unexpectedly casual reaction, Leonid hesitated for a moment. His mouth tightened to a thin line. "It is time to talk."

"Okay." Jessie leaned against the car and folded her arms, regarding him coolly. "Talk."

"Not here." He glanced around at the cars left in the parking lot, at the workers straggling out of the building on their way home. "There are too many people."

"Where, then?"

"Davy's."

Jessie recognized the name of a faintly seedy cocktail lounge not far away. She didn't care for it much, but she could see the advantages to meeting there. No one would pay any attention to them in that noisy, anonymous crowd.

She nodded. "Okay."

"My car is over there." Leonid caught her arm, but she shook him off.

"I'll drive my own. I have errands to run before I go home." Jessie might be new at this spy business, but she wasn't stupid enough to get into a car with Leonid.

"I will bring you back here afterward."

"I'll drive myself," she insisted. Their gazes locked, clashed, and then Leonid nodded shortly.

"I'll follow you."

"I have to stop and get gas."

"I will wait while you do that." A thin smile bent his lips. He wasn't going to give her a chance to contact anyone before their meeting.

"All right." She kept her voice cool. "I'll see you there."

"Very well." He turned and hurried across the parking lot to his car.

Jessie didn't wait until he reached it, but started her engine and made for the exit. If he wanted to tail her, fine, but if she could lose him she would take a moment to phone Sam King. He'd virtually *commanded* her to call him before she met with Leonid or anyone else, and she wanted to follow his instructions. For one thing, she liked the idea of having FBI agents around her in case something went wrong with the meeting.

She could see that Leonid didn't intend to give her an opportunity to call. As she turned left onto Canoga Avenue, she saw him speeding across the parking lot in a dull yellow sedan.

He shot onto Canoga three seconds after the light changed. Brakes squealed, horns blared, and a young man in a pickup shook his fist angrily as Leonid raced after her. He caught up with her in a block, and when she turned into a corner gas station he pulled up behind her at the pumps.

Jessie let the attendant fill her tank while she looked longingly at a pay phone ten yards away, beside the rest room doors. She could hardly call with Leonid watching, which meant there would be no advice from Sam and no gun-toting FBI agents watching over her from the back booth.

So much for the best-laid plans. Jessie sighed. If she couldn't call and get instructions, she'd just have to handle this herself.

"Ma'am? Ma'am?" The attendant's voice brought her out of her reverie.

"I'm sorry." She looked up at him. "I didn't hear you."

"That'll be ten seventy-five, with the cash discount."

She gave him the bills, took her change and pulled out of the station. In her rearview mirror she watched Leonid nearly drive over the attendant's toes in his eagerness to stay close.

It was the same at Davy's. He parked in the space next to hers and grabbed her arm as she walked toward the small, shabby building. She jerked free at the door, waited for Leonid to open it for her, then sailed inside with what she hoped was the grace of a queen.

The dark, smoky bar was a contrast to the bright afternoon outside. A country tune blared from the jukebox, and a raucous crowd clustered around a pool table in the corner. Jessie spared them a brief glance, then led the way to a booth near the door, where dirty sunlight slanted through the front window.

"I'll have ginger ale," she announced in her best society manner before Leonid could sit down. "With a wedge of lime."

She didn't watch to see if he'd fetch her drink, but lowered her head and rummaged in her purse. When she heard him walk away, she pulled out a tissue and quickly blotted her damp forehead. By the time he came back with her ginger ale and what looked like vodka for himself, she was cool and composed.

He set the drink in front of her with a thump, spilling some on the tabletop, and dropped onto the bench opposite her.

"So," he said after a few moments' silence, "what is your answer?"

She looked up slowly, letting her gaze run over his shirt, a loud plaid that clashed horribly with his bright green tie. The light highlighted the sharp bones of his face. His neck was thin, his chin pointed, his lips narrow and unsmiling beneath a straggly mustache. He watched her steadily, his almost-colorless light gray eyes small and cold. She sat back and lifted her chin.

"I'll do it."

There was a quick flare of triumph in those watery eyes, and Jessie had to lower her lids to conceal the anger in her own.

"That is good. That is the smart thing to do."

Jessie didn't want Leonid's compliments. She didn't care if he thought she was smart or not, she just wanted him to think she was a traitor. It hurt her pride to even appear to oblige Leonid in his nasty mission, but she could deal with that by keeping her mind on her ultimate goal—defeating both Leonid and the people he worked for.

She sipped her ginger ale, waiting for his next move. She knew what he was thinking. She could practically see him rubbing his hands together at the prospect of reeling in his catch—her. He looked up, and Jessie schooled her face to an impassive mask.

"When will I have it?" His question was abrupt.

Jessie took another sip, thinking fast. If she'd talked to Sam, he could have told her what the FBI wanted her to say. Instead, she had to figure out the best way to play this herself. Realism was the key. If she made it too easy, they'd suspect something. If she were really a traitor, what would she do?

She set her glass down and looked at him. "A few weeks."

Leonid stiffened. "Weeks? No!" His refusal was quick and angry. "That is out of the question. You must have it for me much sooner than that."

He's bluffing. Jessie couldn't have said how she knew, but she was sure he was trying to bully her, to see how far she could be pushed. Well, she couldn't be bullied, not by him.

"That's impossible. It'll take six or eight weeks at least, maybe more."

"You have a week," he snapped. "Ten days at the most."

She slid out of the booth and stood, picking up her purse. "I've told you, that's impossible. If you can't give me the time I need, then we have nothing to discuss. Goodbye."

Before she'd taken two steps, Leonid caught her arm. "Wait."

Jessie glanced down at his hand, and he released her. She stepped back and looked up, lifting an eyebrow in cool inquiry.

"We will talk about it," he said reluctantly. "Sit down."

She nodded after a moment and returned to the booth.

"Why do you need so much time? Its just a computer disk."

Jessie smiled at that. "You don't know much about computers, do you?"

He stiffened at the condescension in her tone. "I am not a technician."

Jessie let her smile linger for a moment before it faded. "Neither am I. This is a long program, and a complicated one. Security is tight. I don't have a copy of the program, or of the documentation, or even of the notes I made while I was working on it. Everything is locked in the vault with my disks each night."

"So how do you get it for me?"

"I have to reconstruct it bit by bit, and that will take time."

"Six weeks?" he asked incredulously, and she nodded.

"At least. Unless you want the whole world to know what I'm doing, I'll have to take it slowly. I'll give myself away if I try to rush." She met his frown with a level gaze, and at length he nodded.

"All right."

At his grudging agreement, she had to hide her smile of triumph. She'd called his bluff and won!

"You can have time," he said, "but not too much. You must work as fast as you can."

She nodded, then reinforced her image as a money-hungry American by adding, "When will I be paid?"

"When you give me the program."

"No." She shook her head. "I want part of it up front." He looked confused by the colloquialism, and she explained, "I want part of the money now."

He began to shake his head, but she cut off whatever he might say.

"I want part of it now, and the rest as the program is delivered."

"We will not do that. We—"

"Then I don't deliver the program. I don't trust you any more than you trust me, Mr. Antonov. No money, no program."

He scowled. "How much?"

She considered. "Fifty thousand with the first part, the rest with the final delivery."

"Fifty thousand first, fifty thousand later."

"No, the deal was for one hundred and fifty total. Fifty now, another one hundred as I deliver it." She was beginning to enjoy herself, bargaining like a merchant in a bazaar. The assurance in her manner must have convinced Leonid, for after a long pause, he nodded.

"One hundred fifty thousand."

"I get the first part with the first part of the program?"

He frowned. "You will be notified."

"Okay. But be sure to tell your bosses, Mr. Antonov, that I'm not sticking my neck out for nothing."

Since she gave no choice, he had to agree, and they parted moments later. Jessie waited in the parking lot until Leonid had driven away, then drove in the opposite direction.

She drove slowly, on side streets where the traffic was light, because she didn't trust herself on the busy boulevard. Her hands were shaking and her stomach was churning, but despite everything she felt a growing sense of triumph. She'd done it! She'd gone toe-to-toe with Leonid, and she'd won!

She was still trembling a little when she got home, and adrenaline was surging through her bloodstream. Kerry was full of her own day's events, and the babble about homework and art projects helped to cover Jessie's distraction until she could send her daughter to wash up and set the table.

Alone at last, she picked up the kitchen telephone and punched out Sam's home phone number from memory. He answered on the third ring.

"Hello?"

"Hello, Sam, it's Jessie." Mindful of the bug on her line, she kept her voice light and casual. "I wanted to make sure you were still coming to dinner tonight."

They had made no dinner plans, but he replied without hesitation, and with a smile in his voice. "Sure I am. I've been looking forward to it all day." Since he couldn't ask her what time he was supposed to be coming over, he said instead, "I'm running a little behind, though."

"That's okay. I had a late meeting this afternoon. What time should we expect you?"

"Is seven all right?" His voice wasn't quite as relaxed as it had been. She knew he'd realized what she meant by "late meeting."

"Sure. I'll see you then." She hung up smiling, eager to tell him of her triumph.

"You did *what*?" Sam's voice, though it was pitched low to keep Kerry from hearing, was harsh with barely leashed anger.

"I met with him at that bar," Jessie repeated. She quietly closed the door between the kitchen and the living room. If Sam didn't keep his temper under control and his voice down, Kerry would hear him. "What else could I do?"

"You could have called me! Before you went anywhere with anybody. *That's* what you could have done!" His fury was clear and, as far as Jessie was concerned, unreasonable.

"Well, I couldn't!" she retorted. "He popped up in the middle of the parking lot like a jack-in-the-box, said he had to talk to me, right that minute, and then he followed me to the bar."

"Oh, that's just great! Do you know how stupid of you it was to meet him alone, with no backup?"

"It wasn't stupid. It was necessary!"

"Not if you'd called me!"

"Called from where?" she demanded, her own temper rising. "He followed me in his car, then pulled in behind me at the gas station. If I'd gone to the ladies' room at that bar he would have followed me in! He's not a fool, Sam. He wasn't about to give me a chance to contact anyone."

"Damn it!" Sam punched his bunched fist into his palm with barely controlled violence. "That's not the way you're supposed to handle—"

"Mommy, is Mr. King—" Kerry burst through the door from the living room, and her face lit up when she saw Sam standing there. "You came!"

She didn't seem to notice that she'd interrupted an argument. She ran across the kitchen as if to hug Sam and then stopped short a yard from him in a spasm of shyness. She couldn't quite look him in the face, but bounced on her toes, clutching a sheet of paper in front of her.

"Hello, Kerry." Sam gave Jessie a look of frustrated irritation, then bent down to Kerry's level. "What have you got there?"

His smile was easy and his voice held none of the angry impatience Jessie knew he was feeling, and for that she was grateful. If he'd spoken to Kerry the way he'd done to her, she would have hit him.

Kerry blushed happily, oblivious to the undercurrents around her. "I made a picture for you." She thrust it out, and Sam studied the crayoned flowers and rainbow around a silver-haired stick figure labeled Mr. King.

"Is this for me?"

She nodded and gave him the picture.

"Thank you, Kerry. This is really pretty."

"I can make you another one," she offered eagerly.

"After dinner, Kerry," Jessie said, her tone sharper than she'd intended. She gentled her voice. It was Sam she was angry with, not her daughter. "It's time to eat, sweetie."

It wasn't a relaxing meal for Jessie and Sam, whose unfinished business hung in the air like a stifling fog. Kerry, however, chattered happily to Sam while Jessie took a casserole from the oven and a salad from the refrigerator.

"Mr. King?"

"Yes, Kerry?"

"You can use my special glass if you want to." She proffered the brightly decorated plastic tumbler.

He glanced at Jessie, confused. "Well, I don't know...."

"You can have chocolate milk, too. If Mom says it's okay."

"I, uh..."

Kerry pushed the glass into his hand, and he straightened slowly, flashing Jessie a harried look. She took pity on him, though she didn't think he deserved it.

"It's nice of you to offer, Kerry, but your glass is kind of small for Mr. King." Kerry looked Sam up and down, her eyes round. "How about if you have your milk in that glass and we give Mr. King a bigger one?"

Kerry looked from Sam to her mother. "Can I have chocolate milk?"

Jessie had to laugh. "All right, tonight you can have it chocolate. But don't think you're going to get away with this every time, little girl."

"Thanks, Mommy!" Giggling, Kerry skipped to the refrigerator to get the chocolate syrup.

Jessie passed Sam a plate of salad, spooned some of the casserole onto another plate and handed it to him.

He looked at it, his face dubious. "What is this?"

"Tamale pie." She handed a plate to Kerry, who accepted it eagerly.

Sam prodded the sauce-covered mound with his fork. "What's in it?"

"It's good!" Kerry took a big bite.

"Ground beef, tomatoes, cheese, corn-bread stuff on top." Jessie tasted her own. It was good, as usual, spicy and substantial. Sam was still staring at his as if it might bite him back.

She studied him for a moment, seeing things she hadn't seen before, the heavy gold watch and the fraternity ring, the silk tie and the sport coat that had to be cashmere. He didn't look like a man who would eat tamale pie because it stretched the hamburger a little farther. They must be paying FBI agents more than Jessie would have thought.

She and Kerry lived comfortably now, but old habits persisted. Sometimes they had steak dinners, and other times Jessie fixed the kind of casserole that had stretched not only their meat but their money in the early days. It didn't hurt to watch pennies, even now that she didn't have to. Mr. Sam King might prefer steak, she thought with inward amusement, but it wouldn't hurt him to eat a casserole once in a while.

"It's all the ingredients that go into tamales," she said, taking another bite, "only without the corn husks."

"Tamales." He'd eaten tamales in Mexico City and liked them well enough. "Okay." With the air of a man doing something slightly risky, he tasted it.

Jessie watched him out of the corner of her eye. She managed not to smile at the expression on his face when he took the first bite, or when he finished his first serving and accepted a second. It took some effort, but she kept a straight face.

She needed a few minutes to collect her thoughts before she told Sam why she'd met with Leonid on her own. She had done nothing wrong, but it was obvious that convincing an FBI agent wasn't going to be easy.

In the meantime, Kerry bombarded Sam with questions. When he told her he had a cat, she had to know everything. What was the cat's name, how old was he, what color was he, did he have green eyes? The barrage didn't stop until she'd finished her dinner and raced away from the table to draw a picture of Sam's pet.

She left an echoing silence behind her, and a returning feeling of tension. Though Sam had been patient with Kerry, Jessie didn't sense any of the same forbearance in his attitude toward her.

"I'm sorry Kerry gave you the third degree," she said after a moment. "She's a little excited about your being here."

"No fooling." His tone was very dry.

Jessie glanced up sharply to see if he was criticizing her daughter. He was smiling, and she relaxed a little.

"Would you like any more dinner?"

"No, thanks. But that was very good."

Jessie rose and picked up her plate. "You don't need to sound so surprised," she told him, and walked into the kitchen before he could respond. When he came in after her she was rinsing dishes at the sink, her slender back stiff, straight and very expressive.

"What's the matter?" he asked.

She didn't turn around. "I'll bet you eat a lot of steak, don't you?"

"What makes you think so?"

"You look like the steak type." She put the last plate in the dishwasher and closed it. "And it's obvious you haven't had much to do with casseroles."

"I just don't eat that stuff much."

"You must have when you were a kid. Everybody's mom makes tuna casserole."

"I always liked steak," he said stiffly. Then, impatiently: "Look, are you done with all this?" He pulled the dish towel out of her hand and tossed it on the edge of the sink, keeping a grip on her wrist. "We've got to talk."

"Talk?" Jessie asked tartly. "Do you really want to talk, or are you going to yell at me some more?"

"I wasn't yelling—"

"Not in terms of loud volume, but that was only because Kerry was on the other side of the door. You were browbeating me, and I don't like that, Mr. King."

"So maybe you'll remember this next time and call me before you meet with anybody."

"I will if Leonid gives me the chance. If he doesn't I'll just handle things the best way I can, like today."

"Your 'best way' was damn stupid!"

"I had no choice!" She jerked her arm, trying to free herself from his grip on her wrist, but he held on. "Will you *listen* to me? Leonid stuck with me every minute. I don't know what he thought I'd do, but he made darn sure I didn't talk to anyone else before we got to that bar. He wanted to talk to me alone, and he saw to it that's what happened."

Sam's scowl deepened, but this time his anger wasn't directed at Jessie. "Do you think he suspects that you're working with us?"

"No." She shook her head. "I think he was just being cautious on principle."

"Let's hope so," he muttered. "I don't like to think about what could have happened—" He broke off and pulled her closer, again gripping her wrist with bruising force. "My God, do you have any idea what could have happened to you today?"

"It didn't happen. Sam, I did what I did because anything else would have tipped Leonid off. I know I was supposed to call you, but I didn't have a chance. I did the best I could, and it worked out."

"You took an insane risk."

"As I said, I did what I had to. I kept my end up with Leonid and convinced him I'm only interested in the money. Isn't that what you wanted me to do?"

"What *I* wanted?"

"Yes! If you don't want to catch Leonid and the rest of them, then what *do* you want?"

Sam's gaze flicked from her eyes to her lips. "I thought that was what I wanted," he said in a voice that was low and tense and just a bit surprised, "but now—" With a smooth, strong movement, he drew her against his body. "Now I want this."

He closed his mouth over hers in a kiss that was deep and hungry.

Chapter 6

The shock of delight was still there, the same sensation as when he had kissed her in the shopping mall, that stunning initial moment of passion and recognition—and surprise at both. Sam released her wrist and slid his arms around her, running one hand up her spine to cradle her head and wrapping the other around her waist to pull her against his body from breast to knees.

She couldn't have put into words what was happening to her, but she was conscious of every little detail. She felt the strong muscles flex in his arm as he drew her even closer. She felt his fingers threading into her hair, tipping her face slightly to the side as he slanted his mouth across hers, deepening the kiss.

He stroked his tongue over her lips, and when they parted softly at the touch he stroked again, across the edge of her teeth. She pressed a fraction closer, but that small sign was enough to release Sam from the control he'd held over himself. He plundered her mouth, and as her knees dissolved, Jessie wrapped her arms around his neck and clung.

She hadn't felt this kind of reaction to a man since she had met Charlie. This was the same emotion, and yet it wasn't, for she was no longer the innocent, rather sheltered girl of nineteen. When Sam kissed her she went up in flames, burning with a dangerous, seductive brew of wanting and wariness. It was no longer his surface resemblance to Charlie that made a hash of her defenses, it was the tall, tough, quick-tempered man himself.

He tightened his arm around her waist and tangled his fingers in her hair as he let his lips drift over the velvety skin of her cheek to her throat. Her head fell back, and he stroked his lips to and fro over the spot where the pulse beat frantically beneath the skin.

"Mr. King!" Kerry's shout from the hallway preceded her into the kitchen. "I drew you a picture of a cat, and some flowers and a rainbow, and I colored 'em with my markers."

When Kerry burst through the swinging door three seconds later, Jessie had wrenched herself out of Sam's arms and was standing with her back to the room, gripping the edge of the counter so hard her knuckles were white.

"Thank you, Kerry." Sam's voice was rough, and he coughed before he spoke again. "Is this Cat?" He pointed to a spiky gray creature in one corner.

"Uh-huh." Kerry nodded hard. "I made a flower garden for him to sit in. Are you sure he doesn't have a real name?"

"That is his real name. Cat."

Jessie half listened to their conversation while she concentrated on breathing evenly, on slowing her racing heartbeat, on willing the heated color out of her cheeks.

She didn't turn until she was sure she had her face under control. Then she smiled at Kerry and raked her fingers roughly through her hair to straighten it. She looked everywhere but at Sam.

"It's time to say good-night, Kerry."

"Aww, Mom!"

When Kerry was bathed and tucked in, her story read and good-night kisses given, Jessie returned to the living room to find Sam sitting on the sofa, nursing a cup of coffee. Another cup was waiting on the table.

Jessie sat in the armchair opposite him and took a long sip. After a moment, Sam set down his cup and leaned forward.

"Jessie, in the kitchen, I didn't mean—"

"I don't want to talk about it," she said, interrupting him. When she put her cup down, it rattled in its saucer. "There's really nothing to discuss."

Sam thought of the volcano that kiss had unleashed. He didn't want that any more than she did. He didn't want involvement with any woman, much less one he was working with, but passion was a force he understood. Though he seldom allowed himself to surrender to it, he understood it and he knew that passion, once discovered, could not be so easily banished.

"All right," he said after a moment. "We won't get into that now. We still have some work to do." He took a palm-size tape recorder from his inside coat pocket and set it on the low table between them. "I need a statement, in your own words, of what happened this evening. Are you ready?"

Jessie took another gulp of coffee. "Okay."

Sam switched on the recorder and gave the date and time and both their names. "We're speaking in Mrs. Ames's living room," he said. "Mrs. Ames, will you tell me what happened when you left work this evening?"

She cleared her throat. "Well, I left my office a little after five today—"

"Can you be more specific about the time?"

"Between five-fifteen and five-thirty."

"Thank you. Go on, please."

It took nearly an hour to give her statement, with Sam occasionally prompting her for details. When it was over, Jessie felt as if she'd lived through all the tension and fear again. She was tired and hoarse, and she drank deeply of her cold coffee, grateful for anything that could moisten her dry throat.

"Okay." His voice was full of satisfaction as he clicked the machine off and took out the tiny cassette. "I'll get this transcribed in the morning, and then we'll see about the next step."

"I assume that'll be Leonid telling me he has a check ready. That's where we left the negotiations."

"That's where *you* left them. Leonid has to report to his higher-ups and get approval for anything he does. Since trying to lowball you on the money didn't work, he'll report in and get his new orders. We may be able to use that to our advantage."

"Use the money?" Jessie was confused.

"Use the fact that Leonid can't make decisions on his own." Sam's smile faded into a frown. "I wish we'd had the chance to put a tail on him. We might have learned something."

"But we *didn't* have the chance." Something in her voice made him look up. "And please don't start again. I did the best I could, and I'm not going to apologize for it anymore."

He held her gaze for several seconds, then nodded. "All right. I accept that you couldn't call, but I still don't like it. It all worked out in the end, but it was a damn dangerous thing to do. I'll have to make sure it doesn't happen again."

That was fine with Jessie. She hadn't enjoyed being on her own with Leonid. She glanced at the clock on the mantel. Sam followed her gaze and swore under his breath.

"It's late," Jessie said as they both stood. "If there's nothing more you need..."

"We've finished with Leonid and his pals." With a casual ease, he caught her arm, halting her on her way out of the room and swinging her around to face him. "But that's not all there is to say."

Jessie looked at him and felt a shiver slide down her spine. She shook her head as she spoke. "Sam, there's no point in getting into that."

"There's no point in pretending it didn't happen." His voice dropped lower, and he drew her toward him. "We both know that it did." With a gentle yet irresistible pressure, he brought her fully into his arms. "And we'll both wonder how it would be..."

"Sam, no..." Her protest was a whisper, easily ignored.

"How it would be if it happened again." His head lowered slowly, and at the last moment her lids fluttered down, her chin tipped up and she met his mouth. The kiss was slow and deep and sweet, so sweet. It went on and on, and when it ended there was nothing at all to say.

Sam traced a fingertip down her cheek and left her standing in the middle of her living room, stunned.

"You've been keeping secrets from me."

When Marcie White greeted her at the door, all Jessie could say was "Huh?"

"Your new *friend*, remember? The one who had dinner with you and Kerry last night?" Smiling broadly, Jessie's neighbor watched her walk inside. From the back of the house came the sounds of children playing.

Jessie stopped, turned and grinned resignedly. "Kerry's been talking." It wasn't a question, and Marcie laughed.

"Kerry never stops talking. She's told us at great length about Mr. King and his cat, and how he ate tamale pie, and she made him some pictures, and everybody had a good time." Marcie waited, her head cocked expectantly to the side. "So what happened that Kerry didn't tell me about?"

"It doesn't sound as if there was anything that Kerry didn't tell you about," Jessie said dryly. "My daughter's better than the Associated Press."

"Oh, come on, Jessie, tell me about this guy. When did you meet him, and where? How did you two get to know each other? What does he do? Does he work at Anchor? How late did he stay—"

"Marcie, come on!" Jessie protested. "He just came to dinner last night, that's all."

Marcie rolled her eyes. "Oh, sure. How did you meet him?"

"We just met, casually. A couple of months ago."

"Okay. What does he do? What's his job?"

Jessie shrugged. "He's a writer. He's working on a screenplay." She couldn't quite meet Marcie's eyes, afraid the lie would show in her own. Talking about a man in her life would have made her uncomfortable in any case, but this felt so artificial, like reading a script.

"A writer? Really?" Marcie's eyes were alight. "What's his name? Maybe I've seen it on a movie or something."

"His name's King. Sam King."

"Sam King." Marcie nodded her approval. "I like it. What's his middle name?"

Jessie shrugged. "I don't know."

"Ahhh." Marcie nodded again, knowingly this time, and said in a voice heavy with innuendo, "You've been too busy with other things to find out."

"*Marcie!* I haven't known him long, but he's a nice man and I like him. That's all there is to it, okay?" She tried to make the assertion convincing, but she could feel a betraying blush heat her cheeks.

Marcie watched her color, her grin widening. "Whatever you say, Jessie, but I think the lady doth protest too much."

Jessie knew that Marcie was right. Her feelings for Sam King weren't something she could treat casually. But he was the FBI agent charged with working on her "case," and she was crazy to have feelings for him. Absolutely crazy.

She was still thinking about those feelings when she put the key into her back door lock. She turned it clockwise, as usual, but something felt different. It moved too easily, and there was no soft click as the bolt disengaged from the door frame.

She pushed the door open, then closed it again and locked it. When she unlocked it this time, she could feel the bolt's movement distinctly. Her mouth went dry, and she swallowed hard.

Kerry stood watching curiously. "What's the matter, Mom?"

"Nothing, honey. I just thought the lock felt funny." Jessie's voice was pitched higher than usual. The door had been unlocked. She opened it again but didn't hold it wide for Kerry to enter. "It's such a nice afternoon, Kerry, why don't you just stay out here and play on the swings while I fix dinner?"

"Don't you want me to change clothes?"

Changing out of school clothes before playing was a firm rule, but this time Jessie shook her head. "Not today, honey. You go on."

"Okay!"

While Kerry sprinted across the yard to the swing set, Jessie turned the knob and slowly, warily, opened the door.

Heart pounding, mouth dry, she moved quietly through the house, looking into each room, each closet. When she finished, back in the kitchen, she knew she was alone. Whoever had been there was gone now.

But who *had* been in her house, and why? There were none of the obvious signs of burglary, no overturned furniture or dumped-out drawers, but something was not quite right. She looked around again, more carefully this time, and she began to see the signs.

Though nothing was overturned or broken, little things were out of place, the kind of things only she would have noticed. A row of glass jars on the kitchen counter that held rice and macaroni were normally arranged in order of the frequency with which she used them. Spaghetti was always closest to the stove, oatmeal farthest away, but now the jars were reordered, the spaghetti and the rice in different places.

What else had they touched? She moved quickly around the kitchen, then through the rest of the house again, noting the tiny differences.

Books had been taken from the shelves in the living room and then replaced, making marks in the light film that had accumulated since she'd last dusted. Bottles on her vanity table had been moved just slightly from their accustomed places, and even the items in the bathroom medicine cabinet were shifted out of place.

When she returned to the kitchen this time, she went directly to the telephone and dialed with shaking fingers.

Sam was sitting at his desk, staring blindly at the transcript of Jessie's statement. It had been on his desk when he'd gotten back from a meeting this morning. He'd turned to the first page, started to read and found that just reading her words brought back the whole evening, the debriefing, the dinner, the argument—and the kisses.

Oh, those kisses. It was hard to believe that something so powerful had been born of a simple kiss. But there was nothing simple about it, was there? He posed the question to himself, half in irony, half in anger. He, who avoided any sort of emotional involvement, had been rocked right down to the ground by a kiss.

Sam knew he was attractive to women. From the time he'd begun to get his growth, at fifteen, girls and then women had looked at him with a sort of unspoken speculation in their eyes. By the time he was seventeen, the early promise of height, strength and good looks had become something that the giggly girls who kissed him in back seats couldn't resist. At eighteen he'd been propositioned by a business acquaintance of his father's, an attractive woman in her mid-thirties.

He had been a fairly sophisticated eighteen, but that had shocked him. It hadn't shocked him enough to keep him from taking what the business acquaintance was so clearly eager to give, but enough to keep him from doing anything stupid. Enough to keep him from falling in love.

Looking back on it from the distance of sixteen years, he had to smile. He'd received his initiation to sex from a woman who'd known exactly what she was doing and who had undoubtedly been relieved when he hadn't insisted on following her around in puppylike adoration after their single night together.

Sam had been too smart for that. He'd seen love, and he knew what it could do. It could make a mockery of a man who was otherwise strong and self-assured, could shred his dignity, shatter his pride, make him weak, despised by friends, shamed before his family. Love could destroy a man. It had destroyed his father.

Sam shook his head at his thoughts. He wasn't going to let love anywhere near him, and he wasn't going to let lust fog his mind, either. The ground might have moved when he had kissed Jessie Ames last night, but it was damn well not going to move again.

He pushed away thoughts of soft lips and soft skin and forced himself to concentrate on the transcript. It wasn't easy, but he had nearly finished reading when his phone rang.

"King."

"Sam?" He didn't need to ask who the tense, scared voice belonged to. She spoke carefully, clearly all too aware that unfriendly ears might be listening to the conversation. "I know you were going to work late tonight, but do you think you could stop by here for a while? Kerry and I made brownies for you."

"Thank you, I'd like that." He tried to inject some natural-sounding eagerness into his reply. "I'm glad you called. My late meeting was canceled, so I can come right over."

"Okay!" Her effort to sound enthusiastic wasn't much more convincing than his, but she was trying. "When should we look for you?"

"Anytime. I can leave now."

"Oh, good!" Her relief was plain. "We'll see you soon."

He must have set some kind of record for getting from Westwood to Woodland Hills in rush-hour traffic, Sam thought as he stopped in Jessie's driveway with a jerk. The trip had only taken thirty-five minutes.

It must have seemed an eternity to Jessie, for she hurried out her front door just as he got out of the car. She was anxious and he didn't want her anxiety to show. He hesitated only a moment before walking quickly to meet her and take her in his arms.

She stiffened as he kissed her, more in surprise than rejection, but then her lips softened and her hands came up to cling to his sleeves. This was for the sake of the operation, he told himself, a way to mislead anyone who might be watching. The rush of heat, the sudden acceleration of his heartbeat and the urge to hold her close and kiss her until he forgot anything else—that was nothing but biology, and biology was easily ignored.

It wasn't as easy as he'd have liked to loosen his grip and walk her to the front door. He put his arm around her shoulders and bent as though to whisper sweet nothings in her ear. "What's wrong? Why did you call?"

She glanced at him, then took a deep breath, pushing aside her reaction to that kiss. When she spoke, her voice was steady.

"Someone was in my house today." She showed him the details she'd noticed, and then he conducted his own search. He wouldn't have seen the small disorders she had discovered, but he found something more in the living room.

"Well, well." He had tipped a table lamp over and was exploring the inside of the base. Jessie looked around to see him remove a tiny metal disk. "Will you look at this?"

She looked and shivered, then watched, puzzled, as he pulled a tiny wire out of the disk and dropped it in his shirt pocket. "Sam, what are you going to do?"

"Nothing—for now. How about getting pizza for dinner? I doubt if you feel like cooking."

She held up trembling hands to show him and sighed. "If I turned on the stove tonight I'd probably burn the house down."

"Okay. What's the best pizza place around here?"

"Guido's. Sam?" She caught his sleeve when he turned toward the back door to call Kerry who he'd seen playing outside.

"Yes?"

"What are you going to do with that?" She indicated his shirt pocket.

"We'll deal with it after dinner."

After Kerry was tucked into bed Jessie sagged tiredly on the couch beside Sam, leaned back, then glanced at him. "Can we talk?"

"Without being overheard, you mean?" he asked, and she nodded. "Yes, we can. I went over the room with a fine-tooth comb while you were putting Kerry to bed, and I didn't find any other bugs."

"What about the one you found? Are you going to put it back in the lamp?"

"No, I have plans for this one." He grinned at her like a boy planning a prank. "But right now we can talk without being heard."

She nodded slowly, and he saw her swallow. "But they'll want to hear, so they'll come and put more bugs in." Her voice wobbled, and she turned her face away, blinking hard. "Do you know how much I hate this?"

"Jessie . . ."

"They walk in and out of my house whenever they want. They look in my closets, go through my things. They plant bugs in my house, in my phone." She took a deep, shaky breath and turned dark, frightened eyes on him. Her hands were clenched into fists in her lap. "I have to live here, knowing they can violate my home, my privacy, any time they want to, and I hate it, Sam. I hate it!"

Her voice cracked on the words, but before she could turn away again he reached across to her. "Come here." He pulled her close, her face against his shoulder, his warm, comforting arms around her. "I know," he murmured. "I know you hate it, anybody would, but you're not in this alone. I'm going to be with you all the way."

"I know, but—" She bit her lip. "It's just times like today, coming home and finding that someone has been in my house. . . ."

"I know." He hesitated. "But you don't have to be alone, if you can't handle it."

She looked up at him, frowning in confusion. "What do you mean?"

"I could move in here," he told her. "I could live with you until this is over."

Chapter 7

Jessie shoved herself away from him, shaking her head vigorously.

"No," she said quickly. "You don't need to do that. I can handle it. I'll get used to the bugs and things if I have to. Kerry and I are okay. We'll be fine."

Because he knew there would be no physical danger to either Jessie or Kerry until the program was delivered, and because both the local police and a couple of FBI agents were keeping an eye on the house, Sam let her convince him to go back home. He did so with feelings that were uncomfortably mixed.

"Damn!" He flung open his kitchen door with a shove that sent it banging against the wall. Cat shot from his bed atop the refrigerator with a howl of protest and disappeared into the darkened living room. Sam glanced after him and swore again as he dropped his mail on the tile countertop. He was angry with himself, and he didn't like the feeling.

He should have left Jessie Ames's house with nothing more than a deep sigh of relief. He liked the kind of women he could walk away from and forget, but he was already having trouble pushing Jessie out of his mind. The last thing he wanted was to spend every night and most of each day in her house. He should have walked away from her with a load off his mind and a smile on his face.

He shouldn't have hesitated at her door, fighting the urge to kiss her goodbye. He shouldn't have paused at the end of the drive, looking back at the comfortable home with its ruffled curtains and neat flower beds. He shouldn't have thought about how full that house was—full of light and color and love. He shouldn't have thought about how empty his own house would seem after being at hers.

If it weren't for Cat, no one would care if I never came home.

Sam shoved the thought aside. He didn't want anyone to care. That was the first crack in a man's defenses. If he cared, if he lusted, if he loved, he was weakened. He didn't feed Cat because he cared, he fed the animal because it was the humane thing to do. If Cat had been a clingy, demanding pet like a dog, Sam would have unloaded him at the animal shelter and let someone else get sappy and emotional over him.

He didn't need that kind of tie, and he wouldn't allow himself that kind of weakness. It was true he wanted her, and in ways that both surprised and alarmed him, but he would deal with that. He'd keep Jessie safe until this case was wrapped up, but he wouldn't let a big-eyed woman with a problem get under his skin. He damn well wouldn't.

When Cat jumped onto his lap, he absently moved a stack of mail aside to make room. Cat turned in a circle, then settled himself comfortably. He waited a moment, then butted Sam's arm impatiently with his head. Sam responded automatically, dropping one hand to the thick, silky fur. After a moment, a rumbling purr began to vibrate in Cat's chest.

Leonid didn't wait long to contact her. Jessie got a call at home barely a week later.

"Hello?" She tucked the kitchen phone between her ear and shoulder and turned down the flame under the spaghetti sauce, stirring continuously to keep it from scorching.

"The Red Baron Lounge," said a muffled male voice without preamble. "Tomorrow at six o'clock."

Jessie's hand hung motionless over the bubbling pot. "The Red Baron." She had to clear her throat. "At six. I think I can make it."

"You will be there. And you will be alone." There was a click, followed by the buzz of the dial tone.

Sam wouldn't have any cause to complain about her going off on her own this time, she thought the next evening. She didn't see him when she walked out of the building, but she knew he was there, and the knowledge comforted her.

The sky was gilded with late-afternoon sunlight, and the air was unusually smog-free for late September. It was far too lovely a day for the ugly business she was on her way to conduct.

She tried to let the beauty outside calm and encourage her, tried to think herself into her part and steel herself to face Leonid calmly. Somehow it helped to know that he was going to try to frighten her or throw her off balance. It hardened her determination to defeat him.

Leonid was there before her, waiting at a table in a remote corner of the restaurant-bar. She strolled across the room with a queenly air, took the chair opposite his and sat back comfortably.

"When will—" Leonid began, but she cut him off imperiously.

"I'll have a ginger ale."

Leonid's breath hissed between his teeth, but he clamped his lips shut on whatever he might have said. After a moment he nodded and went to get her drink.

Jessie waited, letting her gaze run idly over the other patrons, wondering which of them was her FBI guardian angel. The crowd was about evenly mixed between young gray-suited executive types and more casually dressed students from the community college a few blocks away. None of them looked like her image of an FBI agent, and almost any of them could have been her undercover protector.

Whoever it was, she hoped he or she was keeping a close eye on Leonid. She glanced up as he returned to the table with drinks for them both and accepted his without thanking him.

"So what's the topic this time?" she asked after tasting her drink.

"The topic?"

"What this meeting's about," she elaborated with a touch of impatience. "Why I'm here."

"Do you have the program? You have had some time, as you wanted. What do you have for me?"

Jessie sipped her ginger ale, making him wait a moment for her answer. She lowered her glass and looked coolly across at him. "I have some of it. A small part."

"How much of it?" He spoke calmly, but the quick flare of interest in his eyes gave him away.

"About ten percent." She told him what she and Sam and Mr. Howell had agreed upon. "The beginning. When you have the first payment for me, I'll be happy to give it to you."

"Where is it?" Leonid glanced at the briefcase resting on the chair beside her.

Jessie shook her head, a half smile denting her mouth at his assumption. "I'm not a fool, Mr. Antonov. It's in a safe place, not at my office or my home."

"It's good that you are careful. I would not want it to fall into the wrong hands." He smiled, and not pleasantly. "And, of course, you would not want anything to happen to that pretty daughter of yours."

"No," she said with a sharpness that covered the stab of icy terror she felt. "I don't want anything to happen to her." To regain some advantage, she reached into her purse and took out a small, shiny object. "Here." With a saccharine smile, she dropped the bug into Leonid's hand.

He jerked back, startled and angry. "What is this?"

"Oh, come on, Mr. Antonov. After all, I am familiar with electronic equipment. Finding this little toy wasn't hard." She rose, smiling coldly. "You can get in touch with me when you have the money," she said, and walked away.

She drove several blocks, then turned into a side street, stopped her car and switched the engine off with fingers that shook so hard she could barely grasp the key. The engine coughed into silence, and she pressed her hands to her cheeks as she leaned forward to rest her forehead on the steering wheel.

They couldn't, could they? They wouldn't, would they? Not Kerry. Anything but that. Not Kerry. She bit her lip, squeezed her eyes tightly shut and took slow, deep breaths, fighting for control.

"Miss?" At a tap on the car window she jerked her head up, startled. An elderly man stood on the sidewalk, peering into the car. "Miss, are you all right?"

Jessie sat straight in her seat and swiped her hands over her cheeks. "Yes. Yes, I'm fine."

"Well, I wondered. You looked like you was sick or something."

"I'm fine. Thank you for asking, though."

She managed a smile and reached for the key to start the engine. She had to drive to the end of the cul-de-sac to turn around, and he was still standing on the sidewalk when she drove past. She waved and he waved back, and she drove home thinking that there were still some people out there who cared about strangers. It made her feel a little better, but the core of icy terror lay heavy in her heart.

"Do you want to give up the operation?" Sam asked quietly. She'd told him what had happened and about her resulting fears.

Jessie looked at their joined hands. Her fingers were icy and still trembled a little, while his were warm and strong. She wanted to be strong herself, but his gesture of comfort meant more than he could know. She bit her lip, then shook her head slowly. "I thought about that while I was waiting for you to get here. My first impulse was to give it up, but the more I thought about it, the clearer it became that that's not the solution."

Sam watched her face. "Why isn't it?"

"Because it wouldn't keep Kerry safe. They think I'm going to give them something they want very badly. They don't know I'm setting them up, and they don't know I'm working with you. If I tell them I won't go through with it, all they'll see is that they're losing White Eagle. They'll try to do something to force me to turn it over. Instead of keeping Kerry safe, I'd be placing her in more danger."

He nodded, as if she were a pupil who had come up with the answer to a difficult question. "You're right. Until we have a handle on who these guys are, you'll be safest if they think you're cooperating."

"Yes." She looked up, her eyes dark with anguish. "That makes sense, but what if we're wrong? This is what I was afraid of at the beginning. What about Kerry? How can I keep her safe?"

Sam released her hands and sat back in his chair, putting a little distance between them, both physically and emotionally. When he spoke, his voice was cool, and it was once again Special Agent King speaking. "I'll stay here," he said, "in this house, with you and Kerry, until this is over."

Jessie looked up, her eyes wide and alarmed. Even as she opened her mouth to refuse, he caught her hands, talking quickly.

"I know. I know it's the last thing you want. You don't want to have to make embarrassing explanations to the neighbors. You don't want some stranger in the house. It's an awkward situation, and I wouldn't even suggest it if I didn't think it was necessary. But I'll be here, to prevent any more bugging or burglary, to watch over Kerry, to keep you both secure."

"I don't know." Jessie pulled her hands away and folded them in her lap. "How on earth could I explain to people why I had a man living in my house?"

"We went over that, remember? We'll use the cover story that I'm a free-lance writer working on a screenplay. We met weeks ago, we've gotten close, and if anyone wants to know more than that it's none of their damn business."

He said it without heat, but with a kind of implacability that, unexpectedly, had laughter bubbling up in Jessie where before there had been only fear.

He was right. She owed no explanations to anyone. She was a grown woman, entitled to live her own life. And with him there, she wouldn't be alone with her thoughts, and with the knowledge that evil men were walking in and out of her house whenever they wished.

She looked up at Sam and almost managed a smile.

The relief was so great that it overshadowed all the complications—at least for a while. The complications came rushing back, though, when she opened her front door to find Sam standing there, suitcase in hand, carrying his clothes and toilet things, prepared to stay the night.

"Hi." Wishing her voice wasn't so high and thin, she unlocked the screen door and pushed it open for him. He bent and picked up a good-sized wicker basket fastened shut with a metal clip and followed her in.

"I hope you don't mind, but I brought Cat. There was nobody I could ask to go in and feed him. I won't let him bother you, though. I can put him in the garage."

Jessie dropped to her knees beside the basket, from which a protesting "Rowr" arose. She glanced up at Sam, her face lit by the first honest smile he'd seen since Leonid had threatened Kerry.

"Are you kidding? Do you know what kind of grief I'd get from my daughter? She'll want him to sleep on her bed and wear her doll clothes."

Sam smiled at the idea. "I don't know how he'll react to that. If he doesn't like something he just disappears. I don't think he'll hold still for being dressed up."

"I'll warn her." Jessie poked a fingertip into one of the holes in the openwork section of the cat basket and was rewarded by a soft puffing of air as the cat sniffed, inspecting her.

"Do you know much about cats?"

"No. My dad was allergic to cats and dogs, so we always had birds or fish for pets."

"Like those?" He nodded at the tank bubbling quietly in the living room. Several brightly colored fish swam in lazy circles inside it. "I'd better put him in the garage."

"You don't need to do that," she protested. "It's dirty, and it's too cold."

Sam left the cat basket on the floor and walked over to examine the fish tank. "You know about cats and fish."

"That's a good lid. The man at the pet store said it was the kind that little kids can't get open. I bought the tank when Kerry was three and I didn't want her taking the fishies out to play."

"You sure? I don't want Cat eating the fishies, either."

"He won't." Jessie looked at the basket. "Can we let him out now?"

She didn't look at Sam. It was easier to concentrate on the cat than think about Sam sleeping in her house, in the room next to hers.

He was there to keep her safe, but now that he'd arrived she wasn't sure if her peace of mind would be increased by having him around, or if it would be shattered completely.

Sam crouched beside her, his knee and shoulder brushing against her as he reached down to unfasten the catch on top of the basket. He opened the clasp and folded the two-piece lid open. Cat crouched inside, apparently waiting to see if freedom was really his, or if there was a catch. After a moment of gazing up at them both with a basilisk's stare, he jumped smoothly out.

Jessie watched him pace around the room, peering under the furniture, jumping up to check the magazines and ornaments on the tabletops. "Isn't he pretty?" she asked no one in particular.

Sam looked at the stray he'd taken to the vet in a half-starved and decidedly shaky condition and hid a smile. Cat, with his big, blunt head, ragged ears and solidly muscular body, was hardly "pretty."

On the other hand, that was the perfect word for Jessamyn Ames. Her glossy mahogany-brown hair swung across her cheeks as she leaned forward, watching Cat explore his new surroundings. Her lips were parted in a small smile, her cheeks tinged with pink, and Sam thought he had never seen anyone so lovely. Mixed with the simple lust he felt, though, was another, more dangerous emotion. Tenderness.

She extended a tentative hand toward Cat, unsure whether he would accept the caress or bite her, and Sam reached around her, taking her wrist lightly to hold her hand out, palm up. His chest brushed the slim curve of her back, and he rested a hand on her shoulder to steady himself.

"This way," he said close to her ear. "Just let him sniff your fingers."

She glanced at Sam and found his face very close to hers, his gaze on her mouth. Her cheeks warmed, and she turned quickly back to the cat, her silky hair brushing his lips. Sam felt her stiffen and ease slightly away from him, and he fought the urge to pull her back. Instead he continued to hold her hand.

Cat came over to investigate, and Jessie laughed softly as he sniffed her fingertips. Cat, reassured, put his head to one side and rubbed his cheek along her hand again.

"Does that mean that he likes me?" Sam felt the tenderness welling up inside him again. She might have been Kerry's age, her eyes sparkling with girlish wonder.

"Yeah." Sam's voice was husky, but she didn't seem to notice. "He likes you."

He released her arm and got to his feet, putting some distance between them. Cat wasn't the only one with friendly feelings, but his feelings wouldn't cause the kind of problems that Sam's would.

"It's late," Jessie said and stood. "I'll show you your room."

When she'd finished, she hesitated in her bedroom doorway, looking at Sam standing one door down the hall. "Do you have everything you need?"

"Yes, thank you."

"I put towels in the bathroom. There's a basket beside the sink for Kerry's tub toys. Just dump them in."

"Okay."

There was a moment of taut silence.

"Well, good night."

"Good night, Jessamyn." Sam went into the guest room and quietly closed the door.

Jessie hesitated for another moment, then went into her own room. It was large, sunny in the afternoons, with a nook at the far end where she had an armchair and reading lamp. It had always been her refuge, but just now it seemed very empty. She walked into the smallish master bathroom, flicked on the light and regarded the woman in the mirror with surprise.

Her cheeks were flushed, her eyes were sparkling, and a small smile curved her lips. She looked like a teenager after her first date, bubbling with excitement and new emotions.

"Oh, brother," she whispered, and leaned back against the linen cupboard door. This was crazy. She was wildly attracted to the FBI agent on her case, and now he was living in her house. A recipe for disaster, at the very least.

But it would be disastrous only if he was attracted to her, as well. She'd thought he was, but now she wasn't so sure. She'd felt a distance in him in the last couple of days. He'd said he was going to *act* like her boyfriend, and maybe that was all he was doing. She was interested, but there was no reason to assume that he was, too.

And as for him living in her house, she'd just deal with it. He was there to protect her and Kerry. They were playing roles, and she had to remember that was all it was, playacting.

Easy enough to say. Not so easy to remember at one-thirty in the morning.

Jessie heard, with what she jokingly referred to as her "Mom's ears," a small sound from Kerry's room. Kerry frequently tossed off her covers during the night, and if she got cold she would wake up and then be groggy for school in the morning. Jessie was practiced at getting up in the dark of night, walking down the hall to her daughter's room to cover her warmly again and returning to bed, all without ever becoming fully conscious.

She padded down the hall, which was dimly illuminated by the small night-light on the wall about ten inches above the floor. Her eyes were nearly closed, her brain in that comfortable state that meant she could go promptly back to sleep when she returned to her own bed. She didn't really need to wake up for this little task, any—

A heavy hand fell on her shoulder, spinning her around and against the wall. "What the hell is going on?"

For a moment Jessie froze, her heart in her throat. She jumped and gasped, then pressed one hand to her throat and fought to steady her breathing while she waited for the feeling of pure terror to ease.

"What on earth did you do *that* for?" she whispered.

"I thought somebody had broken in."

"After the way you barricaded this house?" He'd insisted on checking all the windows and doors and putting extra locks and alarms on those he deemed less than reliable. That had encompassed most of them, and Jessie hadn't known whether to be relieved or annoyed. Just now, she was annoyed. She'd been scared half to death in her own hallway, and she was definitely upset. "A fly couldn't break in here."

"Then what are you doing up?" The fact that they were talking in whispers in no way muted the angry demand in Sam's voice.

"I'm going in to cover Kerry," she replied with heavy patience. "She kicks her covers off at night and then wakes up because she's cold. Now, do I have your permission to do that?" She glanced at him with an expression that was meant to convey schoolmarmish annoyance, but she knew she didn't pull it off.

She hadn't really looked at him before; she'd been too angry. Now she looked, and she went still.

Somehow, seeing him dressed in business suits hadn't prepared her for the sight of him wearing nothing but what looked to be a pair of running shorts. They were red—what there was of them—and they left a great deal of Samuel King uncovered.

She tried not to look at the deep, broad chest liberally dusted with hair, the heavy shoulders and powerful arms, the strong neck, the long, tanned, muscular legs.

She tried not to look, but she wasn't blind, not to the size and strength of him, and not to the sudden stillness of his face as he looked down at her. Her nightgown was thin cotton, washed and worn until it was sheer, nearly transparent, barely concealing breasts, hips and waist. Jessie saw the quick blaze of heat in his eyes and felt the sweet heaviness low in her stomach, the tension and the heat.

The hand on her shoulder tightened, drawing her fractionally closer. Her treacherous body softened and swayed.

"Jessamyn," he whispered thickly, and kissed her mouth.

Chapter 8

Their lips touched, lightly, hesitantly. Then Sam lifted Jessie's chin with his hand and slanted his mouth over hers, deepening the kiss with a kind of desperation that was all the more intense because it had to be silent. He didn't wrap his arms around her or pull her into an embrace. He simply kept one hand beneath her chin, tilting her face up.

His other hand drifted from her shoulder to her collarbone, then lower, to the wide, scooped neckline of her gown. He traced along it, ruffling the narrow eyelet trim, making her shiver with a fingertip's touch. Then he brushed the eyelet aside, slipping his fingertip beneath the thin cotton and over the soft upper curve of her breast. Jessie's body began to drift toward his as if it were drawn by a magnet.

She reached for him, but he still didn't take her in his arms. The hand that had rested under her chin slid around to cradle her nape, his fingers tangling in her hair.

He slid his other hand back along the cotton and lace to her shoulder and pushed the strap down. It slid off her upper arm until it came to rest at the bend of her elbow. The fabric clung tenuously to the peak of her breast. Jessie's breathing was quick and shallow, and her heart was thundering against her ribs with such force that she thought it might break free.

Sam stroked her naked shoulder, then let his fingertips drift very slowly across her upper chest. Jessie couldn't breathe. Her heart hammered, the blood roared in her ears, and she wanted him to touch her so badly that she nearly cried out with need. He slipped his fingertip beneath the lace, lifted it away from its one source of support and let it fall.

The gown sank down, and Sam's hand followed to cover her small breast. Her grasp was muffled by his mouth, but the response of her body was unmistakable. Her back arched, her breasts swelled, her nipples tightened to aching buds. The skin he caressed was hot, and it heated still more as he stroked his fingertips upward, lifting the slight weight of her breast, then releasing it, her nipple brushing across his fingers with tantalizing effect.

This time she gasped aloud. He'd lifted his mouth from hers and leaned back slightly, looking down at her in the uncertain glow of the night-light. It highlighted the shape of her breast, throwing the erect nipple into stark relief. Jessie's instinctive shyness warred with arousal and lost. She reached for Sam again, her hands on either side of his waist, and pulled him close.

The soft, electrifying caress of his body hair against her single naked breast was followed immediately by the press of powerful muscle as he gathered her in his arms at last, kissing her with a passion that made nonsense of her idea that the attraction between them might not be mutual.

Jessie strained to stand on tiptoe, pressing her body up into the curve of his, digging her fingers into the hard mus-

cle at his waist as she clung to him, their mouths searching,
seeking, inflaming.

The sound that tore them roughly apart was no more than
a rustle and mutter from Kerry's room. Jessie shoved herself out of Sam's arms, yanking her nightgown back onto
her shoulder even as he tensed and pushed her behind him,
all his instincts telling him unexplained sounds meant danger.

"It's Kerry." Jessie pushed at the arm holding her against
the wall. It was rigid as steel. She pushed harder. "Let me
go, before she wakes up."

His arm relaxed a bit, but he still didn't release her. "Are
you sure nothing's wrong?"

Jessie half smiled into the darkness. "I'm sure. Kids kick
their covers off all the time."

"All right." He dropped his arm and stepped away.

The night air felt cool on her skin, and it helped clear her
head. She took a quick step back, deeper into the darkness,
her arms crossed protectively over her breasts, her head
down so that he couldn't see her face.

"You can go back to bed," she said quickly as she slipped
past him to Kerry's door. "There's nothing to worry about."

"I'll wait until you're finished."

Wait for what? Jessie glanced warily at Sam as she
reached for the doorknob, but his face was in shadow, and
she could read nothing there. She turned away and went to
Kerry. She had kicked the bedclothes off one side of the bed
and was hanging half off the mattress herself. Jessie put her
back in the center, covered her up to her chin and tucked her
stuffed dog in beside her. She stroked Kerry's hair lightly,
gave the quilt a final pat and padded back to the hall.

Sam was standing in the shadows, but he stepped forward into the light when she pushed the door quietly closed.

"Do you do this every night?" His face was that of a
stranger, empty of anything but a distant courtesy.

"Just about." Jessie stood facing him across three feet of hallway and fought the urge to cover herself with her hands. She wouldn't have been embarrassed in front of the man who had kissed and caressed her, but this was a different person.

She might have asked what he expected to prove by ignoring what had happened between them, but it was two in the morning, and she wasn't up to it. "Sometimes Kerry gets up for a drink of water, or because she's had a bad dream."

He nodded. "I thought about putting pressure sensors in the house, but if you're up and around at night that's no good."

"Pressure sensors?" she asked, but he had already turned back to his own room.

"Don't worry about it," he said, almost curtly. "I'll see you in the morning." He disappeared into his room, closing the door quietly but definitely behind him.

And good night to you, too. Jessie went back to her own cold bed, to lie wakeful and wondering.

"Mom?"

"Hmm?"

"How come you're all dressed already?"

Jessie looked up from her coffee and the newspaper. Kerry was regarding her with acute interest, comparing the mother she saw neatly dressed in a skirt and tailored polo sweater with the one who usually ate breakfast in her slip and a light robe.

"We have company, Kerry. Mr. King is staying here."

"*He is?* Can I go see him?" She bounced eagerly out of her chair.

Jessie caught her arm and steered her back to the table. "Finish your breakfast. You can see Mr. King when he gets up."

"But where is he?"

"I'm right here," Sam said from the doorway.

"Hi!" Kerry turned to kneel on her chair, grinning at him. "Are you visiting us? Mom said that's why she's got her clothes on instead of her robe. Because we have company."

"I see." Sam glanced at Jessie, and for a moment she saw a flicker of amused warmth. Then it was gone, replaced by distant courtesy. He went to the counter, poured some coffee into the cup Jessie had set out for him and started drinking it black.

"Would you like eggs, or bacon, or cereal?" Jessie asked. "I can cook something for you."

He glanced at her plate, which had a single slice of toast on it. "Toast and coffee is fine. I don't eat much in the mornings."

"I can fix it for—" She was half out of her chair when Sam held up his hand to stop her.

"I can make toast," he said, almost sharply. "Just tell me where the bread is."

"In the box." Jessie sank back onto her chair. "Over there."

"Right."

"What kind of jelly do you want?" Kerry put her empty cereal bowl in the sink and opened the refrigerator, revealing a row of jam and jelly jars.

"You got strawberry in there?"

"Yeah." She took out a fat jar and carried it over to him with great care. "Mom likes strawberry. She looks pretty, doesn't she? She put her clothes on for breakfast because you're here."

That got Jessie out of her chair. "Kerry, that's enough about my clothes, all right? I know Mr. King isn't interested in what I'm wearing." She steered Kerry toward the front door. "It's time for you to get your things into your backpack for school. The bus will be here any minute."

"Aww—"

"Scoot!" Kerry scooted, and Jessie turned to Sam, her cheeks warm with embarrassment. "I'm sorry about that. Kids find the strangest things interesting."

"It's all right." He looked her up and down as he put his plate on the table. "She was right, you know. That's a nice outfit."

Jessie glanced sharply at him. His words could have been complimentary, but his tone had been curt, as if he begrudged the admission. "Thank you," she said, her tone as cool as his, "but it's nothing special." She walked out of the room.

She'd calmed down by the time she put Kerry on the school bus.

"I'm going over to the office," Sam said, rinsing his cup at the sink. "I've got to finish some paperwork and report on what I'm doing here."

"Yes." She brushed a few crumbs off the table into her cupped hand. "We need to talk about that."

"There's no need." He turned away, looping a deep red tie over his head. "Nothing to talk about."

She watched his broad back. "You know better than that."

"Do you really think talking is going to accomplish anything?"

"I think it's better than trying to sweep things under the rug. They have a nasty way of sneaking back out again."

"So what do you have to say?" He turned around, adjusting the knot on his tie.

"We can't—" She flushed and looked down for a moment, then took a deep breath. "We can't pretend that it didn't happen. It did, and we need to talk about it."

He gave the tie a jerk. "We were in the hall, in the dark. Nature got the best of us for a minute."

"Nature, meaning sex?"

He frowned at her bluntness, then shrugged. "Sex, yes."

"And that's it?" Jessie's tone was mild, light and cold. "Just sex?"

"What else?"

"Just sex." She nodded after a moment. "I see. We're playacting at being lovers, and last night was nothing but sex." She considered. "In that case, Mr. King, you can save the playacting for the public and skip the sex."

Sam watched her, his eyes hard. "Nobody made any promises here."

"No." She managed a smile, but her eyes were bleak. "We didn't. We're here to catch Leonid and his bosses, and that's something we'll both have to remember."

It wasn't until she'd left and Sam was alone that he realized he wasn't relieved. He *should* have been relieved but instead he felt alone, almost lonely, as if he'd been close to something important and lost it.

When Jessie's phone buzzed, she had a thick printout unfolded in several big sections on her desk. She rummaged beneath one of them and found the intercom button. "Yes, Sally?"

"Phone call for you, Jessie. On line two."

"Okay, thanks." She unearthed the phone from beneath a stack of paper, punched the button and picked up the receiver. "Mrs. Ames."

"Tonight," said a brusque, male voice with a hint of a foreign accent. "At eight."

It was the message she'd been waiting for. Jessie felt her heart begin to pound, and her hand shook a little as she reached for a pencil and a notepad. Her voice was steady, though. "Where?"

"The Crazy Fox."

Again Jessie knew of the place, but she'd never been there. She didn't look forward to going to a hangout like that in the evening, but there wasn't a lot she could do about it, since someone else was picking the meeting places.

"All right," she told the anonymous caller. "I have to work late this evening, anyway. I'll go directly from here."

"Alone."

"I'm hardly likely to bring a bunch of friends," she retorted with heavy sarcasm. "I don't want an audience any more than you do. How will I know who I'm meeting?"

"You will know." There was a pause. "You will bring it?"

"The introduction."

"Bring it."

"Yes."

"You will be watched," he said, and there was a note in his voice that sent a chill over her skin. "Do not do anything foolish."

"I'm not a fool," Jessie said coolly.

"Good." She heard a click, then the buzz of an open line. Jessie took a deep, shaky breath and dialed a number quickly. It only rang once.

"Sam King."

"He called." She didn't bother to introduce herself. "It's tonight."

"What time?"

"Seven."

"I'll meet you." And he hung up.

In the days since Sam had moved into her house they had gone over their plan again and again. Jessie knew it inside out and backward, in all its variations, but still, as she packed her briefcase and locked her office, her hands were shaking.

She left her office at five-thirty, but instead of taking the elevator to the ground floor with everyone else, she went to the ladies' room, and stayed there. A couple of other people came and went, washing hands and refreshing lipstick.

She waited until she'd heard nothing from the hall outside for ten full minutes, then opened the cubicle door and tip-toed out. She peered outside, saw no one in the hall, and darted toward the service stairs.

It was a long climb to Mr. Howell's penthouse office, and she met Sam three flights up. She didn't hear his approach over the clatter of her heels on the metal stairs, and when he caught her arms from three steps above her, she nearly jumped out of her skin.

She started and jerked back, away from the hands that grasped her, and her feet slipped off the narrow steps.

Sam swore as she nearly pulled free, and grabbed at her upper arms. He was nearly overbalanced, himself, as he staggered down two steps before he could stop Jessie's backward fall down the stairs and bring both of them to a halt. He braced himself against the wall and hauled her against his chest, her feet an inch above the step as he wrapped his arms around her.

Jessie clutched his waist for dear life, her face against his chest, and above the pounding of her own frantic pulse, she could hear Sam's thundering heartbeat. Below her dangling feet, the stairs wound endlessly around and down. She didn't know how far she might have fallen before she stopped, but her imagination was having a field day with falling and tumbling and crashing into the unyielding steel posts and rails.

She felt the rumbling vibration in Sam's chest, but didn't realize he was speaking to her until he reached down to lift her face from his shirtfront. He still had one arm wrapped around her, hard as a steel bar, but though he was holding her securely, Jessie gasped and clutched at his back.

"It's okay. I've got you." He shifted his feet on the narrow, slippery stair tread, turning them both. "I'm going to set your feet on the step, okay?" Jessie nodded, but her fingers tightened on the small of his back as he eased her around until they were both standing securely. She didn't let go. "Are you okay?"

"Yes." Her voice was breathless, and she repeated herself, more firmly this time. "Yes. I'm okay."

"Well, what the hell did you nearly jump down the stairs for?" Remembered fear sharpened his voice. "And don't tell me you thought you could fly!"

"No, I didn't think I could fly! And what the hell did you grab me like that for? You scared me half to death!"

"I was just coming to get you. You didn't have to jump like that."

"You sneaked up on me. Of course I jumped." Jessie's voice was tart, but something warmed inside her. Sam might not be smiling at her, but at least they were talking, for the first time in days, for the first time since their bitter little confrontation in her kitchen.

Sam had done as she'd asked, dropping the loving act when they were alone and keeping his distance with such determination that Jessie was beginning to feel like a pariah. Though he was living in her house, they might have been miles apart. He barely spoke to her, and he hadn't touched her in days, not even in the most casual way. He avoided taking her arm while they walked or her hand to help her into a car.

He had done as she'd asked, and in doing so he'd managed to make her feel as if she were being punished. What her crime was, she didn't know. Or was she really the one he was punishing?

"Let's go up," she said abruptly, and started climbing again. Sam stayed two steps behind her, so his head was on a level with hers. She glanced at his profile from time to time, struck by a thought that had just occurred to her.

Was he punishing her, or himself? He'd kissed her with a passion that was almost desperate, that made a lie of his assertion that the only thing between them was sex. Did he really believe that? Was he fighting her, or his own feelings?

What she felt for Sam King went deeper than hormones. She hadn't been looking for a man when she'd called the FBI that night, but she was coming to realize that she'd found one, a man who could be both strong and tender, a man she cared about.

Though he'd been cold to Jessie, his coolness hadn't extended to Kerry. He had played games with her, read storybooks and listened with a seemingly bottomless patience to her chatter. He listened patiently when Jessie just couldn't face another list of what Kerry's friends' dolls had worn to school or another knock-knock joke.

Sam was patient with it all, though. He listened, he laughed, and he helped Kerry make friends with Cat, who now, to her delight, slept on her bed.

He wasn't a cold man, however hard he might try to be. He had feelings for Kerry, she knew. Did he also have feelings for Jessie, feelings he was trying to deny?

"What are you smiling at?" he demanded into the silence.

She looked back at him, startled. "Smiling?"

"Yeah. You're smiling to yourself. Care to let me in on the joke?"

She shook her head. "It's nothing. Just a thought." She reached the penthouse landing, and Sam motioned for her to step back. He eased the door open, peered out and then waved her through. Mr. Howell was ready for them. He held his office door open and ushered them inside. He closed the door quietly behind them and left the lights off in the outer office.

"I have the disks you said you needed, Jessie." He showed her to his desk, and seated her in his deep leather chair. "Can you do everything you need to here?"

She nodded. "I've been working on the changes at home. I just have to transfer them to the White Eagle disks."

"You only have half an hour," he reminded her.

"That's okay." Her smile hardened, and Sam could see the cold determination in her. "Half an hour is all I need."

Chapter 9

As she worked, Sam knew he was seeing a new side of Jessie.

In Marshall Howell's office she greeted the two agents who would provide backup, one of whom was a computer expert himself, then booted Mr. Howell's computer and got to work.

While she worked, the other men in the office talked quietly among themselves and Sam just stood back and watched her. His own understanding of computers was rudimentary at best, and what she was doing was as far removed from his sphere of expertise as astrophysics. It seemed to confuse even Mr. Howell.

Sam was more interested in Jessie herself. He had met her at a time when she'd been angry and fearful, had come to know her while she'd been under enormous stress and had failed utterly to see the real Jessie inside the woman made fragile by pressure and fear.

As she worked at the computer she outlined what she was doing in brief, staccato sentences. Sam could see that she worked with a combination of talent and logic, and with an intuition that allowed her to bypass them both and arrive at answers to seemingly insoluble problems. When Howell questioned her on a point, she explained, as a teacher would to a pupil, what she was doing. Howell accepted the reversal of roles without a murmur. She was the expert, after all. He was merely the boss.

And she was brilliant. Sam, possessed of a higher-than-average IQ, dean's list graduate of Harvard Law School, watched and listened and realized that while he was intelligent she was something more. He found himself both intimidated and intrigued.

He wasn't accustomed to being in the presence of such a powerful mind, and the fact that he'd come damn close to making love to the woman with that mind was even more odd. It had been easy for him to see her as a desirable female, a homemaker, a good mother, and then to dismiss her as just another woman. Adding genius to the mix made her unique, an intriguing puzzle.

"There." She sat back and studied the screen with satisfaction. "It's finished."

"That's all you're going to do to it?" asked John Kelley, one of Sam's fellow agents, the computer expert. He leaned closer to read the amber letters on the monitor.

"That's all I need to do. Nothing else in the introduction to this program is unique, and a lot of it is already on the market in one form or another. I set up the way the system will operate a piece of machinery, the plane, just as computers operate robots in factories."

"So even if they can't fly planes with it, they can take this back to the Eastern bloc and use it to operate robots?" Kelley wondered.

Jessie shook her head, smiled and punched a series of buttons. The machine hummed as it copied her altered program onto a blank computer disk. "I fixed that. It looks as if it ought to work, but it won't. It won't execute a long enough series of commands."

John nodded, and Jessie took out the disks and put them in paper envelopes. "That's it, then. This one's for you, Mr. Howell—" she handed it to him "—and this one's for Leonid."

She laid the disk aside and pressed her hands to her lower back, stretching to ease muscles stiff from sitting too long in one position. Her back arched, and her small breasts pressed against her thin sweater in a movement that Sam knew wasn't deliberately seductive. Seductive it was, nonetheless, and Sam stiffened when he saw John Kelley watching her with frank appreciation.

"If that's all, then we'd better get going," Sam said brusquely. He stepped forward to pull Jessie's chair away from the desk, shouldering Kelley rudely aside. "She has to get moving if she's going to meet Leonid at seven." He kept a possessive hand on Jessie's shoulder while she stood and helped her solicitously into her jacket.

Jessie didn't look at Sam's face, but the expression on John Kelley's said a lot. He was half smiling as he watched Sam. When the men looked at each other there was a moment of recognition and male challenge.

Was Sam jealous? Sam? Jessie kept her face a careful blank and moved away to collect her purse and the disk.

"See you at the bar." John Kelley smiled warmly and shook her hand for just a moment longer than was necessary.

She felt Sam come closer, but she stayed just out of his reach as she walked toward the door and said goodbye to the others. If he was jealous, if he had feelings for her that he was uncomfortable with, she would just let him be uncomfortable for a while.

He didn't speak until they were in the stairwell, walking back down to the fourth floor and her office. "I don't like this."

"Don't like what?"

"Your meeting with Leonid on your own." He rounded a corner and started down the next flight. "I don't like it."

"I won't be on my own. John and the other man—"

"Terry. Terry Gold."

"They'll both be there with me, and you'll be outside."

"Don't forget, there may be other people watching the two of you. If anyone sees you make the exchange, you're apt to have the LAPD arresting you."

"You're such a comfort to have around."

"I'm not trying to be a comfort. I want you on your toes."

"I know what to do, for heaven's sake! You've gone over it with me enough times!"

"Something can always go wrong."

"I'll be careful."

Sam muttered something she didn't catch, then ran lightly down the last flight and stopped at the fourth-floor door. He rested his hand on the bar, but didn't push it open.

Jessie joined him on the landing, standing close to him in the small space. She was breathing hard with exertion, and her hair was ruffled. Sam brushed the sweep of glossy dark hair away from her face, then took her chin in his fingers and lifted her face to his. His eyes were dark, his face grave, as he looked down at her.

"I worry about you," he said softly.

"I'm tougher than I look."

A slight smile twisted the corner of his mouth. "I know you are." He bent his head, and his lips brushed hers lightly, then lifted for a moment. "You're going to do fine," he murmured, and kissed her again.

Jessie's lips trembled and parted. She rose on her toes as he slid his arms around her, kissing him with all the pent-up emotion, and with a need that was heightened by fear. When he released her, her cheeks were pink, her breathing had quickened, and every cell in her body was singingly alive.

"You'll do fine."

"Yes." She nodded firmly. "I will." She pushed the door open, then looked up at him. "You'll be there, won't you?"

"Right outside." Sam bent down so that his face was only inches from hers. "I'll be waiting for you." He quickly kissed her on the mouth and sent her on her way.

She reached the bar at five after eight, turned off the car and tucked her keys inside her purse, along with a paperback mystery she'd bought a few days ago. She forced herself not to clutch the bag to her as she walked inside. It would be a mistake to call undue attention to it, so she let her hands swing naturally as she walked while the purse hung on its shoulder strap.

Leonid was sitting in a booth, glowering at his glass. He made a stab at behaving naturally when he saw her, though. He rose, and he even managed a stiff attempt at a smile.

With better manners than he usually showed, he remained standing until she was seated. "What do you wish to drink?"

All this gallantry was too much. Jessie blinked at him in surprise. "Ginger ale," she replied after a moment. "Thank you."

As he walked to the bar, she watched with a mixture of curiosity and suspicion. Was he being polite because she'd made it clear she disliked his rudeness, or did he have an ulterior motive? She didn't know the answer, but she wasn't going to be disarmed by courtesy.

He set her ginger ale in front of her and sat down again. She drank, put her glass down and waited. The silence stretched into half a minute.

"Do you have it?" he asked at length.

She shook her head at him in mild reproof, then slid the paperback out of her purse and laid it on the table. "You ought to read this. It's a good story."

Leonid's chilly gaze flicked from her face to the book and back. She gave an almost imperceptible nod, and he picked it up. "You have studied this?"

"Yes." She didn't smile. "You should find it interesting."

He riffled the pages, and though his face remained perfectly still his pupils widened when he saw the disk. "I think I will." He slid the book into his pocket and took a long swallow from his glass. "Do you want another drink?"

"I'll get this one." She moved quickly, reaching for her wallet, and clumsily knocked her purse off the table. "Oh, rats!"

It wasn't fastened, and the contents spilled onto the floor as nicely as she could have wished. A couple of men at the bar looked around at the noise, but all they saw was an open purse, with change and a compact and lipsticks rolling across the floor.

She and Leonid bent to clean up the mess, dropping each item back in. The last thing Leonid picked up was a slightly crumpled brown envelope that looked as if it had been in the purse with the grocery lists and the key chain for a long time.

"Is that everything?" he asked, tucking the envelope deep inside the soft leather bag.

"Why don't *you* tell *me* if that's everything?" she asked quietly as she rose.

Leonid made a pretense of checking the floor under the table. He looked at her and nodded. "It's all there."

She understood. "I really don't want another drink," she said, zipping her purse closed. "Will I hear from you?"

"When the time is right."

"Okay." She said goodbye and walked calmly out of the bar. There was a prickling between her shoulder blades and a quivering in her stomach, and she had to fight the urge to break and run. Her leg muscles were tensed, her breathing was quick and shallow, and only rigid self-control enabled her to walk quietly into the parking lot.

Her car was parked under a lamppost, but she checked inside before opening the door and getting in, tossing her purse casually on the passenger seat as if it didn't contain an envelope full of cash.

She started the engine and drove away, staying carefully within the speed limit, not driving home but going in the opposite direction, to a quiet residential neighborhood a mile away. She drove slowly down a side street, then swung into an alley and turned off her headlights. Behind the third house on the left was a small garage, and she parked beside it in a pool of deep shadow.

She picked up her purse and stepped out, her footsteps crunching on the gravel as she walked farther into the shadows, her eyes straining against the inky blackness. Without warning, strong hands seized her, and she gave a stifled yell of surprise. A hand clapped over her mouth to silence her, and she was pulled farther around the shabby little building, into a cluster of enormous oleander bushes.

"It's okay." Sam took his hand away from her mouth but kept a strong arm around her waist. "It's just me."

"Did they follow me?" She clung to him, her arms wrapped around his waist and her face against his chest, feeling safe at last.

"I don't think so." He spoke softly into a small radio and received a crackling reply. "Doesn't look like it. Come on."

He put the radio back in his pocket and took her hand, leading her to a small garage door. "Let's get going."

A service van with no windows on its sides waited in the garage. Sam slid the side door open.

"There's a blanket back there, since you'll have to sit on the floor. Sorry, but I want you to stay out of sight." He closed the door on her while she got settled on the blanket folded behind the driver's seat. The dome light flashed on as he opened the driver's door and climbed in. He pulled a grubby baseball cap over his hair, covering the unmistakable silver, and peered around the seat at her. "You okay?"

"I'm fine." She leaned against the back of his seat, her legs extended, her ankles crossed. "This is actually pretty comfortable."

"Good." He flashed her a grin, then slammed his door. The light went out, and darkness like thick black velvet closed around them.

Jessie heard his seat springs squeak and his keys jingle. She waited for him to start the engine, but nothing happened.

"Sam? Is something wrong?"

"Huh? No. No, nothing's wrong." The seat squeaked again, and his fingers brushed her hair, then her shoulder. She turned to peer up at him in the darkness, and he cupped her chin in his hand. His fingertips touched the pulse in her throat, which was still beating fast. "Are you scared? Did Leonid frighten you?"

"Leonid?" She shook her head and her hair slid over his hand like warm silk. "He's a weasel. He doesn't have it in him to scare me. I was scared, mostly, of something going wrong. Of my dropping the disk or the money and blowing everything."

"You did well." Sam stroked her cheek, and she turned her head so that his fingers brushed across her lips. "Terry said the exchange was a pro job. Looked very natural, very smooth.''

"Oh, good!" she breathed thankfully. "I didn't know if I'd be able to do it."

"You did fine."

He tightened his fingers on her chin, lifting her face a fraction higher. "But don't get overconfident. Leonid himself may be fairly harmless, but the people he works for are another story. Never forget that."

She swallowed and nodded. "Okay."

"Good girl. Now let's roll!" He used a remote control to raise the garage door, then drove to the end of the alley before turning on his headlights.

"Terry said you got an envelope."

"Yes." She pulled it out of her purse and held it up near his right elbow.

"Have you looked inside it?"

"Looked inside it?" she repeated blankly. "No, I didn't open it."

"Well, open it now and make sure there's money in there. Not cut-up newspaper or something."

"What?" That hadn't occurred to her. Jessie ripped the envelope open and examined the contents in the flickering glow of the passing streetlights. "It's money, all right."

"How much?"

It took her a few minutes to count the bills while the light swung and shifted inside the van. "It's all here."

Sam gave a low whistle. "Fifty thousand in one little envelope, huh?"

"Not such a little one." Nervous at the idea of having so much cash in her hands, she stuffed the thick stack of bills back inside the envelope and tucked it in her purse again. "What would someone do with this kind of money, Sam? You can't just walk into the bank with a roll thick enough to choke a horse and say, 'Hi, I have a little deposit to make.'"

"It'd definitely get the bank's attention." He signaled and turned onto a freeway ramp. "You can do a number of things with large amounts of cash, though. Launder it, spend it a little at a time, put it in a safe-deposit box. Or just stick it under the mattress." He glanced over his shoulder and grinned again. "But you don't have to worry about that, since Gold's going to take that little problem off your hands in about fifteen minutes."

"And we can both relax," Jessie added softly, and subsided onto her blanket for the rest of the trip.

Sam took Mulholland Drive past the overlook where they'd parked to elude the KGB agents to one of the dirt roads that were used during emergencies by fire-fighting vehicles.

He drove about a quarter mile up the winding road, the van bucking and twisting over ruts and bumps, until the curve of the hillside and a cluster of huge boulders concealed them from the highway below.

He parked the van with the nose facing the road, killed the engine and lights, climbed out and opened the door for Jessie.

"I want to see if anybody's followed us. We'll wait outside."

"Okay." She scrambled to the doorway.

"Where's the money?"

"Right here." She tucked the fat envelope in her pocket, then slid out of the van and stretched. A gust of cool night air hit her, and she shivered.

Sam turned toward her. "Come here." He shrugged out of his worn leather jacket and swung it around her shoulders, pulling it closed under her chin. "You're gonna freeze out here."

"Not anymore." The jacket felt wonderful, soft and supple and warm from his body, and it carried his scent. She snuggled deeper into it. "Do you think anybody followed us?"

"I don't think so." He looked past her at the road below them. "I don't take chances, though. When you get sloppy, you get into trouble." He drew her closer, into the lee of the largest boulder, then pushed her back until she was leaning against the smooth stone and rested his hands on her shoulders.

Jessie watched his shirtfront move slowly up and down with his untroubled breathing. How could he be so calm? Her heart was tumbling along in a nervous rhythm, her breathing was shallow and quick, but Sam stood steady. She shivered again and felt him shift slightly to look down at her face in the moonlight.

"Are you still cold? C'mere." He slid his arms around her. "That better?" He stooped down to look into her face, and his breath feathered her hair.

Jessie turned so that her mouth was very close to his. The breeze lifted a strand of her hair and wafted it across her lips. "Yes," she breathed. "That's nice."

"Yes." Sam reached up to brush the strand away. He tucked it behind her ear, then trailed his fingertips over her lips again, lightly, almost experimentally. They parted, just a bit, and he bent slowly until his mouth had replaced his fingers.

Jessie closed her eyes. Soft and sweet, the kiss went on and on, building slowly in intensity as their bodies pressed together and strained to make close into closest.

Jessie clutched Sam's shoulders, pulling him down to her and pressing her body up into the curve of his. She made a little sound of want and need deep in her throat, and as if that had broken the rein he'd kept on his hunger, Sam bent his head and slanted his mouth across hers. His lips bruised hers with passionate force, and his hand tangled in her hair to lift her face to his.

Jessie met his demand with her own, her hands touching his throat, brushing over the hair that grew to his collarbone. He was big and strong and warm, and she'd waited for days to touch him this way and now she couldn't get enough. She needed more than just a kiss, needed all of him, mind and heart and body. She moved her hands down, pushing his shirt open to the second button, spreading her fingers over the heavy muscles of his chest.

Sam stiffened at the caress, as if he wanted to resist but couldn't. Almost tentatively, his arm tightened around her and one hand slid down her back, paused at her waist and then drifted around to slip inside the leather jacket and cover her breast.

His warmth struck Jessie through the thin sweater she'd put on that morning, heating her blood as her nipple tightened. She strained against him and felt his body quiver slightly with barely controlled tension.

She knew she was the cause of that tension, and she sought, with little inflaming movements, to push him further, to break the control he was still maintaining. When he found the buttons on her sweater, opening one, and then another and another, she caught her breath and went lax in his arms.

Jessie was so lost in the wonder of his embrace that she didn't at first realize what the long beams of brilliant light meant. They swung in a huge arc across the dark hillside, sending shadows leaping wildly over the rugged terrain. Then light grazed the rocks behind them, and Sam's head snapped up. He swore violently, his body tightening with another kind of tension.

Suddenly frightened, Jessie pressed closer, but he jerked her hands away from his shirt and swung her roughly behind him, pushing her into the shadows. He pinned her against the rock with an arm that was hard as iron.

Jessie fumbled with shaking hands to button her sweater, cold with shock and dawning fear. "Who is it?" she asked in a whisper that shook from more than the cold.

"I don't know." He reached behind his back and drew a small but deadly looking revolver from a waistband holster. "Not yet."

Chapter 10

Sam could see over the rocks to the hillside below them, but Jessie couldn't. Facing the other way, she could only look up the hill, where the headlight beams bobbed and swung wildly as the oncoming car bucked its way up the rutted road. As it approached, she heard the sound of a powerful engine snarling in protest as it climbed the steep slope.

The car paused for a moment as its driver downshifted and then ground its way up the last rutted stretch of gravel and dust. Sam tightened his arm, pushing Jessie out of sight in a curve of the rock, his body in front of hers.

Her heart raced as the car stopped only a few yards away. The headlights flicked out, and she blinked blindly in the dark, listening to the ticking of the cooling engine. She caught her breath and held it, her eyes stretched wide, staring up at the black hillside.

A door squeaked open, gravel crunched beneath a heavy foot, and Jessie pressed against Sam's back, straining to see in the moonlight.

The footsteps stopped. There was silence for a second, and then a quiet cough. "I'm looking for a king with a ransom."

At that unorthodox statement, the rigid tension left Sam's body and he lowered his gun, flicking the safety back on before he tucked it into the holster again.

"The king's here, and so is the ransom."

"Yeah," said the other voice, full of laughter, "but where are you? I can't see a damned thing."

"You need cat's eyes, man." Sam walked around the boulder, with Jessie following just behind.

She peered around him and saw a heavy-duty pickup truck and a tall, lean figure silhouetted against the moonlit sky. He stepped forward, and the silhouette became a man in his mid-thirties with thinning blond hair and a wide grin. She'd last seen him a couple of hours before.

"Hi, Terry."

"And hello to you, too." He grinned boyishly at her. "You had yourself quite an evening, didn't you?"

She tried to laugh, but it came out shaky. "That's one way to put it."

"Do you have the money?"

She handed him the envelope, and he hefted it experimentally in his hand before tucking it in an inside pocket.

"Nice piece of change," he said, then glanced at Jessie. "Unless it's nothing but old newspapers?"

"It's money," she said. "I checked. And it's all there."

"He'd be stupid to try and stiff you before he has the whole program," Terry told her. "When will you give him the next installment?"

"In ten days or so. Maybe two weeks. Then another couple of weeks for the last segment."

He nodded. "That's when the risk will be greatest—when you give him the final part."

"Oh." Jessie's voice was suddenly very small, and Sam put an arm around her, pulling her close to his side.

"Nice going, Terry," he said, his voice heavy with sarcasm. "Are you always so full of good news?"

"Hey, I didn't mean anything by it."

"Yeah, sure. Well, is that all you need? We ought to get going before somebody sees us up here and calls the cops."

Terry nodded and walked back to his truck, then paused and looked at them. "Good job, Jessie."

He gave her a thumbs-up, then climbed in and drove away, negotiating the first hundred yards of the road without lights. Sam watched until the car had vanished around the first curve on Mulholland.

"Well—" he looked up and down the highway, but saw nothing suspicious "—it looks like we did it."

"We did, didn't we?" Jessie looked up at him, a smile dawning on her face. "We really did it!" The smile widened, and she flung herself into his arms in a burst of exuberance. "*We did it!*"

She linked her arms around his neck and gave him a smacking kiss on one cheek. Then she drew back to kiss the other cheek and he turned his head so that the kiss landed on his lips.

For an instant he didn't move. Then he tightened his arms and kissed her again. He eased her down until her toes were touching the ground and ran his hands over her back, sliding her soft sweater against her skin as he plundered her mouth. When he raised his head, Jessie clung to him, her heart thundering against her ribs.

"Oh, Sam," she breathed, resting her cheek on his chest. "I'm so glad...."

"Glad?" He murmured the word into her hair, nuzzling gently. "Glad about what?"

She tipped her head back to look into his face. "Glad we did it. Glad nothing went wrong." She paused, and her whisper dropped lower. "Glad you were with me."

He shrugged. "Somebody had to be there. It wouldn't have been safe otherwise."

"Yes." She smiled, her eyes soft. "But I'm glad it was you. You're very important to me, Sam."

He didn't move, not a muscle, but she could feel his withdrawal. "I'm in charge of the case. I'm responsible for anything that happens to you."

There was a pause. "I see," she said in a cool little voice. "And that's all? I'm a part of the case, like the money, or the program?" She pushed away from him as she spoke, and when his arms fell to his sides she walked a few steps away, stumbling on the rough ground. "Is that what you think?"

"That's how it is." His voice was light and hard.

"I don't think so."

"It's the way it is. You and I would never have met if you hadn't been approached. The only thing we have in common is this operation."

"Oh, no." She tried to see his face in the deceptive moonlight. "You're wrong. We have a lot more in common than that."

"We have nothing in common!" He swung away, striding over to the van and yanking open the door. He looked back at her. "Well? Are you coming?"

Jessie waited a moment, then walked across to the van. "I'm coming." She climbed into the back again. "And you're wrong."

By the time they entered her living room, the silence had gone from chilly to oppressive. Jessie didn't switch on any lights. She stopped short in the center of the room and turned to Sam. "You're wrong," she said again.

"Huh?" He was checking the alarm system he'd rigged to let them know if anyone had been in the house while they were gone, and he had his back to her. His voice sounded tired and bored. "Wrong about what?"

"About us, you and me." He straightened sharply and turned to look across the room at her. "We are more to each other than this operation, and when it's over there will still be something between us." She spoke calmly and surely, moving slowly toward him. When she stopped, a scant yard separated them. "I know it's true, and so do you. Why are you fighting it?"

He moved his head involuntarily, not quite shaking it. "No. You're making proximity out to be something more than it is. That's all."

Jessie sighed and reached out to touch his arm. He stiffened, almost flinching away, and she let her hand fall to her side.

"Why do you say that? It's here, Sam, between us, all the time. I want—" She swallowed. "I want to kiss you, to hold you, and you—"

"You know damn well what I want to do!" His face twisted into a bitter mask, and his hands shot out, catching her shoulders in a punishing grip. "You know what it is, but you don't want to call it by its right name, do you?" He pulled her closer, his voice low and harsh. His grip on her shoulders tightened until he was almost shaking her.

"You're like any other woman, you want to dress it up with pretty words, want to put strings and conditions on it, but when you get right to the bottom of things, you know and I know that the only thing between us is sex!"

If he'd meant to frighten her, it hadn't worked. She rested her hands on his arms and looked up at him calmly. "You're wrong, and—"

She never got to finish her statement. It was cut off by his mouth crushing down on hers in a kiss that was empty of any emotion save anger and the need to hurt. He held her with an arm wrapped around her waist, and with the other hand he jerked her sweater up and ran his hand roughly over her back and ribs. Jessie stood rigid for a moment, shocked by the barely leashed violence she felt in him. Then she began to struggle.

"What's the matter?" Sam lifted his lips and looked down at her, his eyes glittering in the dim light. "Isn't this what you want?" He covered her breast with his free hand, but there was no tenderness in the touch.

"Not like this." She pushed against his chest, but he held her with an ease that was almost insulting. "Please, Sam. Not like this."

His hand moved on her breast in a caress that was far from rough, despite his anger. She stiffened, bracing herself, but with a muttered oath he pushed her out of his arms and swung away from her, gripping the edge of a bookshelf, his head lowered, his shoulders hunched. His breathing was harsh in the silence.

Jessie backed warily away from him. "Sam?"

He straightened, and she tensed. "Is Kerry spending the night next door?"

"Yes. Marcie said they'd love to have her."

"Okay. I'm going to have a cup of coffee or something. You go to bed."

"But I should—"

He looked around at her, his face bleak. "Go to bed, Jessamyn."

She went, and she locked her door.

Jessie sat in the chintz armchair in the corner of her bedroom, gazing out at the backyard, which was washed to silver and black by the moonlight, and tried to think. She'd had two days to reason it out, two days since Sam had peremptorily sent her to her room.

That should have rankled, because she wasn't the type to meekly obey an order. Something in Sam's voice, though, or in his eyes, had convinced her that at that moment discretion was the better part of valor. He'd reached his limit, whether from her pushing or from the emotions he was dealing with, and it would be dangerous to them both for her to go any further.

What, she wondered as the clock's hands slid past midnight, was happening to Sam?

A few days ago, even two days ago, she would have sworn that he felt something for her, something more than lust, or sex, or whatever he wanted to call it. But what she'd seen in his eyes when he'd sent her away had been closer to hate.

Since then he'd been gentle and generous with Kerry, while he'd treated Kerry's mother with polite distaste. He acted as if the sight of her, her mere presence, was repugnant to him. Did Sam King care for her, did he hate her, or was he wrestling with some demon she didn't understand?

And what about her feelings? She shifted in the chair, pulling her knees up to her chest and tucking her feet beneath the hem of her nightgown. She'd begun to think she wanted Sam in her life, but did she really? Did she want the man who had ordered her out of his sight?

She knew that she liked, maybe even loved, the funny, gentle, strong man she'd thought she was getting to know. But the angry, bitter person who had sent her away was a stranger. Which was the real Sam? The cruel man? She didn't want *him* in her life. If he was Sam, she had to deal with that, had to protect herself from her feelings for him.

She hadn't been looking for a man. Her life had been going along just fine until Sam King entered it. But fate had thrown her a curve—a man who had shattered her first defenses with his eerie resemblance to her late husband.

She'd lost the chance to put a wall up between them, and she had begun to care for him and to think he might care for her. She'd even begun to think there might be room in her life for a man, after all, and then Sam had changed.

He was pushing her away, as if he hated her, or, she realized in surprise, as if he *feared* her. Whatever was going on in his mind, she had to keep her distance, in the interests of self-preservation.

"Edwards? The air force base? Up in the desert?"

"That's right."

"And they're going to let this program fly a fighter plane?"

"That's what it's for, after all." She pushed a bit of steak across her plate with her fork. "It's been tested in simulation. Now it has to be tested in a real plane."

"When do they want to do it?"

"Next weekend."

"Okay." Sam considered that. "We don't want Leonid and his buddies to know anything about this little excursion. They've had the second segment for three days now and we haven't heard anything from them, so they must be satisfied with it. And if they're satisfied, they'll be anxious to have it all." He rolled his wine around in his glass, watching the color change from garnet to ruby and back again. "I think we'll let them wait and wonder for a few days. You can just disappear for the weekend."

"With a wave of my wand?"

"Oh, we can come up with a way to get you out of town without them knowing where you're going."

"I see. I'm sure you and the rest of the FBI will find a way to deal with it." They'd both been concentrating on being punctiliously polite during dinner, but suddenly Jessie couldn't tolerate it anymore.

The constant tension was eating away at her. They'd had another smooth-as-silk exchange with Leonid only three days ago, but there had been no celebration this time, no laughter or kisses, only a rather grim acknowledgment that the easy part was over. The last exchange would be the difficult one, the dangerous one, and they had to plan carefully for it.

She shoved her chair back with a screech, picked up her barely touched plate and took it into the kitchen. She rinsed it, put it in the dishwasher and stood at the sink, gazing blindly out the window.

Edwards. The famous base out in the high desert had been such a part of her life once. Her memories of it were fragments of time and sensation. The feel of dry, dry air on a sunny November day, a dusting of snow on the Joshua trees on a cold winter morning, the summer's scorching, relentless heat. Edwards. The thought of going back there both attracted and repelled her.

She'd known that the flight tests would be conducted there, but now that the moment was at hand, she felt no joy.

"...coffee?"

She came out of her trance to the realization that Sam was in the kitchen with her and that he'd asked her a question she hadn't even heard.

"I'm sorry. What did you say?"

Sam looked at her quizzically. "I wondered if you'd made coffee."

"Not yet."

"I'm going to have a cup. Do you want some?"

"Yes. Thank you." Her manner as polite and distant as his, she walked toward the door as he began to fill the machine. At the door she paused. "Sam?"

"Yeah?"

"When will you know what the plans are?"

"In a day or two. I'll come to Edwards with you, though, along with a couple of other agents. We'll work the details out with the air force. Will Kerry stay with your in-laws in Bakersfield?"

"Mm-hmm. They've been complaining that they don't see enough of her. She's gone to school there before, when

I had to work in Hong Kong for a month, so she can stay as long as—'' Jessie's voice faltered. ''As long as she needs to.''

''That's good. We'll see that she's safe.''

Jessie was counting on that.

''Do I *have* to?''

''I thought you liked to stay with Grandma and Grandpa. You'll get to see all your friends in Bakersfield, and go to school there, like you did before.''

''Are you going to Kong Kong?''

Kerry had never been able to get Hong Kong's name quite right, and for a time she had referred to the crown colony as King Kong. The thought still made Jessie smile, but she was careful not to let her amusement show as she replied to Kerry's question.

''No, honey, but I *do* have to go away for work again. That's why you're going to stay in Bakersfield for a while.''

''Because I can keep on with school there so my brain doesn't get too lazy.''

''That's right. So why don't you want to go this time?''

Kerry frowned as she worked out how to express herself. ''I want to see Grandma and Grandpa, but . . .''

''But what, honey?'' Jessie stooped down to look into Kerry's face and smoothed her hair back.

''Well.'' Kerry glanced at Sam, then looked at her mother's face. ''Sam's here now, and Cat's here, and they'll miss me.''

''Oh, honey,'' Jessie pulled Kerry into her arms for a hug. It was Kerry who would miss Sam and Cat. ''I know they'll miss you. I will, too. But they'll be okay.''

''Will you take care of them?''

Jessie wondered silently if unwise promises made to innocent children always had to be kept. She took a breath. ''Yes, sweetie, I'll take care of them.''

''And give Cat his yummies?''

"I'll make sure he gets them." Jessie agreed to all of Kerry's exhaustively detailed list of tasks and duties, wondering if, with her promise to take care of Sam and Cat, she hadn't agreed to something much more difficult than feeding a pet.

Kerry left for Bakersfield on Thursday evening, in the company of Charlie's parents. Jessie's mother-in-law was curious about Sam, and she plainly wasn't satisfied by the brief explanation that was all Jessie could give her.

"He's with the government," Jessie said. "You know that I'm working on a government project."

"I know. But are you sure you're all right, dear?" Elaine Ames glanced at Sam, who was putting Kerry's small suitcase in the trunk, then looked back at Jessie, frowning.

"I'm fine, Elaine. Please, don't worry about me."

"I do worry. You know that. And I can see that you're worried, too." Her gaze slid to Sam again.

Jessie watched her mother-in-law's face for a moment. "It's weird, isn't it?"

Elaine nodded. "At first glance he could almost be Charlie, but then—"

"Then you see that he's someone else entirely," Jessie finished for her.

"Yes," Elaine agreed thoughtfully. "I think your Mr. King and Charlie would have had a lot in common, though."

Jessie shook her head sharply, but the men chose that moment to return to the house, and her chance to speak privately with Elaine was past.

She and Sam left the next day, and Jessie had a performance to give before they departed. She said nothing to any of her co-workers about weekend plans, but if her preoccupation was misinterpreted as having to do with romance, that was all right.

She went down in the elevator with a crowd of people she knew, walked in their midst across the lobby and made certain there were at least twenty people around when she came out the door and saw the car waiting for her.

Sam got out as she left the building and came around the car to open the door for her and tenderly assist her in. She smiled happily, for all the world like a woman going to meet her lover. Before he closed the door, Sam bent down, his face close enough to hers to kiss her, and murmured, "Nice job, Jessie. Everybody in the building must be watching."

"Everybody?" Jessie sat back, her cheeks pink, her tone faint, still smiling gamely. She'd done what she was supposed to, but she wasn't a bit comfortable being stared at. She kept her eyes away from the building's entrance as Sam climbed into the driver's seat again.

He fastened his seat belt, started the engine and glanced at her set face. "Think you can stand to put the icing on the cake?"

"What?" Jessie turned to look at him, still smiling as convincingly as she could. He leaned over, caught her chin in his fingers and kissed her. He let his lips linger long enough for hers to soften, then sat back and drove away from the crowd of riveted spectators.

They were three blocks away before Jessie spoke. "What—" Her voice emerged as a breathless squeak. She cleared her throat and tried again. "What was that for?"

"The kiss?" Sam glanced at her, a half smile curving his lips. "Icing on the cake, like I said. Give them all something to think about over the weekend."

"I see." She turned away from him, looking determinedly out the window. "I hope it worked."

"It worked." His voice was rich with amused satisfaction. "Jaws were dropping all over the sidewalk."

"Oh." She sighed. "Well, I suppose I should be glad, but I don't like deliberately setting myself up to be gossiped about."

Sam sobered. "It's in a good cause. Keep that in mind."

She nodded, her smile fading, then turned to look out the window again. Los Angeles was unrolling past her, but she was blind to the panorama of traffic and palm trees and mountains. They traveled in silence for a time, both of them lost in their own thoughts.

"Did you tell anyone about our weekend plans?"

"Hmm?" She looked around, startled, when Sam spoke. "Well, I didn't actually tell anybody anything specific."

"But you were supposed to let—"

"Don't worry," she said interrupting him. "I got the message across. I don't talk to the people at work about my private business, so simply telling people my plans would have been too obvious."

Sam nodded. "So what did you do instead?"

"I kept that brochure in my purse, the one you gave me on things to do in Santa Barbara. It fell out in the middle of lunch one day, right in front of the biggest gossip in the company."

"Did she ask about it?"

She smiled. "Are you kidding? She practically fell over out of her chair grabbing it before I could put it back. She wanted to know what I had it for."

"What'd you say?"

"I stammered for a minute and said I'd thought about going up there some weekend. And then I got it back from her as soon as I could."

"So as to arouse just a little more suspicion?"

"With her, it doesn't take much. The less I say about what's going on in my life, the more she assumes there is. It's been driving her nuts for years that I don't account to her for every single minute. She was in the elevator with me just now."

"So she saw?"

"She couldn't have missed it. She'll be telling everybody she can think of that I'm going away to Santa Barbara with a man."

Something in her tone made him look at her. "Do you mind?" he asked after a moment.

"Yes, I mind!" The words burst out of her. "I mind a lot!"

"Hey, I don't mean—"

"It's okay." She took a deep breath and spoke more calmly. "It's okay. I don't like it, but I understand why I have to do it. We can't let them know where I am this weekend. I suppose I can deal with gossip for the sake of national security."

The dry note in her voice made him smile. "National security, huh?"

"National security," she repeated firmly. "If I didn't think it was really that important, I wouldn't have gone through any of this."

Chapter 11

He hated to wake her. Sam glanced down at her sleeping face in the glow of the dash lights. She'd dozed off after they'd left the freeway that would have taken them to Santa Barbara and turned inland to take a roundabout route to Edwards Air Force Base.

Night had fallen while they'd still been in the mountains, and Jessie had begun to yawn. She'd drifted off to sleep slumped uncomfortably against the door, and after she'd shifted her position a couple of times Sam had pulled her over to rest against his shoulder.

He didn't like to wake her, but they'd passed the exit sign for Rosamond, and she needed to show her credentials for them to be allowed on the base.

"Jessie." He shook her gently, but all she did was mumble under her breath and burrow closer. "Jessie, come on. It's time to wake up."

"Mmm, no..." she muttered. "Sleepy."

"I know you're sleepy, but we're almost there, and you've got to wake up." He steered the car along the freeway with one hand and used his other to shake her again, harder this time. "Jessie, wake up!"

"Huh?" She yawned, began to stretch and opened her eyes wide when she realized where she was. She caught her breath and pulled herself quickly away from Sam.

He was surprised to find that he missed the feel of her soft, warm weight against him. He put his right hand back on the wheel and told himself his shoulder was aching from her leaning on it. When he spoke, his voice was gruff.

"Do you have your pass? They aren't going to let anybody on that base without credentials this weekend."

"I've got what the Defense Department gave me, and my regular ID. The one I use at work."

"Good. While you're getting them together, would you dig out the car registration and the insurance stuff?"

"In the glove compartment?"

"Yes."

She rummaged for a moment and found the papers they would have to present to drive onto the base. "Here they are."

"Thanks." He extracted his wallet from his hip pocket and tossed it to her. "My pass is in one of those little slots somewhere."

Jessie looked down at the wallet in her hands but didn't open it right away. She was glad the darkness hid her face. It was bad enough that she'd fallen asleep, but to drape herself all over him was too much. She really didn't want the added intimacy of searching through his wallet.

"All right," she said after a moment. He was waiting, and they were nearing the guard post, so she opened the wallet and looked in dismay at all the spaces for cards and papers and photographs. "Do you know what slot it's in?"

He shrugged. "I just stuck it in there somewhere. You'll find it."

"Okay." With the unpleasant feeling she would have gotten from prying through someone's dresser drawers, she began looking for the authorization slip.

"I'll have to show my driver's license, so why don't you get that out, too?" Sam signaled and turned onto the off-ramp.

"All right." She slid the license out of its plastic envelope and glanced at the picture. It was an old one, taken when his hair had been longer. It had been gray even then, though a slightly darker shade, and he'd been just as handsome. She laid the license in her lap and searched for the pass among all the little things he kept in his wallet—credit cards, his FBI identification, slips of paper and, oddly enough, only one picture.

It was a photograph of an older man, with hair that was pure white. The photo was creased and worn from being carried in a wallet, and the pass was behind it.

"Sam?"

"Hmm?"

"Who's this?" She held the picture out so that he could see it in the glow of the dash lights.

"What?" He sounded deeply startled, and angry, as well. "Where did you get that?"

"It was in your wallet, on top of the pass."

He grabbed it from her hand and stuffed it roughly into his shirt pocket. "I didn't know it was there."

"But who is it?"

He braked, rolling to a stop as the MP at the checkpoint stepped out of the guard hut. "Give me the stuff." She handed it all to him as he rolled down his window, and she barely heard his reply to her question. "My father."

Jessie didn't have the chance to ask any more questions. The MP leaned down to look in the window. "You'll have to get out of the car, sir, and come with me, and you, too, ma'am.''

Jessie waited while Sam accompanied the soldier to the guard hut, where his papers were scrutinized, then went herself while Sam waited. When they returned to the car the MP gave her back her identification. "Welcome to Edwards, ma'am."

"Thank you, sergeant."

"Sir." He stood back while Sam got in, then sent them on their way with a snappy salute.

"They're expecting us at the O-Club. You turn up there."

Jessie pointed, and Sam put the car in gear. The Officers' Club was only a short distance along the road she indicated, and "they" were indeed waiting.

Inside the club they were met by an airman who directed them to a private dining room. Dinner was already over, and the assembled group were lingering over coffee and waiting for them. Several men and a woman in uniform sat around a large table, along with three men in civilian clothes.

Jessie glanced at them all, but her attention was focused on a stocky, powerfully built man with swarthy skin, curly dark hair and a thick mustache. He was a full colonel now, she saw, but the smile and the dark, laughing eyes were still the same. He rose slowly from his chair and walked around the table, quickening his pace at the same moment she did.

"Mick!"

"Jessie!"

She ran the last two steps, flung herself into his open arms and let herself be swung in a circle and hugged until she could hardly breathe while she happily hugged him back. Colonel Michael Davis set her on her feet at last, gave her a sound kiss on each cheek and held her at arm's length to study her with a smile.

"You're looking good, Jessie."

"So are you." She smiled back at him. "And can I guess what you're doing here?"

"Hey, I came just to see you."

"And maybe to fly a plane?"

Mick gave a shout of laughter and pulled her close for another quick hug before he released her. "I can't put a thing over on you, can I? Yes, I'm going to fly the plane. You think I'd let somebody else have all the fun?"

She shook her head, smiling. "I should have known you would be the one."

"I couldn't miss the chance to see you. You look good," he repeated. "Really good. Better—" He stopped himself, his expression stricken. The last time he'd seen her had been at Charlie's funeral. He looked as if he'd give anything to call the word back.

Jessie kept smiling, and she shook her head fractionally in a "never mind" sort of gesture. "It's okay, Mick. And thanks." His hand in hers, she turned to Sam, who was standing behind her. "Sam, I'd like you to meet a very special friend of mine, Mick—" She stopped and grinned. "Oh, excuse me, *Colonel* Michael Davis, USAF."

As the men turned to each other, Mick paused, his hand half lifted, his gaze fixed on Sam's face. Watching, Jessie saw his pupils widen and his facial muscles still. She knew that he was seeing a face from the past, his old friend Charlie.

"Mick," she said into the suddenly tense silence, "this is Sam King, with the FBI."

Her old friend glanced at her, and at her barely perceptible nod he extended his hand again.

Jessie looked at Sam and was startled to see the blankly hostile expression on his face. He shook Mick's hand and muttered civil words of greeting, but all the while his eyes were as hard as flint. He wasn't quite glowering, but his expression was a long way from being warm and congenial.

He and Mick regarded each other coldly for a moment, and she could see a brief test of strength in the handshake, as shoulders stiffened and biceps bulged.

Then their hands dropped apart. Jessie couldn't see that anything had been accomplished by the odd male ritual, but there was a perceptible lessening of tension when she and Sam turned to be introduced to the others.

The civilians were people she already knew: Mr. Howell from Anchor, and the two FBI agents, Terry and John. Mick presented her to the base commander, General Al Walters, a tall, lean, gray-haired man who greeted her with grave courtesy and almost managed to hide his surprise that a woman had authored the program that was to land his airplanes. Major Ted Kovak, younger and slimmer than Mick, with a quick grin and laughing eyes, was the backup pilot, and two young sergeants, Cathie Johnson and Fred Timmons, were the air traffic controllers who would be in the tower for the test tomorrow.

When Jessie sat down to a very belated dinner she found Mick sitting beside her. Sam was at the other end of the table.

"So." Mick passed her the breadbasket and watched her take a roll. "What's with the G-man?"

"What do you mean?" Jessie asked with her mouth full. She hadn't been able to eat lunch, but her appetite returned with a vengeance when she tasted the air force's roast beef. She took another bite.

"Your man from the FBI." Mick glanced down the table and found Sam's cold, level gaze fixed on him. He leaned closer to Jessie, speaking quietly. "If looks could kill, I'd be in little pieces all over the floor, and he damned near wrung my hand off."

Jessie tried to stifle a giggle and nearly choked on her roast beef. "Poor little Mickey, almost got his hand smooshed by the big bad FBI man."

"Cute, Jessie, but he's not laughing."

She followed Mick's gaze to the other end of the table and met Sam's eyes. They were dark and cold. She stared back at him for a moment, then, very deliberately, smiled at Mick.

"I don't know what his problem is, and I don't especially want to. So how have you been, Mick?"

"And you don't want to talk about him?" Mick grinned. "Okay. I've been doing all right, just flying along."

While she finished her dinner Mick told her where he'd been and what he'd done since she'd last seen him.

After they'd eaten, General Walters made a toast and welcomed all the civilians to the base. "Each of you already knows what you're to do," he said in conclusion "so I don't think we need a briefing tonight. Get a good night's sleep, everyone, and I'll meet you on the flight line at 0530 hours."

On that note the meeting, such as it was, was adjourned. They drifted out of the room, Mick with Jessie and Sam.

"I'll show you your quarters, Jessie." He nodded coolly to Sam. "King."

"Where did they put us?" she wondered. "BOQ?" Visitors were usually housed in Bachelor Officers' Quarters.

"Not this time," Mick said. "Too public. We're keeping a very low profile on this test. As far as anybody's going to know, I'll be doing a few takeoffs and landings, just for fun."

"They let you take an F-15 up for fun?" Sam asked.

Mick gave him a flinty glance, and for a moment his age and years of hard experience showed. "If I want to, yeah."

Sam's reply to that was a noncommittal grunt. As they neared the parked cars, he caught Jessie's arm and pulled her away from Mick's side. "We'll follow you."

Jessie looked up at Sam in surprise but didn't protest as he dragged her across the gravel. "If it's not BOQ, where are we going, Mick?"

"We've got an empty house. It'll be safer for you."

He climbed into his dark blue official car and pulled out with a spurt of gravel. Jessie sat in silence while Sam followed Mick down the street. They passed a movie theater and an ice-cream store and then drove into a neighborhood of winding streets and smallish houses.

Officers with families lived in these houses, whose cookie-cutter sameness was relieved only by plants and decorations. When Sam had parked at the curb behind Mick, Jessie climbed out and stood in the street, staring at the small house, reluctant to walk up to the front door and go inside. She shivered and rubbed her hands over her upper arms.

Mick didn't let her stand there for long. He caught her arm and marched her to the door, talking briskly all the time.

"As I said, we thought this would afford more privacy...and anyway a bed's a bed." It was clear he was trying to make her comfortable. He unlocked the door and reached in to switch on the lights. Two table lamps illuminated a small living room furnished with a sofa, an armchair and a television. The kitchen was beyond that. There was a coffee maker on the counter, and Mick showed them food and dishes in the cupboards. "Which suitcase is yours, Jessie?"

"The blue one." She pointed, and he grabbed it as he passed, switching on more lights.

"You're in the big bedroom, Jessie, with your own bath." He dumped the suitcase on a luggage rack someone had squeezed in between the double bed and the overlarge dresser. "And you're in here, King." He turned on the lights in the smaller bedroom across the hall. "There's towels and soap and stuff in the bathrooms. Anything else you need?"

"No, Mick, thank you. You seem to have thought of everything." She reached up to hug him and received another bearlike squeeze.

He released her slowly and looked past her at Sam. "Will you be okay?" The question was for her alone.

"I'll be fine, Mick, and thank you. For everything."

Mick studied her face for a moment more, then nodded briefly, turned on his heel and left. Jessie turned around, more slowly, to find Sam watching her. His face was in shadow, and she couldn't read his expression. He was blocking her path to her bedroom, but she couldn't shove him out of the way, so she waited.

"Who is he, Jessie?"

"An old friend. Will you let me by, Sam? I'd like to wash my face."

"How old a friend?"

Anger and exasperation suddenly bubbled up inside her. "Very old!" she snapped. "And since we have to get up at four-thirty, I'd like to get some sleep. I'm tired, even if you aren't!" She pushed her way past him, stalked into the bedroom and closed the door with a bang. She really was tired, and she was darn well going to sleep.

To her surprise, and in spite of her agitation, she actually did manage to sleep for a time. When she woke, abruptly and completely, she lay staring wide-eyed into the darkness. Her travel clock informed her it was 3:00 a.m. Not yet time to get up.

Maybe a drink of water. She slid out of bed and, without thinking about it, padded through the darkness into the bathroom, reached out to fill a glass and froze. The glass clattered against the faucet as her hand began to shake and, without drinking, she set it on the counter with exaggerated care.

She hadn't turned on the light, because she hadn't needed to. She knew exactly where the bathroom cold tap was. Her feet could carry her with ease to the kitchen or to the front door or the other bedroom. She had lived in a house identical to this one for nearly a year, until the day the chaplain and the wing commander had come to tell her her husband was dead.

She walked silently out of the bathroom and down the short hall to the kitchen. The little dinette table stood where hers had stood—there was really nowhere else to put one— and she let her fingers drift over the polished surface as she walked past. She touched the countertop, the sink, the edge of the stove, then pulled open the back door and stood looking out.

A late-rising moon showed her the shapes of nearby trees and distant mountains, and the cold air of the desert night poured in through the screen. She breathed deeply, remembering the smell of dust mixed with the scents of the neighbors' flowers and occasional whiffs of jet fuel.

She remembered arriving on a scorchingly hot day in November, remembered her amazement at the heat, the dryness, the endless vistas of desert and mountains. She remembered the wonder of winter snow, the sudden, drenching rains and the flowers that carpeted the desert floor afterward.

She remembered driving out into the desert with Charlie in the Jeep, and she remembered coming home to cook a simple meal and going to bed to make love through the night. And she remembered coming to the empty house with a folded flag in her hands and nothing in her heart.

"Jessie?" She hadn't heard Sam approach, and when he laid gentle hands on her shoulders she jumped, starting violently. He caught her arms and held her, lightly but surely. "Jessie, are you all right?"

"I'm fine." Her voice cracked. She tried to turn away, and the moonlight fell on her face.

"You're crying!"

"No, I'm not. I—" She reached up to touch her cheeks and fell silent. They were wet with tears. She scrubbed the dampness away roughly with her palms, but her eyes filled again.

Sam pulled her into his arms despite her feeble resistance, cradling her gently against his chest. "What's wrong, Jessie?" His lips were on her hair, and his voice was soft and gentle. "Tell me. Tell me what's wrong."

She didn't want to. She wanted to push him away, to shout that she didn't need his help or his concern, that she didn't want cold, callous Sam King to do anything for her. But this man who was holding her securely in his arms was different. This was the other Sam, the man she'd first come to know, the man who cared for her, and she couldn't resist the comfort he offered. In his arms she was warm and safe. When he held her she was no longer alone.

He hadn't bothered to put a robe over the cotton running shorts he slept in. She let him draw her face down against his shoulder. His skin was warm and smooth under her cheek. Muscles flexed as he brought her closer, his warmth striking her through her thin nightgown, heating her chilled body. Of their own accord, her arms slid around his waist, and she tucked her head under his chin, rubbing her cheek over the hair that curled thickly at the base of his throat.

"What's upset you?" he murmured. "Was it something I did?"

"No." She shook her head against his chest and sniffed. "It's not you."

"If it isn't me, then what?"

She waved a hand in a helpless gesture at their surroundings. "It's not you or anybody else. It's this house."

Chapter 12

This house?'' Sam looked around at what he could see of the darkened kitchen. ''What's wrong with it?''

Jessie shook her head, pulled out of his arms and turned away, putting her hand out for the towel bar beside the sink. It was where she'd known it would be, with a towel on it. She wiped her eyes quickly. ''There's nothing wrong with the house,'' she said, her voice little more than a croak.

''Then what—''

''I knew where the tap was. In the bathroom.''

There was a moment of confused silence. ''The tap?'' Sam followed when she walked into the living room, touching things lightly as she passed them. His night vision was good, but he fumbled a moment at the doorway leading from the dark kitchen to the darker living room. Jessie never paused.

''The tap,'' she repeated. ''I didn't need to turn on the light to find it, because I knew just where it was. I used to live here.''

He could see her silhouette faintly against the windows when she sat down on the sofa. He made his way carefully over to her, feeling his way past furniture and other obstacles. He felt rather than saw her turn toward him when he finally settled himself beside her on the small sofa.

"Here?" he asked softly. "In this house, you mean?"

"Not this one. In a house just like this. Over there." She waved vaguely toward the west. She lifted her face, looking at the shadow that was Sam. "We lived here. Charlie and I."

He made an involuntary movement, offering comfort, sympathy, something, but she shook her head, and he lowered his hand. She took a deep breath for courage and straightened her back until she was sitting very tall and stiff on the sagging cushions.

"We were lucky when Charlie was stationed here. We got a house right away, because they had one empty just then. It doesn't always happen, you know. Lots of times you're put on a waiting list and you get an allowance and live off base, somewhere terribly expensive, until base housing comes up. But this time we got into a house right away."

She lifted the curtains aside to look out at the street, which was dimly illuminated by the lamp on the corner. "I liked it here, way out in the desert with the heat and the dust and the rocks and the Joshua trees. We were settled, I had my first job, Charlie was doing work he loved."

"What did he do?" Sam asked softly.

"He was an instructor at the test pilot school. It was what he'd always wanted to do. He loved it, and we had a—" She faltered, then caught herself. "We had a home. And then, one day—"

She broke off again, gazing out the window. Sam knew she was looking not at the street outside but into the past. She bit her lower lip and drew a long, shaky breath.

"Then, one day—"

"Jessie—" Sam caught her hand "—you don't have to do this."

She ignored his words but gripped his fingers fiercely. "One day, the chaplain and Charlie's commanding officer walked up to the front door." Her grip tightened until her nails were digging painfully into his hand, but Sam didn't move.

"I heard the car pull up. It was just past noon, and I was sitting in here, finishing my lunch and trying to knit a bootee for Kerry. She was due in eight weeks. I never did get those bootees knitted. In the end I just bought her some. I heard the car stop, and I looked out, and—and I knew. Every pilot's wife knows what that means, the uniform walking up to your door. I didn't need to hear them say it out loud. They wouldn't have been there if Charlie hadn't been gone."

"He crashed?"

"Mm-hmm. He blacked out, from pulling too many Gs. If it had happened at thirty thousand feet, he would have been fine, but—"

"But it didn't?"

She shook her head, and Sam felt a tear drop onto his hands. "He was no higher than a thousand feet. It happened so fast, he never knew a thing."

There was a long moment's silence. Then Sam cleared his throat. "And you've told yourself time and again that at least he didn't suffer, to be grateful for that. You tried to be glad for small favors, when you were mad as hell at fate for taking your husband away."

Another tear fell on their hands. "How did you know?"

He said nothing, just continued to grip her hand with his.

"I left," she said after a moment, "and then Kerry was born, and I never came back here. Not until now. I didn't want to."

"And now?"

"I don't know." She took a ragged breath. "It's been so long. It's been years. I thought I could deal with it. But being here... It's like I never left, like I'd gone back and everything was the same." She paused. "It's like living it all over, the happiness, but all the while knowing—how it ends."

"It's over, Jessie." Sam took her other hand and drew her close. "The shock and that first awful pain, it's all over. What you're feeling now is just the memory."

"I know that. I know!" she cried, shaking her hair back out of her face as she looked up at him. "I know all that, but being here, in this house, makes it seem so *real*! I know it's in the past, but as soon as I close my eyes, if I relax even a little, it all comes rushing back." Her voice shook, the hands that clutched his trembled, and her teeth dug into her lower lip.

"Come here." With a smooth movement, Sam pulled her across the few inches that separated them and into his arms. "It's not crazy, not at all. It'd be crazy if you didn't feel something, coming back here where it all happened. It's all right, sweetheart." He cradled her in his arms, rubbing a hand in circles over her back as if he were soothing a child, crooning soft words of comfort. "It's all right to feel the way you do. It's perfectly all right."

He went on murmuring to her until the rigid tension in her began to ease, until the tears she'd tried so hard to suppress finally began to flow. She needed them and the release that she wouldn't have allowed herself.

And so he held her close, until the sobs slowed and the tears stopped. Even when the last little shaking sobs had ceased and her breathing had steadied, she didn't push away from him. She wiped her hands over her wet cheeks, then subsided back into his arms, her face resting against his chest. Sam stayed as he was, content to hold her, her body lax and easy against him.

He had meant only to comfort her in her distress, but now he was becoming aware of other things. Like the fact that she was cuddled against his naked chest, her breath warm on his skin. Like the fact that she was wearing only a nightgown, the same thin, pretty one, he thought, that she'd had on that night in the hall outside Kerry's room.

He was too conscious of the feel of her light, soft body in his arms, of the scent of her hair and the lingering fragrance of her perfume. The sudden upsurge of desire caught him by surprise.

He continued smoothing his hands over her back, searching now, trailing his fingertips up her spine, sensing the contours of her body beneath the thin cotton. She shifted with a soft, inarticulate murmur, then relaxed again, leaning heavily against him.

Sam frowned into the darkness and bent his head, trying to see her face.

"Jessie?" he breathed. Her only reply was to burrow more deeply into his arms. "Jessie?"

She sighed, and then her breathing resumed the slow, deep rhythm of sleep.

"Well, I'll be damned!" Sam sat back again, suppressing his laughter to keep from waking her.

He probably deserved this. His libido was coming to life, and Jessie was sound asleep. Served him right. She hadn't gotten up in the small hours to come to his bedroom. She'd gotten up because she was haunted by the ghosts of the past. She'd needed comfort, which he'd given, and now she needed rest.

He was aware that she hadn't been sleeping well lately. He'd heard her moving restlessly around her house, but since that first night he hadn't repeated the mistake of getting up himself. He'd listened to her, watched the glow of the kitchen light on the hallway walls and kept very carefully to his own room and his own bed.

Now the insomnia, stress and anxiety were catching up with her. But he could stay with her, sit with her and hold her while she slept, keeping the nightmares at bay.

Dawn tinted the topmost peaks of the mountains to the west, leaving the wide expanse of desert floor in cold, blue shadow.

"Ma'am?"

"Yes?" Jessie turned away from watching Mick do his preflight checks on the F-15. The young controller, Fred Timmons, was offering her a fleece-lined flight jacket.

"It's kinda cold this early in the morning," he said in his soft Southern drawl. "Would you like this?"

"Yes, thank you." She took the jacket with a grateful smile and pulled it on over the thin sweater and windbreaker that were all she had brought with her. The jacket was wonderfully warm when she zipped it up and snuggled her chin into the collar, feeling better immediately. "Thank you, sergeant. It's wonderful."

He nodded. "Colonel Davis said you looked cold."

He turned away to return to the tower, and she looked down at the jacket. The name tag pinned to the pocket read Col. M. Davis. Smiling, she looked across at the plane. Mick ducked under the wing and then straightened, giving the belly of the plane a friendly pat. He looked over at Jessie, and when he saw her bundled into his jacket he grinned and beckoned to her.

"What do you think?"

She looked up at the aircraft. "I think it's an F-15. What else?"

"But ain't it pretty?"

She shook her head, smiling. "You guys and your planes. A plane's a plane, Mick. I just hope this one's in good shape."

"No more than I do," he retorted. "I'm glad you put the jacket on. You were turning blue."

"I know." She nodded ruefully. "Silly of me. I forgot how cold it gets out here at night."

"Yeah, well, I guess you had other things on your mind." Mick dropped an arm around her shoulders. "Were you all right, staying in that house last night?"

"Of course." Her smile was natural and her voice was light, but something came through.

Mick frowned. "I thought they ought to put you in BOQ, but the big guys wanted something more private."

"It's okay, Mick. I know what you mean, but maybe it was best." She bit her lip. "I felt kind of funny walking in there, but it had to be faced."

"You sure?"

"I'm sure." She nodded firmly. "I made a mistake staying away so long. I feel like a weight is off my shoulders now."

"Good." Mick brushed a kiss over her cheek, gave her shoulders a squeeze and released her. He strode toward the chief of the ground crew. "Okay, folks, it's showtime!"

Things began to move quickly as the ground crew bustled around the plane. Sam had been talking to the general and Mr. Howell, but he came to Jessie when she turned toward the control tower.

"Come on." He caught her arm and pulled her along at a trot. "You don't want to be out here when he starts that thing, do you?"

"'That thing' is an F-15, and Mick's not an idiot. He won't start it until we're ready."

Sam glanced at the plane and frowned. He held the door for Jessie to enter the tower, then paused and looked her up and down. "What's this?" He flicked at the sheepskin collar with his fingertips.

She pulled the jacket higher under her chin. "Mick thought I looked cold."

Sam read the name tag, and his mouth tightened. "I see." He let the door swing closed and indicated the stairs in front of them. "Better go on up," he said coldly, "if you want to see everything."

Jessie glanced at his face and walked calmly past him to the stairs. By the time they reached a smallish control room that was separated from the main air traffic control center by a wall of glass, she was no longer thinking about whatever was bothering Sam. That could wait, but the test couldn't.

Out on the apron below them, the plane's powerful engines whined and then roared to life. Unrecognizable behind his helmet and gear, Mick lifted his hand in a thumbs-up, then taxied to the main runway.

Jessie watched the plane roll off into the distance, pause and turn. Mick stopped again, waiting for clearance, and then the plane began to move, slowly at first, then faster, until it thundered past them, lifting into the dawn sky.

It swung into a wide, shallow turn over the desert, was briefly gilded by the rising sun and then disappeared into the distance.

Jessie stepped back from the windows to watch a monitor while the loudspeakers transmitted Mick's conversation with Fred, the controller. Mick swung around in a circle over the desert and mountains to approach the main runway again.

He had deliberately positioned the plane so that it would have to change course for the landing. He would rely on Jessie's program to turn the plane, make the descent, lower the landing gear and bring the F-15 to a stop. Mick could override the program at any time simply by putting his hands on the controls again.

"Hands off the controls," he said, and Jessie held her breath.

Mick calmly and crisply recited the readings on his instruments as the plane descended, slowed and turned on a heading that would bring it safely to the runway. Sam stood behind Jessie, looking over her shoulder as she watched the numbers on the screen, columns of them, changing second by second. The figures meant nothing to him, but he could sense her intensity in the stiff set of her shoulders and the tension in her back. His only clue to what was going on was Mick's calm, almost bored-sounding reports to Fred.

Airspeed, altitude and all the other parameters were correct, and off in the distance they could see a dark speck against the sky.

"There he is!" Terry Gold pointed out the window, but only Mr. Howell and his fellow agent looked. The others were absorbed in the computer and radar displays.

"Flaps?" Fred asked. They were down. "Gear?"

Mick's voice crackled through the radio. "She's coming in, but the landing gear are up."

Jessie jerked around to look outside. The speck in the sky was closing on them fast. She turned back to the monitor. "They'll be down in a minute," she whispered to no one in particular, watching the rapidly changing figures intently. "In just...a...minute."

Her fists were clenched at her sides. Sam caught one of her hands in his, and she gripped his fingers tightly.

One number on the screen began to blink. "Now," she whispered. "Come on!"

The radio crackled again, giving Mick's altitude, then, "The gear are going down!" He paused, then, "Gear down and locked."

Jessie's fingers tightened convulsively on Sam's, and she turned to look out at the runway. They could see the plane clearly now, approaching fast. Mick's words came quickly, reading figures off his altimeter and airspeed indicator as the plane descended. They had already decided the altitude at which Mick could still make the decision to land the plane himself, and as he neared that level the group in the control room tensed.

"Do you wish to override?" Fred asked. There was a moment of taut silence.

"Negative. Repeat, negative. I will not override." There was silence while the altimeter figures counted down—three hundred feet, two hundred, one hundred.

Jessie stared out the window, her gaze riveted on the F-15 as it angled toward the ground. The nose came up just a bit as the rear landing gear touched the runway with a puff of smoke, lifted and touched again. Then the nose gear settled gently onto the runway. The engines reversed thrust to slow the aircraft, the roar reaching them through the thick windows, and the plane rolled to a stop almost directly in front of them. The engines whined into silence as Mick shut them down, but no one moved or spoke until the canopy lifted.

"All *right*!"

Fred's yell was the start of a great shout of relief and approval that filled the room. Jessie sprinted recklessly out the door, taking the stairs two at a time, pulling Sam along by the hand. She let go of him when they got outside and dashed across the apron.

Mick, grinning hugely, was climbing down from the cockpit. He clapped the crew chief on the back, then turned to Jessie. She flung herself into his arms, and he swung her off the ground in an exuberant hug.

"It worked!" she cried, and kissed him hard. "Mick, it really worked!"

"Of course it worked!" He gave her another bone-crushing squeeze. "You're a genius!" With his arm around her, Mick drew her over to receive the congratulations of the others.

Sam said the right things to her, that the program was great, that he was truly glad that the test was successful and Colonel Davis was okay. But he stepped back to stand on the fringes, watching the congratulations and waiting out the lengthy debriefing that followed, carried on in a private room near General Walters's office.

The debriefing process, complete with charts and graphs, and with stenographers recording every word, took most of the day. Lunch was brought in, and finally, late in the afternoon, they began winding things up.

General Walters's chair squeaked under the strain as he leaned back and tented his fingers in front of him. He looked across the table at Mick and Jessie, who were sitting side by side.

"So we can consider this morning's test a success?"

"Absolutely." Mick grinned.

"Essentially," Jessie replied at the same time, and the general regarded her quizzically.

"Would you care to clarify that, Mrs. Ames?"

She glanced at Mick, then spoke to the general. "I'm glad . . . I can't really tell you *how* glad I am that the program landed Mi—Colonel Davis's plane safely this morning, but I'm not totally satisfied with—"

"It was perfect!" Mick protested.

She shook her head at him. "Not quite. I still have to finish the involuntary takeover for pilots who aren't able to flip a switch or push a button, and there were a couple of minor problems with other elements. I can work on those with Colonel Davis and the control tower personnel."

"Those are specifics. What's your overall view of the test?" the general asked.

"Overall?" A slow smile spread across Jessie's face, "Overall, general, I think it went well. Really well."

"Oh, come on." Mick elbowed her gently. "You know it went perfect."

"Almost." She grinned. "Almost perfect."

"In any case, I think we have everything we need." Smiling like a genial uncle, the general pushed his chair back and stood up. "So we can adjourn for the day. I'd like to thank you all for an excellent effort."

Outside in the scorchingly hot afternoon, with the autumn sun hanging low over the western horizon, everyone drifted in different directions, calling goodbyes as they went. Jessie walked slowly toward the parking lot, lost in thought.

Mick caught up with her and dropped an arm around her shoulders. "I'd take you to the O-Club for a gourmet dinner, Jessie, but—"

"But the O-Club doesn't serve gourmet dinners!" She laughed as she supplied the punch line.

"And I have duty tonight."

"That's okay, Mick. I don't think I have the energy for it, anyway. I'd just as soon go take a cool shower and loaf around for a while."

"You'll be okay?"

"Of course." She smiled.

He kissed her cheek and turned away toward the flight line while she and Sam continued to the car. He said nothing, just held the door for her to get into the bakingly hot interior. While he walked around to the driver's side, Jessie wound the window down, fanning herself with her hand. If he wanted to give her the silent treatment, that was up to him. She was too tired to care.

The five-minute drive to the house was accomplished in silence. Sam followed her inside, closed the door and stood in the middle of the shadowy living room.

"Jessie?"

"Yes?" She paused on her way to the cool shower she was longing for.

"What is Mick Davis to you?"

Chapter 13

What?"

"What is Mick Davis to you?"

Jessie dropped her head and studied the carpet beneath her feet for several seconds. When she looked up, her face was calm, concealing her thoughts. "He's a friend, a very good friend. I'll tell you about it if you want, but I'm hot and hungry and tired, and I want to clean up and have some supper."

"Oh...well, sure." He released her arm and stepped back. "What do you want for supper? I can start fixing it."

"I think—" She looked out the hall window at the desert landscape. "You know, I think I'd like to have a picnic. Did they leave us something to make sandwiches with?"

"They must have. You have your shower and I'll see what I can put together."

He put together enough for an army—roast beef sandwiches, fruit, chips, soda and containers of coleslaw and potato salad he'd found in the refrigerator. He even included a bag of cookies, packing it all, along with a blanket, in a couple of good-sized paper bags.

When Jessie joined him she was wearing jeans and a short-sleeved white shirt, sneakers and sunglasses and carrying a jacket. Sam glanced over his shoulder, then hefted a bag in each hand.

"Here it is. Do you know where you want to go?"

"Mm-hmm." She looked at his chinos and sport shirt. "We'll have to walk a mile or so," she warned him, "and it'll get cool. You'll need a jacket."

He brought one, and she directed him to drive to a spot a couple of miles from the cluster of huge hangars that marked the flight line. They parked the car and hiked to the top of a smallish hill. It wasn't a mountain, by any means, but the desert floor around the base was so flat that they felt they could see forever.

Sam said so as he spread a blanket over the dusty ground.

"I know. I don't know whether it's the air or the terrain, but you feel like you can see the ends of the earth from here." Jessie sat down cross-legged with Sam beside her, his long legs stretched out in front of him.

"How far away are the mountains?" He gestured toward the south. "Those ones over there?"

"I don't even know. Miles and miles. That's why it's such a good place to land the space shuttle." She took the sandwich he handed her, and a plate with salads and fruit on it.

"That and the dry lake. An ideal natural runway."

"Unless it rains and the lake isn't dry anymore," she said around a mouthful of roast beef. "Mmm. This is a good sandwich."

"Glad you like it." They ate in silence for several minutes. When Sam finished and set his plate aside, he turned toward her, his thigh brushing against her knees. "Jessie?"

"Hmm?"

"Can you tell me about Mick Davis?"

She set down her plate and took a long drink of her cream soda. "Mick," she said thoughtfully. She put down her can and drew her knees up to her chest, linking her arms around them.

"Mick is my friend. He was Charlie's friend, even though they weren't in the same squad or anything. They spent a lot of time together, and we used to plan dinners with Mick and Penny."

"Penny?"

"Mick's wife." Her voice was soft with reminiscence. "She was a doll, tiny and redheaded and sweet."

"I thought Davis was single."

"He is." She raised her head, and the evening breeze ruffled her hair, lifting it away from her face. "Now. A drunk driver wandered over the center line when she was driving back from Lancaster one day. She didn't always take the freeway. She liked the little desert roads. She was killed instantly." Jessie paused, and Sam could hear her swallow hard.

"Charlie and I were all Mick had. He took her home to bury her, but he'd never been close to her family, and he had none of his own. When he came back after the funeral, he was...empty inside. We tried to help."

"Most people don't like to be around grief. It makes them uncomfortable."

"We were his friends. We had to help." She fell silent and looked out over the desert landscape, which was gilded now by the sun sinking low in the western sky.

"I hope we did help. I don't know. But when Charlie was killed a few months later, Mick was there. The chaplain asked if there was anyone I wanted him to call. I said no. I couldn't think of anybody. I couldn't think at all. Everything was a blank. When they left, I just sat in the living room, staring at the wall, thinking that it was all a nightmare and I would wake up and it would all be gone. Only I didn't wake up.''

She looked up at Sam, her face bleak with remembered pain. "I was sitting there when Mick came. He—'' Her voice cracked, and she took a couple of slow breaths to steady herself. "He took care of me. I don't know how I would've gotten through those first weeks without him.''

"And yet you two never got . . . close?''

She looked out over the desert again, a half smile tugging at her lips. "We were, and maybe we still are, as close as two people can be. But not the way you mean. He's like the brother I never had. I love him, but I'm not in love with him, if you see the distinction.''

"I see.''

Though he didn't move or change his position, Jessie could sense an undefinable relaxing of the tension in him, and she was amused by the reason. Sam was jealous! Who would ever have believed it? The man who insisted he felt nothing for her but lust had comforted her in the night and was jealous of Mick Davis. He might call it lust, she thought with the kind of tender indulgence she usually saved for Kerry, but it was more than that.

And he wasn't the ogre he'd made himself out to be, either. That realization left her with a startling sense of relief. The man she had been falling in love with wasn't as cold and cruel as he'd wanted her to think. She hadn't misjudged him, and she hadn't deluded herself.

Feeling herself relax, too, she leaned back and watched the sky fade from pink to purple as night fell over the distant buildings. On the flight line, a jet taxied down the runway and lifted off, disappearing into the distance to the east. The sound of the engines reached them faintly, then faded again.

"Where do you think he's going?'' Sam asked softly.

"He might be going to Nellis, over in Nevada," Jessie replied, "or he might just fly in a loop and then come back." The silence that fell between them was a comfortable one. The dusk deepened, and somewhere nearby a coyote yipped mournfully.

"Does it still bother you? Being here?"

Jessie glanced at the man sitting beside her. She couldn't read his expression in the dim light, but she could hear concern beneath his carefully casual tone of voice.

"It did. Last night." She could talk about that now, with introspection rather than deep pain. "I didn't want to come back. When I heard the test would be here and not at Nellis, I wanted to back out."

"But?"

"But it's my program. I had a responsibility. I told myself I was a big girl and I wasn't going to be a baby about this. Then, that house." Her voice dropped, until he could hardly hear her above the soft rush of the breeze. "Now I think I *had* to come back. I had to face the past, and say goodbye to it, so I could go on without the old shadows hanging over me."

"It doesn't upset you?"

"Not anymore." She smiled at him. It was a broad flash of relief and freedom. "I'm glad. I'm free to come here now, and I'm glad, because I always liked it."

"I can see why." Sam looked out at the purple desert, at the darkening sky overhead, dotted with a growing galaxy of stars. "It's awesome and beautiful."

Jessie turned and found him looking at her rather than the scenery. His face was very close to hers, his breath feathering her cheek. Her heart skipped a beat, then began to pound in slow, heavy thumps.

"Beautiful," he repeated, and bent his head to kiss her.

His lips were gentle, searching rather than demanding, moving softly as he persuaded her lips to part. Gentle persuasion, where she might have expected a sudden rush of passion. Gentle persuasion, where he might have tried sweeping her off her feet.

But she responded. Though he touched only her lips, warmth flowed through her, the remnants of grief and bitter memories melting like ice cream in the desert sun. She moved before he did, turning toward him, balancing on one hand and reaching up with the other to clutch his shoulder as she strained up toward his mouth.

When he knocked away the last vestige of her balance by wrapping his arms around her and pulling her down as he lay back on the blanket. She sprawled across his chest, her hair falling around her face and her arms closing around his neck as they kissed. She could feel passion in him, but she also felt caring and something that was almost shy, something that meant much more to her than simple, uncomplicated lust.

She knew the secret he was hiding even from himself, and the knowledge warmed her in the moment before she gave herself up to his kisses. They went on and on, long and deep, until they no longer satisfied, until she wanted more, needed more. She twisted in his arms, pressing her body closer, her movements seeking, inciting, demanding.

Sam kissed her, hard. Then, with an effort that she could sense, he tore his lips away and buried his face in her hair. She could feel his muscles bunch and tense before he rolled away, putting a slight distance between them.

"We—" His voice was a hoarse rasp. He drew a deep breath and cleared his throat. "We should go back."

"Yes."

They packed up their picnic without speaking and returned to the car in silence. They walked quickly and tossed the picnic things into the trunk, and then gravel sprayed from beneath the spinning tires as Sam made a ragged turn and headed back to the house.

She walked inside, and he closed the door very deliberately, locking them in and the world out.

He turned slowly away from the door to look across at her. She stood in the center of the living room, looking back at him with a message in her eyes that made his heart pound. She stayed where she was, waiting for him, knowing he would walk across to her, knowing he would lead her down the hall to the bedroom, where they would be alone.

She didn't know he would sweep her into his arms and carry her there, cradled against his shoulder. She gasped when he scooped her up with an arm behind her knees, and she clung tightly to his neck as he carried her down the narrow hall and into the darkened bedroom. He laid her across the bed with exquisite gentleness and stood looking down at her as he shrugged out of his windbreaker and shirt and tossed them aside.

A shaft of light from the streetlight outside slanted between the curtains, sliding across his chest and shoulders as he came to her, eased himself down on the bed and slid his arms around her.

A little shy of him, she looked not at his face but at her hands, which were resting lightly on his chest. His body was as big and lean and muscular as she remembered, his skin warm and smooth, the hair on his chest soft yet crisp against her palms. She stroked her fingers across his body, savoring the feel of him, learning curve and line and texture. He stood it for a moment, then pulled her firmly against him, kissing her with the passion that he had earlier kept under tight control.

He teased her lips apart and plundered her mouth with a kind of desperate hunger while his hands roved restlessly over her back, stroking and caressing, then tugging her blouse free of her waistband. She shivered in pure pleasure as he stroked her skin and wriggled slightly away to help him strip her blouse off.

The time for patience and delay was past. They were trapped in the passion they had built and then postponed, and their hands were clumsy with haste as they pulled clothing away, their mouths hungry, demanding. When Sam tossed the last scrap of her clothing to the floor, Jessie wrapped her arms around him, twined her legs around his and let passion take her. Sam kissed and stroked and teased, and her body seemed to melt from within, lax and boneless and alive in every nerve and vessel.

It was both a discovery and a rediscovery, and it was even more wonderful than she had remembered. She had been a widow for so many years, and she had remained celibate due to a combination of initial grief, single motherhood and innate distaste for the casual taking of lovers. She'd known what it meant to have a marriage based on interwoven love and friendship and passion, and she had no desire to settle for the emptiness of passion alone.

Now, though, with this man, she had the passion, the love and even, she thought, the beginnings of friendship. Sam's every gesture gave him away—his jealousy of Mick, his protectiveness of Jessie herself, his tenderness as a lover.

He loved her with strength and gentleness, exciting her more than she would have thought possible. He taught her again the magic and excitement of feeling a man in her arms, the roughness of hair against her smoother skin, the strength and contours of hard muscles against her softer body, the touch of firm lips on her breasts, the exquisitely exciting rasp of a day's growth of beard.

Her own touches and kisses and movements drove Sam to the same peak of need, drove him until he could wait no longer, until he turned with her in his arms and covered her body with his. He heard her gasp of mingled surprise and pleasure as their bodies joined, and she clung to him tightly as the magic began, powerful and overwhelming.

The need and the wanting grew and built, the world narrowed to only them, and then it spun away in an explosion of light and heat and release.

Jessie came back to earth slowly, reluctant to leave the limbo of delight they had reached. Sated and drowsy, she clung to Sam as he pulled the bedcovers over them.

There was no way he could have disentangled himself, even if he'd wanted to, so he settled her in the circle of his arms and slid down comfortably to sleep.

"Jessie?" he murmured.

She could barely summon the energy to reply. "Mmm?"

"Are you okay?"

"Mmm." He could feel her smile as she nestled even closer. "Wonderful. S'wonderful." She relaxed against him, her breathing deepening and slowing. Sam thought she was asleep, but then she moved again, curling into his side and sliding one leg across his. She yawned hugely and rubbed her cheek against his cheek.

"I love you, Sam," she murmured as sleep claimed her.

She woke alone.

Her first thought was of the night before, and she was smiling before she was fully awake, secure in her newfound happiness. She kept her eyes closed and reached for Sam but found only an empty bed. She opened her eyes and looked, but he wasn't there, and the sheets were cold.

Jessie lay back on her pillow, fighting a disappointment that she told herself sternly was silly. She would have liked to wake in Sam's arms, but men probably didn't think of things like that. She closed her eyes and stretched luxuriously, conscious of a few aches but still smiling. She didn't mind the little twinges. They were memories of something special. She rolled out of bed, yawning, and padded to the bathroom to brush her teeth and her hair and pull on a robe.

He was making coffee. The scent reached her as she entered the living room, along with the smells of bacon and toast. So that was why he'd left her alone, to fix breakfast for them both. Or was he fixing breakfast in bed? They needed to get going fairly early, but they had a little time before they had to leave. She smiled and pulled her slipping robe higher on her shoulder before she pushed open the swinging door and walked into the kitchen.

Sam stood at the stove, forking bacon out of a skillet, and it was obvious he wasn't planning to rejoin her in bed. He was shaved and dressed in jeans, shirt and shoes, and his hair was neatly combed.

He didn't hear her open the door, so she padded silently over to him and slid her arms around his waist for a hug. His reaction was not exactly what she had expected.

"What the hell?"

He jerked roughly away before she could link her hands around him. Several strips of bacon slid off the plate in his hand, landed on the edge of the burner and began to smolder. He slammed the plate down on the counter and tried to pull the bacon away from the flame with a fork before it caught fire.

"Dammit!" he muttered irritably. The last strip of bacon burst into flames, and he tossed it into the sink. It flared brightly before Jessie turned on the water to put it out with a sizzle and a puff of smelly smoke.

"What did you do that for?"

Jessie stared at his back for a second before answering. "To say good morning," she said mildly. "That's all."

"You shouldn't sneak up on a person."

Another moment of silence. "I didn't mean to sneak. Sorry." She turned away to pour herself a cup of coffee.

"I'm having bacon and toast." Sam set his cup and a filled plate on the table. "You want eggs?" His tone was just short of rudeness.

Jessie looked at the food waiting on the counter. "Bacon and toast will be fine."

It was clear he wasn't going to fix breakfast for her, so she put some of the bacon and toast on a plate and took it to the table. She didn't know what to think. Rudeness, especially this kind of deliberate rudeness, wasn't like Sam at all. Even when he had been angry with her, he hadn't been purposely hurtful. Last night he'd been loving and tender and passionate, but this morning...

What could have changed so drastically since last night?

She let him get away with it for ten minutes, while he ate his breakfast and she picked at hers. When he pushed his chair back to rise, she caught his wrist and held on.

"What do you want?" He tried to pull free, but she didn't let go.

"We need to talk." She didn't ask if he wanted to, because that wasn't the issue. "Now."

"There's nothing to talk about." He didn't jerk away, but he didn't meet her eyes, either.

"There is." She waited for him to look up, and when he didn't she swallowed and made herself go on. "Sam, please tell me what's wrong this morning. Something has changed since last night, and I have to know what it is."

Sam glanced up, his eyes cold. "There's no point in discussing this. We have a long drive ahead of us, and we need to get going."

"We have time enough." Jessie tipped her head to one side, trying to see into Sam's face. "Last night was..." She faltered, searching for the right words. "Last night I gave myself to you in love, Sam. This morning you're like a stranger. I have to know what's gone wrong."

He shoved himself out of his chair, striding across the small kitchen to stand facing the sink.

"Look," he said, his voice clipped and curt, "there's nothing to talk about. What happened— Well, it happened, but it didn't change anything."

Jessie stood, too, and walked across the room, stopping when she was an arm's length away from Sam. His back was stiff, the muscles rigid beneath his thin cotton polo shirt. She wanted to touch him, so she locked her hands together in front of her to prevent herself from reaching out.

"Sam, it changed everything. We made love. We shared something precious and wonderful and intimate, and it can't help but change things."

"It didn't change me. I'm no different." Sam turned his back to the counter and clamped his hands on the edge on either side of him. His face was stony, and he bit out his words. "What happened last night didn't make a difference to anything."

Jessie flinched as if he'd struck her. "Sam, I *love* you! Doesn't *that* make a difference?"

"No!" He didn't shout, but his angry vehemence was worse than a shout would have been, and Jessie winced in spite of herself. "No! It doesn't make any difference. I told you before, I'm not looking for love. I don't want the strings and complications. I don't want love forced on me, and I don't want somebody expecting me to give love to them, because I'm not going to. I like my life the way it is, and I don't want to change it. I'm not going to change it."

She stared at him in disbelief. "You don't want love?"

"No." The absolute certainty in the single syllable was like a slap in the face.

There were several long seconds of silence. Then Jessie drew a deep breath and spoke very, very calmly.

"I see. Well, I *do* want love, Sam. I had it once, and I know what it brings to life. I want love, and I'm not going to settle for something as empty as sex without it.'' She brushed past him, put her plate and cup in the sink and continued toward the door. ''I'll be ready to leave in half an hour.''

Chapter 14

The engine rumbled into silence. Jessie pushed open the passenger door and was climbing out before Sam had the key free of the ignition. She was glad to be out of the car, to escape the suffocating tension that had ridden with them for more than six hours.

She was confused, angry and hurt. She'd shared something wonderful with Sam—or at least she'd thought they were sharing something wonderful. Now she didn't know what to think. Was she crazy, or was it Sam who wasn't thinking clearly? He didn't want love? How could anyone not want love?

At the front door, she set her overnight bag down while she unlocked the bolt and chain, then picked up the bag and pushed the door open. She stepped inside and froze.

Behind her the wind caught the door and swung it back to bang against the side of the house, while in the entryway the canvas bag slipped out of her nerveless fingers and thudded to the floor. Pressing a hand to her mouth, she walked slowly into what had been her living room, nausea rising in her throat.

The room was a shambles. Furniture was overturned, knickknacks and books swept off the shelves, drawers dumped out, papers and magazines scattered. Nothing was as it had been when she'd left, nothing was undisturbed, nothing was whole.

"What the hell?" Behind her, Sam closed the front door and crunched across the shattered remnants of a lamp.

"What happened?" Jessie whispered brokenly. "What happened to my house?"

He looked around the room, his face grim. "Maybe a burglary. Or maybe something made to look like a burglary."

"What?"

Jessie bent over a pile of her books, which had been thrown from the shelves. They had fallen helter-skelter, corners crushed and bindings ripped. She picked one up. It was her favorite book of poetry. The pages were crumpled, and many were torn. She tried unsuccessfully to smooth them out, then gave up and gripped the book between her hands as she gazed helplessly around her, seeking someplace to put it. She couldn't even put the book back on its shelf, because the bookcase had been flung to the floor.

She didn't try to right it, couldn't find the energy. The destruction was so comprehensive that she couldn't see where to start in cleaning it up. She turned, not wanting to see any more of the breakage and mess, and looked at Sam.

"If it wasn't burglars, who did this?"

He surveyed the room. "Can you tell if there is anything missing?"

"In here?" She looked around and shrugged helplessly. "Even if things were missing, I wouldn't be able to tell."

"But you don't see that anything's obviously gone?" He'd already noted that the TV and VCR were lying in a corner, damaged but not stolen. "Did you have any silver or valuable paintings in here?"

"No paintings. There were a couple of things on the mantel, a tray and a pitcher. Wedding-present kind of things."

"How about the rest of the house? Silver, money, cameras, do you have any of that?"

She shrugged. "My regular flatware is stainless steel. I've got a couple of silver serving pieces. There's some money in my dresser drawer, and the camera's in the den."

"Let's see if they're still here, then. Real burglars wouldn't miss that stuff. You said you had the money in the dresser drawer? Where was the silver?"

"In the kitchen. In a drawer."

He shook his head in weary disgust. "Burglars would clean you out in about six minutes."

They stopped in the kitchen doorway. The floor was deep in broken glass and crockery and food. All the cupboards were open, and even the refrigerator's contents had been swept out. Judging by the smell, it had been that way for at least a day. Jessie clutched the door frame and made an inarticulate sound of distress.

Sam caught her hand and led her away to the bedrooms. Kerry's room was messed up, but not as badly as Jessie's, where the mattress had been flung off the bed and all the drawers emptied. The cash she kept there, three hundred dollars folded in a money clip, was under one of the piles. Sam handed it to her without a word and went on into the den.

It was in the same state as the rest of the house, but when they righted her overturned desk the camera was there, beneath a broken drawer. The lens was cracked, and the back was open. Sam picked it up carefully, catching the shattered lens as it fell from its mount. He handed the camera to her. "Was there film in this?"

"Yes, there was." She cradled the camera sadly. "I had almost finished a roll that I started a couple of months ago."

"What was on that film?" The note of urgency in Sam's voice brought her gaze up to him. He was searching through the debris that had been under the desk.

"Just pictures. Kerry, the neighbor kids, the pink hibiscus in the backyard. Why?"

"There's no film here, which means they took it. Which means they think you might have information on that film that they want."

"But what would they want with pictures of Kerry?"

"They don't. But suppose you made notes on the White Eagle program, and rather than leave incriminating sheets of paper lying around you photographed them and then destroyed the originals?"

Jessie frowned in comprehension but said nothing.

"They took the film, but they didn't bother with the camera. They tossed the house, but they didn't take the TV, or the money, or the silver." He led her into the hallway, where they at least had a clear floor to stand on. "Real burglars might make a mess, but they'd take the goods. These weren't real burglars."

Jessie stared up at him with dark, worried eyes. "Who were they?"

"I think you already know. And I think it's time to get out of here." He pointed her back toward her bedroom. "You can't stay here. Go pack some things, enough for a couple of days, at least. I've got some calls to make while you do that, and then we'll leave." He started toward the living room, then paused. "And don't go in the bathroom. There's glass all over the floor. We'll stop at a drugstore for toothpaste and stuff."

Jessie went to pack. Almost in shock, her anger forgotten, she obeyed him automatically. Whatever had happened last night, she needed his strength right now. When she rejoined him, she was carrying a small suitcase in one hand and had the pieces of a lumpy clay figurine in the other. She was biting her lip, trying to hold back tears.

"Why?" she asked brokenly. "Why did they have to break things?"

"What is this?" Sam gently took the pieces from her hands and tried to fit them together.

"A bird. Kerry made it in art class last spring."

Sam managed to fit the pieces into a creation that resembled an overweight turkey with a big smile on its face. "I think we can fix it."

"You do?"

"Yes. We'll try, anyway." He took the bag from her hand but didn't start for the door. "When you were packing your stuff," he asked, "did you see Cat"

"Cat?" Her eyes opened wide. "Oh, my gosh, I forgot he was even here!"

"You had other things on your mind," Sam said easily, but his worry showed. "I looked around the living room while I was calling, but no Cat."

"Would he be hiding somewhere? Surely all this—" her gesture encompassed the devastated house "—would have scared him."

"Yes, it would have scared him, and yes, he'd probably hide, so we'd better find him. I don't want him here if they come back."

Jessie bit back a startled protest. Of course. If they'd already done this much, why wouldn't they come back for more?

"We'll find him" was all she said.

They searched together, through closets and cupboards and piles of belongings. The kitchen came last, because of the difficulty of even entering the room. Jessie cleared a path through the debris with a broom, but glass scrunched under her shoes, and she slipped and almost fell in a gory-looking pool of ketchup.

"Watch it!" Sam caught her hand and hauled her back to her feet. "If you fall in here we'll spend all night getting you stitched up."

"I know." She got her footing again. "Thanks."

She stooped carefully and opened the cupboard under the sink while Sam explored the broom closet. She leaned forward until her head and shoulders were inside the space, which went from the sink back into the corner. Jessie usually stored cleaning supplies there, and she sneezed as she leaned farther in, her eyes stinging from the aroma of spilled window cleaner.

"Whew, it stinks in here! I wish I hadn't just bought ammon—" She broke off. "Sam." Her voice was low and urgent.

"What?" He backed out of the broom closet.

"He's in here." She gazed into the depths of the cupboard, where she could see two unblinking eyes gleaming in the dim light. "I can see his eyes, but I can't reach him. He's back in the corner."

"Let me try." Sam took her place, wedging his shoulders into the cabinet opening with difficulty. "I see him," he grunted, and stretched an arm into the cupboard. "Come here, Cat. Come on, old boy."

Cat wasn't eager to come, but a lot of crooning and the offer of a chicken leg that hadn't spoiled finally got him out of his safe spot. He inched forward until Sam could grip him around the chest and lift him out. Sam had the cat almost through the cupboard door when he reached in to support his hindquarters and Cat gave a shrill howl of pain. Sam drew him quickly out onto the floor, still hissing in protest, and then the reason for his distress became obvious.

There was blood on his fur from several cuts, and he was guarding his back leg, holding it tucked up against his belly.

It was clearly broken, the foot sticking out at an unnatural angle. Jessie gasped, and Sam swore quietly and viciously.

"I'll get a towel," she murmured. She found a couple of clean ones in the chaos that had been her bathroom, and she and Sam gently but securely swathed the cat.

"Should we put him in a box, or will you hold him?"

Sam looked at Cat. Only his head was showing. "I'll hold him. If I let go he's going to try to get out, and then he'll hurt himself."

"Okay." Jessie held her breath while Sam lifted Cat, who was steadily growling his objections, into his arms. "Where are your keys?"

Sam handed them to her, and she led the way without a backward look at her ravaged house. The vet worked on Cat for over an hour, setting his broken leg and cleaning and stitching his cuts. While Cat was coming out of the anesthetic, he joined Jessie and Sam in the waiting room.

"Do you know what happened to him?" The veterinarian, Dan Conrad, was a youngish man, tall and thin, with a shock of curly dark hair and a grim expression on his friendly face.

Sam shook his head. "The house was burgled. He was there. When we got back, he was hiding inside a kitchen cupboard."

"Cats do that when they're scared or hurt." Conrad nodded slowly. "He didn't look as if he'd been hit by a car."

"What *did* he look like?" Sam asked, too softly.

Conrad glanced at them both, and directed his answer to Sam. "Like he'd been abused—kicked, maybe. I've seen it before in cats and small dogs. I've set his leg, and it should do fine. The cuts were minor, and I checked him for internal injuries and bleeding, but apart from some bruising, he's okay."

"Really?" Jessie asked.

"Yes, really." Conrad smiled. "He's had his shots, and I gave him antibiotics to handle any infection. You can take him home anytime."

"Is there anything we need to do for him?"

"Just keep him quiet, give him water tonight, and light food tomorrow. I'll give you a sheet of instructions. He'll worry at the cast, but that's normal. He won't be able to get it off. He'll sleep a great deal for a few days, but all he really needs now is lots of love."

There was a moment of silence. Jessie glanced at Sam, but his face was angled away from her. She turned back to Dan Conrad. "We'll take good care of him."

Cat rode on her lap this time, nestled snugly in a box padded with Jessie's towels. He was still too sleepy from the anesthetic to make any attempts to climb out, but she stroked his head soothingly anyway as Sam pulled onto the street.

"Where are we going?"

Sam glanced at her. "We can't go back to your house, so we're going to mine."

She was torn between curiosity and apprehension, but she knew it was the logical solution. Her house was uninhabitable, and they could hardly take an ailing cat to a hotel. And she had to admit that she was curious to see where, and how, Sam King chose to live.

They entered the house through the kitchen. Jessie held the door open so that he could carry Cat inside. "Lock it, would you?" he asked as he passed.

"Sure." She fastened two locks and a dead bolt and followed him into the living room. While he set Cat on the sofa and bent over him, Jessie walked over to the long windows that looked out on a spectacular sunset over the ocean beyond the Pacific Palisades.

"Sam, this is beautiful!"

"Yeah." He glanced out at the splendor in the sky and grinned. "You ought to see it on those foggy Santa Monica mornings."

"When you can't see out of your backyard, right?" She walked over and sat down carefully on the other side of Cat. He was lying comfortably enough inside the box, and he looked rather blearily up at them.

"That's fog for you. Should we take him out of the box, do you think?"

"Probably, if only to keep him from trying to jump out on his own." She looked down the short hallway into the kitchen. "Why don't we make him a bed on the kitchen floor?"

They did, piling the towels and a pure wool blanket that Sam took from a linen cupboard in a warm corner between the refrigerator and pantry. Cat submitted to being carried in and laid in the soft nest, making little rumbles of protest but no longer yowling in pain.

Sam crouched beside him, murmuring and stroking him until he put his head down and went to sleep.

Jessie sat cross-legged on the linoleum a yard away, leaning comfortably against the cupboards, watching—watching and learning that Sam had been lying that morning.

He'd told her he didn't want love, that he wouldn't accept it if given and wouldn't give love in return, but that wasn't true. He loved Cat, and he accepted the love Cat gave him. It showed in the gentleness of his touch as he stroked the furry cheek and in the anger she saw in his face when he didn't know she was looking.

She lowered her eyes to the floor, following a line through the pattern in the linoleum, remembering the things he'd said. She'd been too angry and hurt to fully understand then. Now she was thinking more clearly. He didn't want a woman expecting him to give affection. She'd understood the bit about being tied down, but now she realized that it was the expectation of love that he most objected to.

He wouldn't allow a woman to pressure him into caring for her. While she saw love as a gift, Sam seemed to see it as a demand, perhaps an endless series of demands that he act a certain way, or feel a certain way, or *be* a certain way. He was afraid of the expectations. He wouldn't or couldn't be something he wasn't, and that was what he thought love would do to him.

And what, or who, had made him feel that way?

Jessie lifted her head and gazed blindly out the kitchen windows. She was lost in her thoughts, and when Sam finally moved, she jumped.

"Do you want dinner?" He pulled open the refrigerator door. "I don't know what I've got in here, but we didn't eat much at lunch."

Jessie got to her feet. "Do you have eggs and cheese or mushrooms or something? I can make an omelet pretty quickly."

He grunted his assent and rummaged in the depths of the refrigerator, finally producing an egg carton. He passed it to her. "There may even be some cheese in here that hasn't turned fuzzy yet." In the end he found everything they needed.

They were both hungry, since they'd barely touched their take-out burgers at noon, and the simple cheese omelet Jessie divided between two plates tasted wonderful. She concentrated on her food, and for a few minutes she stopped worrying about feelings and emotions and what she was going to do next.

When she was halfway through her coffee, though, she could no longer ignore all the hovering problems. She set her cup down and looked across the small kitchen table at Sam. As if he could feel her gaze on him, he looked up.

"What is it?"

"What will happen to my house?"

She could tell from the look on Sam's face that she hadn't kept her feelings out of her voice. He reached out and took her hand.

"We'll get it cleaned up."

"I know we will, but it'll take days. And so many things are broken!"

"No. no." He kept her hand in his. "I don't mean 'we' as in you and me. I mean 'we' as in the bureau. The police will be notified, and the bureau will get a cleanup crew to take care of the mess."

"They will?"

"Uh-huh."

"But how will they know where to put things away? They don't know where everything goes."

"They'll figure out that the books go on the bookcases." He smiled. "Mostly they'll be there to clean up the debris, pick up the furniture, wash the floor, that kind of thing. They'll put stuff away in the logical places, but you can move things around when you get the time."

"When I go back there."

"Yeah."

She looked down at her plate for a moment. "When can I go back, Sam?"

He considered his answer. "Not right away. When this is over, I'd guess."

"How long does Kerry have to stay away?"

"How long can she stay with her grandparents?"

"As long as she needs to, I guess."

"She shouldn't have to stay away all that long," Sam said reassuringly. "We'll let Leonid know you're ready to make the last exchange, and then we'll set our trap."

"How long will it take?"

"Just a few days."

"And after that things will be back to normal?"

"Yeah. Back to normal."

Jessie pulled her hand away and got up. "I didn't know."

"Know what?"

"When I started this I knew it would be hard, but I didn't know what it would do to my life. My house is a wreck, and I can't live there. Kerry has to stay with her grandparents. I'm not doing any real work at the office because I'm spending all my time dummying up a fake White Eagle program. I look over my shoulder all the time, I'm afraid to answer the phone—"

"The phone! I forgot all about it!"

"Forgot what?"

"Forgot the answering machine tape. Look, I'm sorry, Jessie, you don't know how sorry I am that your life has been turned upside down this way. I never wanted it to happen. Sometimes these operations go smooth as silk, but sometimes—I'm sorry. I'd hoped we could wrap this up without putting you and Kerry through anything like this. I promise you, we will do whatever we can to get it over with soon."

He caught her hand and squeezed it, then led her to the living room, where he picked up his jacket and searched quickly through the pockets. He produced a small cassette tape. "And getting it over with is why I want this. I took it out of your answering machine."

"It wasn't broken?"

He shook his head. "It was on the floor with all the stuff from your desk, but it was still working, and the light was flashing. Come on. Let's see who called you this weekend."

He led the way down the hall to his study, a cozy den of a room with oak woodwork at the windows and an entire wall of well-stocked bookcases. A big mahogany desk occupied the center of the room, and papers and books covered the top of the desk. Sam extracted a phone with a built-in answering machine from beneath the mess, took out his own message tape and put Jessie's in.

He pushed Play, and Marcie spoke into the silence.

"Jessie, I want you to know I'm sorry about the mess."

Sam and Jessie looked at each other, startled. Did Marcie know something about the people who'd wrecked her house?

"We put out your cans along with ours, but Morrison's damn dog got into them again."

Jessie stifled a laugh and let out the breath she'd been holding.

"He strung your garbage and ours all over the drive. Bill and the kids cleaned it up as well as they could before the truck came, but I'll have to try and hose down your drive before you get home. Sorry about that. Hope you had a nice weekend."

A click, followed by a beep.

"Good afternoon. This is Phillips Photo Studios. We are running a two-for-one special—"

Jessie pushed the button, fast-forwarded, then pressed Play again.

"So, Mrs. Ames, you are not at home."

Jessie's head jerked up, and she stared at Sam, her eyes very wide. It was Leonid.

"Why did you not tell me you were leaving? I am anxious to hear from you when you return. I will expect you to call—" he paused, and his voice dropped "—if you and your pretty daughter are not too busy cleaning your house."

"Sam! He wouldn't—"

"He's trying to scare you." Sam caught her hand. "He wants you to think he'll hurt her, but he can't. He doesn't have any idea where she is."

"He won't find her?" She gripped his hand hard.

"He won't find her," Sam assured her. "Jessie, was your father-in-law in the military?"

"Yes. He was a captain in the marines."

"Then if we have to we'll tell him what's going on. He'll understand what has to be done."

"He'll take care of her," Jessie said to reassure herself. "He wouldn't let anything hap—"

"Wait!" Sam stabbed the Stop button on the machine. "Did you hear that?"

"Hear what?" She frowned down at the machine.

"Listen." He ran the tape back, then played the same segment again.

". . . cleaning your house," Leonid repeated.

Another click, followed by a beep.

"J-Jessie?" The hesitant voice was male, and she recognized it. Bernie Martin. "I, uh . . . I need to talk to you. I thought you were gonna be at home this weekend, and, well . . . I need to talk to you. So call me when you get in, will you? I'll be at home. But call me, okay? Call me right away. Right away." The line stayed open for a moment longer, and they could hear rapid breathing before Bernie hung up.

"That's Bernie." Jessie frowned at Sam. "Why's he calling me at home?"

"Probably because Leonid told him to. He must have gotten in touch with Martin to see if he knew where you were and then put some pressure on him to get you into line."

"But Bernie can't do anything to 'get me into line.'"

"Yeah, but Leonid doesn't know that."

She looked into his eyes for a long moment. "I think I'd better call Bernie. He sounded scared."

Sam nodded. "Call him."

She dialed quickly, listened, then glanced at Sam. "It's ringing." She listened tensely through a dozen rings, then lowered the receiver. "He doesn't answer, Sam."

"It's still ringing?"

She listened for a moment and nodded. "What's going on?"

"I don't know." Sam took the receiver from her hands and set it back in its cradle. "But we'd better go see."

Chapter 15

Bernie didn't answer his doorbell. His condo was in a large complex, but no one showed the least interest in the two of them when Sam rang the bell again and knocked hard. He received no response.

"Sam, he said he'd be at home. Why would he leave, if he wanted to talk to me so badly?"

"I don't know. Maybe he's still here." Sam tried the knob, which turned easily, and pushed the door inward. He looked at Jessie and raised an eyebrow.

Sam pushed Jessie behind him and held her there while he swung the door fully open. He reached in to switch on the lights, then slowly, warily eased inside. Jessie followed him, her eyes wide. The apartment was tidy and clean, with all the impersonal comfort of a hotel room. Bernie might live here, but it was eerie how he'd left no stamp of his personality on the rooms.

"He's not here." Sam led the way back to the empty living room, where even the magazines on the end table were in a neat dentist's-office stack.

"No kidding." Jessie stayed close to him, trying unsuccessfully to hide her uneasiness.

"No sign of a struggle, nothing out of place." Sam looked around him one last time. "Nothing to indicate that Martin did anything more sinister than go out for a pizza. Come on." He took Jessie's hand and made for the door. "Let's go home."

She held back. "Shouldn't we leave a note or something?"

He shook his head. "We're going to leave everything exactly as we found it." Sam switched off the lights and used his handkerchief to wipe off the switch and the doorknob.

"Aren't you going to lock the door?"

He shook his head again. "Exactly as we found it. Let's go."

Jessie went, looking back over her shoulder at Bernie's door. "What if he gets burgled?"

"Then maybe next time he'll lock up when he leaves." Sam strode away so quickly that Jessie had to trot to keep pace.

"But shouldn't we—"

"Look." Sam opened the car door and stuffed her inside. "I don't want anyone—*anyone* to know we were here, understand? We were never here, got it?"

"Got it," she snapped back, and he glanced at her.

"Sorry. Just don't say anything about being here."

"Not even to Bernie? I'll see him at work tomorrow."

"As far as Martin needs to know, you got his message on your machine, you called and got no answer, and that was that."

When her intercom buzzed, Jessie had to shift a stack of printouts to reach the button. "Yes?" she said distractedly.

"Jessie, can I see you for a minute?" Bernie asked. She sat up straight and pushed her pencil behind her ear.

"What is it, Bernie? I'm kind of busy." Sam had cautioned her not to react to the other man as if she were worried.

"Yeah, well, sorry about that, Jessie, but I just need a minute." He tried to keep the plea out of his voice, but she heard it.

She sighed. "Okay, Bernie. Just for a minute. Can you come up here?"

"Yeah, sure. Sure I can." He was almost babbling. "Thanks Jessie. I'll be right up. Thanks, Jessie."

He got there so quickly he must have skipped the notoriously slow elevators in favor of the stairs. When he rapped sharply on her office door, she was in the middle of putting her White Eagle disks in the concealed file cabinet.

"Just a minute!" She stuffed the disks in the drawer and shoved it closed. "Be right there!" she called over her shoulder. Thanking providence that she'd locked her office door, she jerked the concealing panel closed, flipped the nearly invisible latch and hurried to the door, smoothing her hair. She took one deep breath before she let Bernie in.

The breath came out in a rush when she saw his face.

"Good grief, Bernie. What happened to you?" She didn't have to feign surprise or shock, but she tried to conceal a sudden upsurge of fear.

He gave her a sidelong glance out of one eye. The other was swollen shut. His mouth was swollen, as well, his face scratched and bruised, and he moved into her office stiffly. He stepped inside with a furtive glance over his shoulder. Jessie looked out before she closed the door. There was no one there.

"What on earth happened to you?" She walked around and sat behind her desk. "Did you walk into a door or something?" She tried to inject equal measures of concern and humor into her voice.

"Something like that." Bernie tried to grin, but it didn't come off. His swollen lips twisted crookedly, and a large purple bruise on his right cheek was clearly hurting him. "I... It was a really dumb thing to do, but I slipped and fell into the pool."

"You fell in the water and it did all this?" She tried not to let her disbelief show too plainly, but Bernie gave her another hunted glance.

He shrugged. "You know how it is. I'd had a couple of beers, and I slipped on something by the pool. I guess I hit the cement on my way in, but it all happened so fast...." He let his voice trail away, and Jessie took pity on him. It was clear that Bernie was thoroughly cowed. He wasn't going to try to intimidate her again.

"Sometimes things happen so fast it's all just a blur," she said, letting him off the hook.

"Yeah." He nodded quickly. "That's how it is."

"So. What did you want to see me about? I really do have a lot to do today."

"I called you Saturday—" he began.

She interrupted him. "I know. I got your message, but when I called back you weren't home."

"I was probably at the emergency room." He shook his head and flinched. "The doctor told me to be more careful around swimming pools."

"I imagine so. Now, what was it you wanted?"

Bernie hesitated, and Jessie could almost see him gathering his nerve. "I, uh... Have you heard from Leonid?"

Jessie folded her hands on the desk. "There was a message from him on my machine, too. I haven't talked to him, because he didn't leave a number."

"Yeah, well, he gave me a message for you." He hesitated and his eyes shifted uneasily. "He's getting impatient. He wondered where you were this weekend. He wants to—to meet with you. Soon.''

"Okay." Her easy agreement surprised Bernie. "But since he didn't leave a number where I can reach him, why don't you have him call me?"

"O-okay. I will."

"Good." She bent over the papers on her desk, then glanced up. "Is that all?"

"Yeah. I guess so." Bernie started for the door, but stopped. "Do you . . . have what he wants?"

Jessie shook her head. She wasn't discussing that with Bernie. "Just have him call me."

"Yeah. Okay." He opened the door and hesitated again. "See you, Jessie."

She gave him an absent wave but kept her head bent until she heard him walk out and close the door behind him. When the latch clicked, she finally looked up at the empty office and the closed door. "Oh, my God!" she breathed in a shaky whisper. When she tried to gather up the papers littering her desk, she found her hands were shaking, too—with fear.

When she dropped several sheets, she stopped trying to straighten up the mess. Jessie sagged back into her chair. She stared at the papers, but all she could see was Bernie's battered face. What had happened to him had nothing to do with swimming pools. He'd been beaten, but not quite badly enough to put him in the hospital. He'd been worked over by an expert.

She was playing a game of strategy, move and countermove, like chess. But the game had gone far beyond anything she'd anticipated. There were players in this game who used violence, people who wouldn't hesitate to hurt women and children. Jessie whispered a little prayer of thanks that Kerry was safely off with her grandparents, then another prayer that this all be finished soon.

* * *

"You knew, didn't you?"

Sam glanced over his shoulder, then turned back to the stove. "I had an idea. Martin was obviously scared on the phone, and then he wasn't at home. They were putting pressure on him."

"But beating him up?"

"I didn't specifically know they were in the process of loosening his teeth, no." Sam added a generous dash of wine to the chicken and mushrooms in the skillet. "But something of the kind made sense."

"To you, maybe." She shuddered. "Those people, whoever they are, they scare me, Sam."

He moved the chicken off the burner and walked over to the table where she sat. He didn't touch her. If he had, she knew she would have clung to him.

"They scare me, too. That's why we're going to have men all over this last exchange, and women, as well. They'll be surrounding you. You won't be alone, even in the ladies' room."

"Not even there?" Her laugh was shaky. "You *have* covered all the bases, haven't you?"

"I'm going to make sure you're never alone with Leonid. He can't get at Kerry now, and I want to see that he can't get at you, either."

Jessie's eyes were troubled, and he patted her shoulder once before returning to their supper. It was a casual touch, but that simple caress meant more to her than all the words in the world could have.

Sam might not want anything to do with her, but she needed him. Maybe too much. She needed, but she couldn't tell him, because that would be asking for something Sam couldn't, or wouldn't, give her. She was quiet through dinner, and only forced herself to eat by reminding herself that fainting from hunger wasn't the way to deal with Leonid. She might not want the food, but she'd better eat.

After dinner Jessie tried to read for a while, but it was useless. As early as she reasonably could, she closed her magazine and stood up.

"Something wrong?" Sam glanced up from the brief-caseful of work he'd brought home.

She shook her head. "I can't concentrate on anything tonight. I might as well get some sleep."

"You okay?"

"Mm-hmm. I'm just kind of tired." She looked back as she left the room, but he was bent over his papers again.

Sam's guest room had the same comfortable character as the rest of the house, with lots of warm wood, an Oriental carpet and a bookcase stuffed with books. The bed was a carved mahogany antique, high and wide and almost sinfully soft, covered with a museum-quality quilt.

Jessie couldn't fault either his taste or his selection of antiques, but each time she saw the beautiful things she wondered how he could afford them on his FBI salary. She climbed into the big, empty bed, switched off the bedside lamp, lay back against the pillows and closed her eyes, willing herself to relax.

It didn't work.

She lay watching shadows flick across the ceiling as cars drove past. She listened to night birds in the palm tree outside her window and to Sam moving around the house. He went into the kitchen and ran some water—probably filling the coffee maker for the morning, she thought. There was some rattling of dishes, and then he walked down the hall, past the room where she slept, to his bedroom.

She'd looked in through the open door and seen another large mahogany bed, and a carpet that had glowed like a jewel when the morning sun had fallen on it, but she hadn't walked inside.

She imagined him moving around in the room, getting ready for bed. She had waited for Charlie in bed, watching him undress, enjoying his unconscious masculinity. She missed that. She also missed having a man's arms around her in the night and his warmth beside her.

And she ached for Sam King, for the strong and gentle man who had walked into her life and turned it inside out. The single night she'd had with him had been like a taste of honey, reminding her of what she'd lost, whetting an appetite she'd suppressed in the day-to-day rush of work and home and mothering.

But a taste was all she was going to have. She rolled onto her stomach, wadded her pillow into a ball and pressed her face into it. A taste was worse than nothing. It didn't satisfy and it reminded you of what you were missing.

She wouldn't regret it, though. What she felt for Sam King was nothing to be ashamed of. She couldn't force him to return her love, but that didn't mean the love should be denied.

And anyway, she thought, there was a ray of hope. Sam was capable of feeling love, whether he was willing to admit it to himself or not. He loved Cat, and he showed it. Smiling into the darkness, she drifted off to sleep at last.

The nightmare was of formless pursuers in a shapeless darkness, and it brought her out of a sound sleep with a jerk, sitting up in bed with her heart thundering in her chest.

A predictable enough nightmare, she thought dryly when her pounding heart began to slow and her mind reassured her that she was safe in Sam's guest room. The clock told her it was nearly 2:00 a.m., and her rational mind told her that the source of her terror was nothing but a dream caused by her upcoming meeting with Leonid.

But knowing it was only a dream didn't make going back to sleep any easier. She lay tossing and punching her pillow for half an hour, then gave up. If she wasn't going to sleep, she might as well get up.

Moving quietly so as not to wake Sam, she pulled on the thin silk robe she'd bought in Hong Kong and padded barefoot to the kitchen. Cat greeted her with a purring "Rowr" from his nest beside the refrigerator.

"Hi, Cat. Sorry to bother you." She took the milk out of the refrigerator. "Want a midnight snack?" She poured a little into his dish, then heated a cupful in the microwave and stirred instant cocoa powder into it.

Cat finished his treat and followed her into the living room, his tiny cast making a little clumping noise with each step. When she settled herself on a cushion in front of the floor-length living room windows, he curled up beside her legs.

He wasn't a particularly affectionate cat. Like Sam, he held himself aloof until he felt he knew you. He had treated Jessie with reserve, but now he pushed his head under her hand until she stroked his fur, and a deep, rumbling purr vibrated his rib cage.

"You're just an old softy, aren't you?" She rubbed a fingertip beneath Cat's chin and watched as his eyes half closed in pleasure. "Just an old softy." She sipped her cocoa and looked out at the night.

"What's the matter?"

Jessie hadn't heard him coming. When he spoke she jumped, spilling her cocoa. Cat couldn't jump up, but he meowed his protest when Jessie scrambled off the cushion.

"Good grief!" She mopped rapidly at the spill with her napkin. "Do you always sneak up on people that way?"

"I didn't sneak."

Frowning, Sam walked farther into the room and switched on a dim lamp. Jessie glanced at him, then bent her head and concentrated on her cocoa. He hadn't bothered with a robe, and he was wearing only the running shorts he slept in.

"What are you doing out here in the middle of the night, anyway?"

"I was having some cocoa until you scared me to death and I dumped it all on the pillow. This'll have to go to the cleaners, Sam. I'm sorry."

"Don't worry about that. Are you all right?"

"Yeah." She went to perch on the couch. "I couldn't sleep."

"Nightmares?"

Her head snapped up, and she looked at him for a moment before she gave a brief nod. "How did you know?"

"Makes sense." He sat down beside her. "We've all been worrying about this last meeting. Just keep in mind, it'll all be over very soon."

"I don't know whether that's reassuring or frightening."

"You don't need to be frightened."

He laid his arm along the back of the couch behind her shoulders, and while he leaned back Jessie sat straight on the edge of the cushions, trying to ignore the long, bare legs stretched out next to hers, the deep, muscular chest, the strong arm behind her. He was too close, and his nearness made her all too conscious that she was wearing a thin robe over a thinner nightgown that reached only to midthigh.

"I don't know," she said slowly. "I don't know if I can handle it. This exchange is going to be different from the others, and there are too many things we don't know."

"So we drop back and punt."

She rolled her eyes. "I never played football."

"You'll do fine."

"That might reassure me if I thought you had something to base it on."

She leaned forward to put her head in her hands, but he caught her shoulders and pulled her back into the curve of his arm.

"I know it doesn't do much good to say this, but try to relax." He shook her gently. "You're bound to be nervous, and that's not all bad. Nerves give you that little extra edge of awareness." He looked down at her. "As long as you don't let the edge become the fear that can paralyze you."

Jessie sighed deeply. "I don't know. I feel paralyzed already. All I can think about is things going wrong."

"Well, don't think about it!" He hauled her around to look into his face. "Think of putting Leonid behind bars, along with the people he works for. Think of keeping American secrets out of the wrong hands. Think of making it harder for spies on the West Coast, at least for a while." He looked into her eyes, waiting for her agreement.

"You left one out," she told him gravely.

"What?"

"Keeping the world safe for democracy."

Sam was silent for a moment, but then he gave a shout of laughter. "You stinker!" He wrapped his arm around her neck and gave her a mock-ferocious shake.

Jessie dropped her head against his chest, laughing hard. "I couldn't let you do your whole pep talk and leave out the best line!" She giggled helplessly, the top of her head pressed into his chest.

"Come here, you." He pulled her chin up and grinned into her laughing face. "I can't let you get away with making fun of my best pep talk, can I?"

"I don't know." She laughed. "C-can you?"

He shook his head, and then his smile faded. As he lowered his head to hers, Jessie's giggles died away, and her pupils dilated for a second before her eyes drifted closed. He brushed his lips over her mouth. It was the merest breath of a touch.

She wound her arms around his neck, pulling her body up against his, holding on to him with all her strength, as if he were a rock in a stormy sea. In his arms she was no longer afraid, no longer alone. His kiss was gentle at first, almost hesitant until she tangled her fingers in his hair and pulled his face down to hers.

She needed his closeness, needed his strong body next to hers. When he eased her around so that she lay across his lap, she went pliantly, locked in his arms, drowning in his kiss. He let his fingertips drift down her throat, and her head fell back, her hair sliding across his arm as he traced a line to the point where the lapels of her robe crossed. The belt was lightly tied, and when he pressed his fingers into the opening, the fabric slid apart.

Though the robe was black and opaque, her brief gown was pale pink, sheer and soft. The fabric was too thin to have any form, and it clung to her curves, her skin glowing through in shades of peach. The neckline was low and wide, edged with tiny silk-embroidered scallops. Sam looked down at her in the soft glow of the single lamp, then bent and re-traced with his lips the path his fingers had followed.

Jessie gasped at the first touch, her body arching upward in a bow as his mouth moved slowly lower. He pushed the silk gently away with his lips, then tugged at the narrow strap, sliding it off her shoulder and down her arm. The fabric caught on the tip of her breast, and when he brushed it off he let his fingertips caress her flesh.

Jessie shivered and bit her lip against the languid heat that flowed through her, then shivered again when his lips re-placed his hand, tugging lightly. The heat intensified, melt-ing thought and feeling together into a drowning tide of sensation.

It washed over her, and she pulled his face up to hers, to kiss him again and again, filling herself with the warmth she'd been starving for. And yet it wasn't just warmth and human contact she was yearning for, it was love. And love was what Sam refused to give her.

And yet . . .

He was capable of love, she felt it in his lips and hands as he caressed her gently, giving as much as he took. He didn't demand his own satisfaction, but gave her such pleasure it took her breath away. He didn't just lust for her, but loved her with kisses and touches that spoke of so much more than he would admit in words.

He slid the other strap of her gown off her shoulder, and it fell to the bend of her elbows, where her silky robe had caught. Her shoulders were bared, and her breasts, while the sheer pink gown molded to her waist and belly and thighs in a tantalizing veil. Sam gazed down at her, his eyes dark with passion.

She could feel her breasts swell and tighten, and a full, heavy weight settled low in her abdomen. His gaze was like a caress, but when he brought his hand down her throat to the upper curve of her breast, the breath went out of her in a rush. Her head fell back and her eyes half closed as her back arched, offering more.

He traced his fingertips lightly over her breasts, over nipples that were taut and aching, then followed the same path with his mouth. Jessie gasped and clutched his hair, holding him close as he shifted position, pulling her with him as he stretched his length along the cushions, turning her body beneath his.

As Jessie reached up to him, he slid his hands down her arms, pushing the black silk sleeves and the ribbon straps off her arms. Linking his hands with hers, he held her arms down at her sides as he lowered his body fully onto hers and found her mouth with his again. She couldn't reach for him with her hands pinioned, but she twisted beneath him, inflaming them both.

Chest hair, thick and soft, rasped gently over her naked breasts, soft flesh pressed to firm muscle, and legs tangled together. Her gown and robe had fallen to her waist, and when Sam pressed his knee between hers the silk rode up her thighs. When he could no longer bear the sweet torment of her small, instinctive movements, he released her hands, reaching up to cradle her nape and lift her mouth to his, reaching down to stroke her hip and thigh, then more slowly, the thin, satiny skin of her inner thigh.

When he touched her she gasped, when he touched her again, she wrapped him in her arms and legs, pleading with body and hands and little wordless murmurs. And then he acceded to her plea, making them one, holding her close as the old rhythm began, and the world spun away in a shower of light and sensation and release.

She lay clasped in his arms for timeless moments after the last little shudders of delight had died away. His head rested on her breast, his body, lax and sated, was heavy on hers, but it was a sweet heaviness, and she made no effort to move away.

It was Sam who moved first. As his breathing slowed, she felt tension sliding back into his body, then muscles flexed and he lifted himself away from her. His hands weren't rough as he pulled her silk robe around her, but his touch wasn't a caress, either. As soon as her body was covered, he turned away and dragged on his shorts again.

Cold without the warmth of his body, she sat up slowly, pulling the robe onto her shoulders. "Sam?"

She could see the muscles tense in his shoulders. "What?" He raked a hand roughly through his hair.

"What's wrong?"

"Nothing!"

She rose and walked slowly toward him. "Don't shut me out, Sam, please. I love you, and I know something's wrong."

"No!" He whirled on her. "Don't."

"Don't what?"

"Don't love me, because I won't love you back."

"But Sam, you can't deny—"

"No!" he snapped, and raked his hand through his hair once more. "Don't even say it. I want you. God knows, I want you, but I don't...I won't let myself feel any more for you. I won't love you, Jessie. I can't."

She was silent for several seconds. "But why? Just tell me that, Sam. Just give me a reason."

"Can't you just accept—"

"I need to know why. I think you owe me that much."

She could see the tight-strung tension in his stiff back and rigid shoulders, and when he let his breath out in a hiss, it didn't release the tension so much as prevent an explosion.

"I suppose you're right," he said wearily, then walked over and dropped into a big leather armchair. "Sit down."

Jessie sat, perching on the edge of the sofa.

"To begin with, you have to know that my father is rich."

Jessie blinked. His announcement of wealth was made in such a matter-of-fact way that she was left with the impression that he was talking about someone else's father. She said nothing, and after a second's reflective pause he continued.

"I don't mean well-off, or merely rich, or nouveau riche. I mean old money, Westchester and Newport, *really* rich. I was born with the proverbial silver spoon in my mouth, had a conservative upbringing, prep school, college, and law school, and I confidently expected to get my degree and then join the family business. My father had everything planned before I was even conceived. The only flaw in his plans was picking the wrong woman to marry."

His eyes were closed, his face expressionless, but Jessie watched his fist clench.

"My father inherited the business as a young man and spent years building it up. He was too busy, or so he thought, to have a social life, or to marry. So, when he was nearly forty and a pretty woman showed interest in him, he was an easy mark.

"She was a temporary secretary, just arrived in New York from Georgia, and she knew she'd hit pay dirt when the Chairman of the Board was interested in her. She was twenty years younger than he, and pretty, and she flattered a lonely man who hadn't had much experience with women. He married her as soon a she would agree to it, and never even considered that it was the money she wanted, and not the man."

He glanced at Jessie, his eyes hooded. "And so I was born within the year. There were no more children after me. She put up with pregnancy once, to ensure her position as mother of the dynasty's heir, but she wasn't about to go through it again. She hated being pregnant, and she didn't want anything to do with a child. I was raised by nannies and housekeepers—who were mostly kind to me—and when I was ten, my mother ran off with a polo player."

"Oh, Sam!" Her heart was in her eyes, but he clearly didn't want her sympathy.

"I found out, years later, that she'd had affairs almost from the start. After I was born, that is. She didn't want there to be any doubt about my parentage. Her affairs weren't discreet. They were so blatant that my father, and most of their friends, had known about them from the beginning. But he didn't divorce her, he didn't throw her out, because he loved her. She finally asked for a divorce after she left him to marry the polo player. That lasted about a year, and she's been married four times since then. Four that I know of, that is."

He lifted his head slowly and sat forward again, to look into Jessie's eyes for a long time. Then he lowered his gaze to his hands.

"I had always respected my father. Even if we weren't buddies, even if he didn't play catch with me, I always respected him. But when I was in college, and full of the arrogance and idealism that come with being twenty, I asked him about her. I'd begun to hear things about my mother's younger men, and I asked him if it was true. It was.

"Well, how could he do that, I said. How could he call himself a man when his wife had affairs that were practically front-page news, and still he welcomed her on the nights she saw fit to come home? All he could say was that he loved her."

Jessie couldn't see Sam's face, only his bent head.

"He loved her, so he allowed her to abuse their marriage, to humiliate him in front of his friends and neighbors and finally to leave him for a lover with nothing to recommend him but a dashing image on a horse. How could I respect a man who would allow those things to be done to him? I was furious with him for not having more backbone, and I began to despise him."

"What did you do?"

"What I was supposed to do. I went to law school, and I went to work at King Enterprises, and six months after I started, when I was home at Christmas, I found a letter." He glanced at her. "I didn't open his mail. It was lying on a desk in the library, already opened, and I saw my name."

"So you read it."

"I read it. She was in Santa Barbara, and she'd just broken up with a man, but she'd met an actor, and he was really sweet, but it was so expensive to live there, could my father be a sweetheart and send her just a little money, to tide her over until things worked out. And say hello to little Sammy, she tacked on at the end. Little Sammy, when I was twenty-six. I asked my father about the letter.''

Sam shook his head at the memory. "Actually, I stormed into his office, demanded to know what the hell it was all about, and he told me. He'd already sent her the money she asked for in that letter, just as he'd sent her money many times before, when she was between husbands or didn't have the cash to pay for a divorce. Anytime she asked, he sent money. I couldn't understand that. My mind simply couldn't grasp it. But he didn't apologize for what he'd done. He said he'd send her more, whenever she needed it. Because he loved her.''

Sam remained silent and unmoving for several seconds, then sighed deeply and sat back, leaning tiredly against the cushions.

"And so I left. I resigned from King Enterprises, moved out of the house, and applied for a job with the FBI. They trained me, and I ended up out here, a continent away from my father.''

"Do you see him?''

"I haven't for a while. We write once a month.''

"You don't visit on the holidays?''

He shook his head. "Not for the last couple of years. I've been scheduled to work on Christmas, so I just stayed out here.''

"Don't you want to go home?''

Sam shook his head. "I can't see him without seeing a man who was weak and let love destroy him.''

"I see," Jessie said, and she did. She saw more, perhaps, than Sam knew he'd told her.

"Then you see why I can't give you what you want. You want a man to love you, to give you all of himself. I can't do that. I *won't* do that.''

"Yet you'd make love with me?''

His head came up, his eyes glittering and cold. "I've never denied I want you, Jessamyn. And if your coming out here in the middle of the night was a ploy to make something more of that—"

Anger surged through her at the unfairness of that, and Jessie shoved herself off the sofa. "I had a nightmare, Sam. I didn't come to you, but when you came out here... Well, maybe I needed somebody to hold me, and maybe I need somebody to love me, but you've made it very clear that you don't. It won't happen again."

She kept her eyes on the floor and skirted around him as she made for the hall. She stopped at the doorway her back to him. "I don't want the sex without the love, Sam. I'm sorry if I misled you. Good night."

She walked away, and this time he didn't try to call her back.

Chapter 16

What did he say?"

Before answering, Jessie set her coffee cup on the low table beside her and sat back in the depths of Mr. Howell's office sofa. "He said I should be in my office at 5:15. He'll call me then and tell me what to do."

"Did he say where you'd be going?" Mr. Howell asked.

Jessie shook her head in a negative aimed at them all—Sam, Mr. Howell and Special Agents Terry Gold and Katherine March, who would be part of the surveillance team. John Kelley was already outside, in a van painted like a catering truck and equipped for radio tracking.

They had assembled in Mr. Howell's office after Jessie had gotten Leonid's phone call. He had been curt, as if he were excited and trying to hide it, and their conversation had been brief. Be in the office, he'd told her, and she'd have her instructions. And she was to be alone.

She had blandly agreed with Leonid and then had promptly gone to see Mr. Howell. She now sat with the others in his office, waiting for Leonid to call again. They passed the time drinking coffee and nibbling the cookies Mr. Howell had produced from a cupboard.

Everyone was nervous and trying to hide it—everyone except Jessie. She felt unnaturally calm as she waited in the eye of the storm for the thunder and lightning and wind to resume. She sipped her coffee, nibbled a currant cookie and waited.

Sam leaned against an oak file cabinet on the other side of the room and watched her, wondering what was going on in her mind. She'd thrown him a curve at 4:00 a.m. and then walked out of his living room, leaving him to wrestle with his thoughts. They weren't comfortable ones for him.

This had been his operation from the start, and he should have been looking forward to winding it up. Just this morning he'd spent nearly three hours making phone calls to set his plans in motion, yet suddenly he didn't want to let Jessie go. He wanted to walk across the room, take Jessie in his arms and tell her not to go through with this. He didn't want her out there alone with Leonid and the shadowy, dangerous "others."

He shifted his feet and folded his arms across his chest closing himself in with his thoughts. He wanted to make love to her again.

Last night, though he'd sent her away, Jessie's departure had left him feeling alone and oddly empty.

He wouldn't succumb. He didn't need anyone else. He wouldn't *allow* himself to need anyone else. His father's desire for a woman had destroyed the respect his son had had for him. Sam wouldn't allow the same thing to happen to him.

And if that thought made the emptiness worse, he refused to acknowledge it.

The phone's ring shattered the silence, bringing them all sharply to attention. Sam nodded at Jessie. "Go ahead."

She pressed the speaker phone button. "Mrs. Ames."

"Good evening, Mrs. Ames." Leonid's faintly contemptuous voice filled the office. "Are you ready for your adventure?"

"I'm finished for the day."

"Very good, Mrs. Ames."

"Where do you want to meet?"

"No, no, no, no. That is not the way we will do things today. I will tell you where to go in your car, and you will drive there and wait for instructions."

"You're making the rules." Jessie's tone implied an unconcerned shrug. "Where do you want me to go?"

"To the corner of Vanowen and Fallbrook. There is a row of shops and an outdoor telephone. Go there and you will be instructed."

"A phone at the corner of Vanowen and Fallbrook," she repeated. "I'll be leaving in about five minutes."

"Leave now."

"As soon as I can get the car out of the parking lot, okay?" She let irritation come through, and there was a moment of silence.

"As quickly as you can," Leonid said finally. "Do not stop anywhere. Do not talk to anyone. And make sure you are alone. You will be watched."

"I'm leaving now." She didn't wait for him to say anything else, but pressed the button and disconnected the line. She pressed her palms flat on the desktop for a moment, then straightened and pushed herself away with a little shove.

"So," she said to them all, "it's time to go."

"Yeah." Sam bent down to fish in his briefcase. "Time to get you ready." He nodded toward his female agent, then straightened, his hands full of wires and little electronic gadgets, and glanced at Mr. Howell. "Can we use your bathroom?"

"Of course. It's right through there."

Katherine waited for Jessie to precede her. The bathroom was small but it was big enough for their purpose. "This will only take a minute," she said matter-of-factly.

At Katherine's instruction Jessie slipped out of her blouse. "I'll try to put this where they won't see it or feel it." She tucked the small rectangle of the transmitter inside Jessie's waistband, at the center of her back. "Make sure you keep your jacket on," she said as she pinned it into place.

"Okay."

"And try not to let them touch you."

Jessie shuddered. "Don't worry."

A fine wire was threaded from the transmitter to her bra, ending with a tiny microphone.

Jessie looked down at the little silver cylinder and gave it a tug to be sure it was secure.

"It looks okay. You can put this back on," Katherine said, handing Jessie her blouse.

She stuffed the tails down inside her slacks and the two women left the room.

She walked over to Sam. "I'm done. Does it show?"

He looked her up and down, then reached out and straightened her collar with a flick of his fingers. "No." He patted the back of her waist, and his lips tightened. "It doesn't show, but they'll feel it if they know what they're looking for. Just keep your jacket on and try not to let them touch you."

"I know, I know." She had no intention of letting anybody touch her.

"Okay. I'll walk you downstairs. Are you ready?"

She licked her lips, then nodded. "I'm ready." Her voice wasn't as strong as she would have like it to be. By the time she spoke to Leonid she had to sound more sure of herself. The short walk did little to ease her nerves. She paused with him on the bottom step.

"I should get going."

"Yeah." Sam didn't move away from the door. "You'd better."

He took the one slow step that brought him close to her, rested his hands lightly on her waist and, with the slightest pressure, urged her toward him. She swayed into him, and as he closed his arms around her she clutched his shoulders and lifted her mouth for his kiss.

It went on and on, deep and searching and sweet, blotting out the fear of what she had to do, what she had to face. When he loosened his arms and lifted his head, she looked up at him, her eyes wide and grave.

"You'll be okay," he said.

"Yes." She nodded. "I will."

As she drove to the intersection of Vanowen and Fallbrook, she tested both the body mike and the tracking device in her car, announcing her location at each corner she passed. "I'm pulling into the parking lot. I can see the phone."

She felt a bit funny talking into the air without being answered, but as she parked she saw the catering van pull in at a nearby hamburger stand. She spared it only one disinterested glance, but that was enough for her to see Sam, wearing a baseball cap to conceal his hair, sitting in the passenger seat. He nodded and turned away to give his order.

She got out of the car, and as she walked toward the pay phone it began to ring.

"Hello?"

"It took you too long, Mrs. Ames."

"Somebody stopped me to talk on my way out of the building. I didn't want to act suspicious."

"Be quicker next time."

"It takes as long as it takes."

There was a pause during which she could almost hear Leonid's temper rising. That was just tough, she thought.

She had what they wanted. They would just have to wait for her.

"Very well. Do you have a map with you?"

"I have a street atlas in the car."

"Good. Go to Beverly Hills, where Beverly Drive crosses Santa Monica."

"Santa Monica, or Little Santa Monica?" she asked. The two streets, the old and the new, paralleled each other, separated by some railroad tracks.

"The little one. There is a restaurant there, a Chinese restaurant. The telephone is by the door."

"A Chinese restaurant on Beverly. All right."

"Be quick."

She laughed. "At five-thirty in the evening? In the middle of rush hour? I'll get there when I can."

She hung up and walked back to her car. The van was pulling around the restaurant after picking up drinks and sandwiches. Jessie dropped into her driver's seat. "Did you get that, Sam? Beverly and Little Santa Monica, at the Chinese restaurant?"

He didn't look her way, but he lifted his cap as if to settle it more securely and nodded again. Jessie drove off. It took her over an hour to reach Beverly Hills in the freeway traffic. From time to time she announced her whereabouts to her body microphone.

At the restaurant, diners were standing and waiting to be seated. Jessie couldn't have faced solid food, but her head was starting to ache, so she ordered a cola to go and drank it standing beside the pay phone. It helped.

She only jumped a little when the phone rang beside her. They sent her to one of the television studios on Sunset Boulevard, and from there she backtracked to the international terminal at the airport. She sat by a long rank of pay phones and had to wait several minutes before one of them rang. It was a phone that a young woman had been using, apparently chatting with her boyfriend, and Jessie smiled to herself. They must have gotten only one phone number and then had to wait until that phone was free.

"Hello?"

"Why were you talking on this telephone?"

"I wasn't." She didn't sound defensive, and that seemed to take Leonid by surprise.

"Who was it, then?"

"A teenage girl. This is a busy airport, remember? Lots of people use the phones."

He gave a grunt, neither agreeing nor disagreeing, and sent her to Long Beach. She stopped for gas on the way, and when she reached the strip mall where the phone was located it was already ringing.

"Hello?"

"Next you will go to—"

"Wait a minute." Her interruption resulted in silence on the other end of the line. "Are we going to keep this up all night?" It was nearly nine o'clock. "I understand that you don't want anybody following me, but I don't want that, either. Anyway, only an idiot would follow me all over L.A. County. Can we wind up the dramatics now and just do our business?"

There were several seconds of silence. "Very well," Leonid said at last. "If anyone follows you, it will be very bad for you."

"If anybody was following me, they would've run out of gas by now. Where do you want me to go this time?"

Where was not far from downtown, and not far from USC, and nowhere near as pleasant as either of those. It was a warehouse in a crumbling district where men slept on the sidewalks and dealers sold drugs. Jessie was glad her car doors were securely locked.

"This isn't much of a neighborhood," she said into her microphone as she neared the address Leonid had given her.

"It would be kind of ironic to get mugged while I'm on my way to betray my country."

In the van, Sam chuckled, and John Kelley glanced at him.

"She's a brave lady."

Sam agreed. "She's had to be. Is her house cleaned up?"

"Just about. They're steam-cleaning the carpet tomorrow, and then it'll be done."

"Good. Are your people in position around that warehouse?"

"I'll check." John radioed to the surveillance cars, one by one, and they reported they were either in position or nearing the warehouse.

The receiver tuned to Jessie's transmitter crackled with a burst of static. "Sorry about that," she said. "I just pulled my jacket out of the back seat, and I think I hit this thing. Hope it still works."

"Was it checked?" Kelley asked.

Sam nodded. "It was checked. It won't come loose."

Kelley opened his mouth to make a slightly ribald joke about the placement of the mike, but then he glanced at Sam's face and thought better of it. "That's good" was all he said.

"I'm at the warehouse," Jessie said softly. "It looks okay, but this neighborhood is a dump. I don't see anybody waiting for me outside." She took a deep breath. "Well, I've got my purse with the disks in it, and my jacket's on. I'm not going to button it. That would look funny. Wish me luck."

"Good luck," Sam murmured, and bent his head, listening intently to the receiver as she got out and moved toward the warehouse.

Jessie walked as calmly as she could to a small door in the side of the building. A derelict sitting on the sidewalk asked her for loose change. She detoured around his feet and ignored the request. No one answered her knock on the door, but it opened easily when she turned the knob.

She stepped through, took three steps and gave a stifled scream when a rough hand grabbed her arm.

She was yanked farther inside, and the door slammed closed behind her, changing the gloomy dimness into utter darkness. Jessie bit her lip on that first yell of fright, jerked free of the hand grasping her arm and stood stock still.

Her eyes adjusted gradually to the darkness until she could make out shapes, though she couldn't see details. The form next to her was a man—Leonid, she thought.

"Come this way."

It was him, all right. She felt him move as if to put his arm behind her, and she took a step away from him before he could touch the transmitter.

"Could we have a little light in here, Leonid?" She sensed his jerk of surprise at hearing his name. "I don't want to be seen with you any more than you want to be seen with me, but after all, the door's shut now."

Leonid grunted his assent, then called to someone ahead of them in Russian, "A light, Ivan!"

Jessie understood his words but didn't let it show. If they didn't know she spoke the language, they might talk more freely in front of her.

In the distance a light was switched on, throwing long shadows between stacks of huge crates. The light shone from the far end of the warehouse, and though the aisle she and Leonid were walking down was in shadow, the reflected glow was enough.

She glanced at Leonid and smiled when he looked at her. "Good evening. Nice to see you."

He hesitated only a moment. "Good evening."

"Where do we go?"

"There." He jerked his head.

"Back in that corner, away from the street?" she asked for Sam's benefit.

Leonid nodded. "Follow me."

"How did you find your way through this place in the dark?" she asked with all the naive amazement she could muster. "There's not much room between all these piles of crates. What's in them, anyway?"

"In the crates?"

"Yeah. They're so big."

"Tractor parts, I think." He obviously wasn't interested. "I don't know. We are using this only as a place to meet."

"Oh," Jessie took an ingenuous survey of the cavernous interior. "Well, it's a good place for it. Nice and private."

He replied with another grunt and led her around a final stack to an open space in front of the warehouse office. The office door was closed, but there was a window beside it that looked out on the warehouse. The interior of the office was brightly lit, showing her three men inside, like actors on a stage.

She knew they were waiting for the last scene to begin. Jessie took a careful breath and let Leonid open the door for her to make the entrance that would set it in motion.

Two of the men were older, in their fifties, while the younger was about Leonid's age, thirty or so. He was short and stocky, with thick brown hair growing low on his forehead, and he looked at Jessie with an unpleasant smile, almost a sneer, that held a touch of cruelty.

The older men didn't bother sneering. One was short and wide and wore a fedora, and the other was tall, thin, bareheaded and bald. Their facial expressions, closed and set, were interchangeable.

Jessie stopped just inside the office door, her clutch purse tucked under her arm, her hands resting easily at her sides. She didn't rush to greet them with an ingratiating smile, for she had an idea that these men respected strength more than friendliness.

There was a moment of silent assessment. Then the man with the hat stepped forward. "Good evening, Mrs. Ames." He extended his hand to Jessie for a brief handshake. It was dry and cool. "I am Pavel, and these are my associates, Sergei—" he indicated the taller, bald man "—and Ivan." He nodded to the younger man with the cruel smile. "Leonid, of course, you already know."

He stepped back and, with a courtly half bow that struck Jessie as rather odd, given the business at hand, ushered her to a chair. It stood beside a battered metal desk that took up most of the space in the office. There was a personal computer set up on the desk, already switched on.

"Now, I believe you have something for us."

Jessie smiled. "I believe you have something for me."

"And we must show each other our goods before we trade."

Pavel's smile was as small and as insincere as hers. He nodded to Ivan, who reached behind the desk and produced a briefcase. He set it on the desktop, flicked open the catches and lifted the lid.

Jessie glanced over the neatly wrapped bundles of twenties and fifties. She took out one bundle, riffled the end and saw that it contained nothing but currency. She did a quick count on her head and nodded. If the bundles were all as real as the one she'd checked, then she was looking at one hundred thousand dollars. She replaced the money and looked at Pavel.

He held out his hand. She opened her purse, took out two disks and gave them to him. He looked at the small squares in their paper envelopes and passed them to Ivan, who appeared to know more about what he was holding than Pavel did.

"I labeled the system disk," she told Ivan, who glanced at the labels and nodded. "It'll run on any PC clone, but you may have to copy it onto a disk formatted for that machine."

"I see." Ivan looked at the other disk. It wasn't labeled. "How do I make it run?"

"Pull up the directory after you load the system, and load the files in order."

He nodded and sat down at the computer as Jessie watched. He worked slowly but methodically. She didn't know if he was uncertain of what he was doing or if he was simply trying to avoid making a mistake. As a result she couldn't tell if he knew enough to spot the mistakes and traps she had built into the dummy program. She could only hope the appearance of reality would stand up until they let her go.

"What do I have here?"

She got up and walked around the desk. "The directory. Now load each file. Like this." She pulled the keyboard closer and typed rapidly. "There are menus written in. Once you've started running this introduction file—" she pointed to it on the screen "—the menus will tell you what to do next."

"Like this?" He repeated what she'd done, watching the words and numbers flicker across the screen.

"Yes." She pointed to the screen. "Now you follow this menu to run."

"And to see the actual program? To read it? How do I do that?"

She'd hoped he wouldn't ask, because a knowledgeable programmer might spot the inconsistencies that way. All she could do was show him the most authentic-looking segment and hope he wouldn't spot anything wrong.

"Go back to the system."

"Give her a chair," Pavel said.

He jerked his head at Leonid, who grudgingly brought her chair over.

Jessie had to move out of the way while he maneuvered it behind the desk and then step back into the corner so that he could get out again. He moved to let her pass, and as she sidled around the corner of the desk he put an arm out to help her.

Jessie felt his hand brush the back of her waist, and she flinched. Oh, God, had he touched the transmitter?

She said nothing, and neither did he, for the moment. Every nerve on edge, she pushed the chair into place beside Ivan so that it was between him and the office door. She placed herself on the other side of it so that she was closer to the exit and rather than sit down she rested one knee on the seat of the chair and leaned over to reach the keyboard.

"You're at the system." Her voice was tight with tension, and she struggled to sound relaxed. "Now you tell it to list and the program will come up, line by line."

Ivan mumbled a reply, but she was listening to the others. Pavel asked Leonid in Russian how long Ivan's business would take, and Leonid replied that he didn't know. There was a problem, though, Leonid added. Jessie kept her eyes down, trying not to let even a flicker of her eyelid show that she understood.

"What is it?" Pavel asked in Russian.

"She is wearing a microphone. Someone is listening to us."

Chapter 17

Someone is listening,'' Leonid repeated.

An icy trickle of fear slid down Jessie's spine.

She kept her face still and began easing her foot toward the floor, forcing herself to move slowly, though her every nerve was screaming for action. There was a big, heavy ledger book on the corner of the desk. She leaned on it, wrapping her fingers securely around the spine.

Half a block away in the van, Sam swore viciously.

"What'd he say?" Kelley demanded.

"He knows she's wearing a wire." Sam grabbed the radio handset as he shoved open the van door. "All stations," he said urgently. "All stations. They've made the wire. They've made her. Move in." He threw the handset on the seat and was sprinting toward the warehouse, drawing his gun, before Kelley had his door open.

"You're sure?" Pavel asked, still in Russian.

"I felt it. Shall I take it off?"

"Yes."

Jessie tested her grip on the ledger, staring unseeingly at the monitor. Ivan began listing the second file on the disk, intent on the lines flickering on the screen.

"Mrs. Ames?" Pavel asked from across the room.

"Mmm?"

Jessie didn't look up, but her muscles tensed and she raised her weight onto her toes, gripping the ledger.

"I believe you have something we—"

As Pavel spoke, Leonid began moving toward her. He was less than a yard away when she exploded into action.

She used the chair as a launching pad. It crashed against the wall behind her, and she swung the ledger at Leonid's face with all her strength as she dodged in the other direction.

The book struck his cheekbone with crushing force, and he yelled in fury. He grabbed it away from her, but she used the momentum to shove him aside and slip past. There were still two men between her and the door, though, and that was at least one man too many.

With one hand inside his jacket reaching for a gun, Pavel grabbed at her, catching her arm. She jabbed her elbow desperately at his face and connected with his chin. He swore sharply as he let go.

Sergie was clearly more practiced than Pavel. He caught her arm as she tried to evade him and swung her back with an efficient jerk, wrapping his other arm around her neck. He tightened his grip, pulling her head back until her feet nearly left the ground. She had to struggle to breathe, and speaking was out of the question.

"So." Pavel walked around to stand in front of her, his gun finally in his hand. He looked her up and down. "Where is it, Mrs. Ames?"

Jessie shook her head, unable to speak, and Pavel signaled with a jerk of his head. "Ivan."

Ivan stepped in front of her, smiling, the cruelty evident in his face. He could see her fear, and he was enjoying it. Jessie clenched her teeth. She waited until he was within range and kicked out hard at his groin. He dodged, and the blow glanced harmlessly off his thigh.

"Bitch." The cruel smile darkened to a grimace of rage, and he swung his hand up in a backhand blow to her face. Her cheekbone seemed to explode in a flash of blinding light.

For a moment she sagged, the room blurring and swinging around her, her weight dragging on the choking arm around her throat, before her vision began to clear and she found her feet under her again.

"Find it," Pavel ordered in Russian.

Ivan twisted his hands in the front of her blouse, just below Sergei's imprisoning arm, and jerked hard, ripping it open from collar to waist. Buttons flew off, striking the floor with little clicks, and the silk tore where it caught on her belt buckle.

"Here it is."

With more fumbling between her breasts than was necessary, Ivan took the tiny microphone off her bra. Jessie's flesh crawled when he touched her, and she shifted her feet, planning to kick him again.

Ivan saw the movement. "That would be very stupid, Mrs. Ames." He took a step back, lifting his hand, and Jessie ducked her head, flinching from the blow that didn't come. It was a gesture of surrender. She despised herself for it, but she lowered her foot to the ground again.

Ivan pulled the mike off its thin wire and dropped it to the floor, where he placed his heel on it with great care and ground it into shreds. He followed the wire to the transmit-

ter at the small of her back and pulled that off her waistband. It went on the floor and was smashed like the mike.

"So, Mrs. Ames, you have not been honest with us."
Pavel stepped closer, confident that she was cowed. "Who
was listening to that?" He indicated the debris on the floor.

Jessie shook her head and pulled at Sergei's choking arm.
He loosened it fractionally and she sucked in a big, rasping
gulp of air.

"Who was listening?" Pavel demanded again.

She shook her head and said nothing.

"Who was it?" he shouted, and struck her as Ivan had
done. He didn't hit as hard, but the blow to the already-
injured cheekbone made the room swim around her again.

Jessie bit her tongue deliberately, and the small pain
brought sharp awareness back again. Passing out wouldn't
do her any good. The room steadied and her head cleared,
but she kept her eyes half closed and let her weight sag
against Sergei's hold.

Sergei spoke for the first time. "There is no point in this,
Pavel. Whoever was listening, they know we have found the
microphone. We have to get away from this place."

Pavel's face showed his reluctance to abandon his sport,
and Jessie was relieved when he seemed to see the sense in
that. "Is the program real?" he asked Ivan.

Ivan nodded smugly. "I have looked at it," he said with
the slightly patronizing air of an expert talking to a novice.
"It is all here. It is real."

It's phony as a three-dollar bill, you fool. Jessie kept her
head down and her eyes slitted and felt a surge of satisfaction.

"Take it, then," Pavel told him, "and we will go."

"What do we do with her?" It was Leonid who asked.

"Take her."

"Back to—"

"Of course not, you fool. We'll drop her body in the ocean. Later."

Jessie fought desperately against a wave of nausea and vertigo. *Don't think about it,* she ordered herself. *They won't kill you here. Don't think about it. Think about getting away.*

Sam knew the odds had been against her from the start, because she was dealing with people who had nothing to gain by keeping her alive. Keeping her alive was his job, and he'd screwed it up royally. Now the odds against her were desperate.

He slid around a corner and into the alley behind the warehouse, where a bum sat slumped on the pavement, cuddling a bottle of muscatel. Sam vanished into a patch of shadow, and the man took a long pull at his bottle.

"They don't have any lookouts outside," the bum said softly. "Stupid."

"Inside?" Sam breathed, and the man shook his head, resettling his moth-eaten cowboy hat.

"Four of them, and her. Nobody else in or out. That window up there—" he jerked his head toward a point to Sam's right "—isn't locked."

"Thanks."

Sam slid away, and the bum heaved himself laboriously to his feet. He took another drink of the watered-down soda in his bottle, and lurched on down the alley, unobtrusively loosening his gun in its holster.

The window was a couple of feet above Sam's head and opened by swinging outward at the bottom. He stretched upward and eased it open, freezing when the rusty metal gave a piercing squeak. He waited through several heartbeats of silence, then set the strut that locked it open, reached up to grasp the edge of the window frame and pulled himself up to look inside.

There was a twelve-foot stack of big crates directly in front of him that provided excellent cover as he eased inside and lowered himself the length of his arms. He hung there for a moment, then dropped to the floor and crouched, waiting to see if anyone had heard him. There were no shouts of discovery, no pounding feet, no gunshots.

Gun in hand, he slid into the shadows, moving silently from one stack of crates to the next. Behind him he heard someone else slip through the window, but then the sound was lost in the vast, echoing silence of the warehouse.

He couldn't allow himself to think about what was happening in the office at the other end of the building. He just had to get there in time, had to get there before something happened that he wouldn't be able to live with.

He was nearly at the office when the door flew open, rebounding off the wall with a crash. Sam froze and sent up a silent prayer. He crept along to the corner of the nearest stack of crates, then crouched and peered around them.

There were two men in the brightly lit office, Leonid and an older man Sam didn't recognize. They both had guns. Two others were outside, a stocky, youngish man carrying a briefcase and an older man who was pushing Jessie along in front of him. Neither of them appeared to have a gun, but Sam knew better than to take that for granted.

The older man turned toward Sam, and he felt his throat constrict when he saw Jessie, as a red haze of rage washed over his vision. Her captor had one of her arms twisted behind her back, while his other was hooked tightly around her neck. Her blouse was torn open from neck to waist, exposing her lacy bra and the smooth, lightly tanned skin he'd loved last night.

They had done that to her—and they had hurt her. He could see the blotch across her cheekbone, red and bruised. She looked close to fainting. She was white-faced and slumped against the man who held her. And yet, Sam thought as he looked again, perhaps she wasn't so weak, after all. Her feet were still moving, and when none of her captors could see her face, her eyes opened and she looked sharply around her, searching for an escape route.

He fought the choking rage and forced himself to think clearly. Her life depended on it. Okay, sweetheart, he thought, you just hang on, and I'll get you out of this. Just hang on.

Jessie dragged against Sergi as he urged her along, pretending to be dizzy, hoping he'd lower his guard. She stared desperately around her, searching for an escape route of some kind, awaiting an opportunity to break free and run.

When she looked into the dark space between two stacks of crates and saw someone looking back, she nearly cried out in surprise. Sam. Sam was there.

She stumbled and bit back a cry of pain as Sergei used her twisted arm to haul her to her feet.

"How hard did you hit her?" he asked Ivan crossly. "She can't even walk."

"I didn't hit her that hard," Ivan retorted defensively. "She's just weak, that's all."

Jessie stared wide-eyed at Sam. He was there, slipping along behind the crates while she was pushed past them on the other side.

She wanted to crane her neck to look for him in the next gap, and it took all her control to keep from giving his presence away. He was there to help her. He would free her. He *would*. All she had to do was wait for his signal.

She saw him in the next gap, along with another man. Sam gave her a thumbs-up, and the second man melted into the darkness as she passed. Were there others there, as well? She looked down the central aisle and saw no one, but something flickered on the edge of her peripheral vision.

Sergie and the others would notice if she turned her head, so she slid her gaze sideways, peering up through the screen of her lashes.

Movement flickered again, atop the crates. She scanned the other side and saw another shadow skulking along. How many of them were there? Enough to defeat Sergei and Pavel and the others? She glanced around, looking for Sam.

The only light in the warehouse came from the office, and they were taking her away from there, into the shadowy depths. It was already perceptibly darker, and Sam moved closer to the center aisle. She could see him for a few seconds, long enough for him to mime dropping to the floor.

She hoped she understood what he wanted. When he gave the signal, she would fall. Heaven help her if that wasn't what he meant! Jessie swallowed hard, painfully aware that she wasn't living up to the adventure-heroine standard of behavior. She wasn't plucky and intrepid. She was shaking like a leaf, and she was scared to death.

They walked on, Sergie pushing to speed her up, she hanging back, moving as slowly as she could. "Move!" he snarled in her ear in Russian. Then he repeated it in English. "Move!"

"I'm trying." She didn't have to feign the catch in her voice, or the rasp of suppressed tears. She made no effort to strengthen her voice when she added, "I can't—can't breathe."

"If you'd stop choking her," Pavel said in Russian, "she would be able to walk."

"If I let her go, she will run."

"Hardly." Pavel's laugh was scornful. "She's too weak to run. Let her breathe, let her walk, and we can get out of this place."

Sergei tightened his arm around her throat, pulling her head up and back. "You cannot get away," he muttered in her ear. "They will shoot you if you try. Do you understand?"

Jessie made a sound he seemed to take for assent, and bit by bit he relaxed the strangling arm around her throat. When he shifted his grip to her arms, she stayed limp in his grasp, gulping air while she gathered her strength and waited for Sam's cue.

The signal came from the far end of the warehouse. A gunshot rang out, echoing deafeningly in the large, hollow space.

The little group moving along the center aisle froze for an instant, staring toward the far corner. A second shot followed before the disorienting echoes of the first had died away from the opposite end of the warehouse. The echoes boomed around them, and the four men spun to see where this new threat came from.

Sergei's grip on her, already relaxed since he'd removed the choking arm around her neck, loosened even more as he fumbled for his gun. A third shot cracked from yet another corner of the warehouse, and from the darkness behind her Jessie heard Sam shout, *"Now!"*

She flung herself at the nearest gap between the crates, ripping out of Sergei's grasp. He yelled as she half crawled, half scrambled away, while a fusillade of shots exploded over her head and men's shouts filled the air.

Jessie winced as a bullet whined beside her, and she screamed in desperation when strong hands grabbed her. She'd gotten away from Sergei, and she wasn't going to let him drag her back. She screamed again and fought desperately to get away.

The hands around her tightened. Her struggles had no effect. "Relax," said a familiar voice in her ear. "Sweetheart, it's me. It's me!"

As she went limp with surprise and relief, Sam yanked her bodily into the darkness. She bumped along on her knees past several crates and into the deepest darkness behind them.

Sam pushed her behind him, shielding her with his body while he crouched at the corner of the crates, his gun trained on the fracas going on out in the light. His face was lit in strong angles, and he looked nothing like the man she loved. He looked, with the gun in his hand, every bit as dangerous as Pavel and the others.

The gunshots seemed to go on for hours, the booming, echoing sound battering at Jessie like fists until she cringed behind Sam, gripping his shirt, her face pressed against his back. And then the gunshots stopped.

"Don't move!" shouted someone on the other side of the warehouse. Jessie heard running footsteps on the floor and then on the crates above her. She looked up just in time to see a man leap from one stack to the next directly over her head. Then his steps thudded away.

"I said, don't move!" A single shot cracked and thudded into the wood above Sam's head, sending a shower of splinters onto them.

"That's the way," said the man overhead. "Lie down, face down on the floor." He repeated the instructions in Russian, his voice sharp. "Now, slide the gun over there." Jessie heard the scrape of metal on concrete.

"Kelley, check 'em out."

Jessie heard murmurs and the sounds of movement. She started to move around Sam.

"Stay back!" He put an arm out and pushed her back into her corner. "Stay there."

"But aren't they finished?"

"Not quite." Sam's gun was leveled on the scene out in the aisle.

"What about him?" one man asked another. She couldn't see either of them.

"Sam, I'm scared." She stood and craned to look around the crates. "I just need to see..."

"I'll take a look," John Kelley said as she leaned out far enough to see him. He was bending over a man lying face-down on the floor, and she watched in growing horror as he turned the man's limp body over. Kelley straightened, shaking his head. "He's dead."

The man lying on the floor was Leonid.

Jessie gasped, and Sam turned quickly. "Damn it, Jessie!" He pushed her behind the crates again.

"But that's Leonid." Her eyes were huge, her face white. "He's..."

"I know." Sam shoved his gun into the holster and pulled her into his arms. "I know. But are you okay?" He leaned back so that he could see her face. "What did they do to you?" He touched the livid bruise on her cheekbone, his face twisting in anguished rage. "They hurt you."

He looked down at her open blouse, at her bra, and her skin, gleaming pale in the half-light. Jessie followed his gaze and tried with shaking hands to pull the ripped edges together. Sam unbuttoned his own shirt quickly and shrugged it off.

"Here." He put it around her shoulders, helped her thread her arms through the sleeves and buttoned it to her throat. It was far too big, but it covered her.

"Thank you." Jessie bent her head, making a production of turning the sleeves back from her hands. Sam stopped her with gentle hands on her shoulders.

"Jessie?"

She looked up after a moment.

"Did they hurt you? Did they do anything to you, besides this?" He touched her face. "And this?" He indicated her blouse.

"No. But they were—" She swallowed. "They talked in Russian. They didn't know I understood. They were going to—to kill me."

"You knew, when they were marching you out of here, that they meant to— Oh, God, sweetheart!" Still on his knees, he reached out, and she went into his arms to be enfolded in a hard embrace. "God, Jessamyn," he murmured against her hair. "I'm sorry I got you into this. I'm so sorry. I never meant for anything to happen. I never meant for *this* to happen."

Jessie clung tightly to him, and when he lifted his face from her hair she reached up for his kiss. Their lips met in an explosion of need, nothing tentative or shy, only emotions rubbed raw, with nothing left for masks or pretense.

It went on forever, and when it ended Jessie was gasping for breath and Sam's breathing was as ragged as hers. He pressed her face into his shoulder, stroking her hair with a hand that trembled. The arm he wrapped around her was rigid with tension.

"God!" His chest heaved beneath her cheek. "God, Jessie, I didn't—"

"Sam!" John Kelley shouted from the center of the warehouse. "You and Jessie okay?"

"Yeah! Yeah!" he called back.

"Good. The local militia's on the way. You want to stick around?"

"No." Sam stood up, pulling Jessie up with him, safe within the curve of his arm. He kept her back where she couldn't see Leonid's body on the floor and waited for John to come to them. "We'll go to the office. She can give her statement there."

"Okay." John looked Jessie up and down, noting both her bruised cheek and Sam's enormous shirt. "You all right, Jessie?"

"Yes." She nodded, and Sam pulled her a little closer. "I am now."

"Yeah." John looked at them both, and his mouth curved in the beginning of a grin. "I guess you are."

Chapter 18

Giving a statement seemed to take forever.

For the benefit of tape recorders and a stenographer, Jessie recounted everything that had happened since she'd walked out of Mr. Howell's office in exhaustive detail.

When she described Ivan taking the body microphone off her, her voice began to shake. Sam, who was sitting on a hard chair beside her, reached out and took her hand in both of his. She glanced at him, then turned back and focused on the stenographer, continuing with her story while she gripped Sam's hand tightly.

The mantel clock was chiming 4:00 a.m. when Sam let them into his house. Cat came to greet them, meowing and winding himself around Jessie's ankles. She picked him up and held his furry warmth to her face, listening to the purr rumbling in his chest.

"Do you want a cup of coffee?" Sam stood rather uncertainly in front of an open cupboard. "Or would you rather have something stronger?"

Jessie shook her head, rubbing Cat's chin. "Coffee's fine."

While it was dripping, Sam made sandwiches, and he brought them to the table along with two mugs of coffee. "Here." He set a plate in front of her. "You need to eat something."

Cat was more interested in the sandwich than Jessie was, and she set him gently on the floor before he could snatch a bite. "I'm really not hungry, Sam."

"It's just roast beef. You can choke down a little."

As if by way of encouragement, Sam took a big bite of his sandwich, then fed a bit of beef to Cat, whose reaction was just short of ecstatic. Jessie added milk to her coffee and sipped that, wondering if it would relax the knots her stomach was tied in. The thought of the sandwich was almost too much.

"Go on, at least eat a little of it." Sam was halfway through his, munching with every indication of enjoyment. "I know you didn't get dinner."

"I couldn't have eaten it anyway." She picked up the sandwich and tried a bite. It might as well have been cardboard, but she chewed determinedly for a while and finally swallowed. She set the sandwich back on her plate.

"Come on, Jessie, you need more than that."

She shook her head. "I can't—not right now. Coffee is fine."

"Not if you pass out from hunger and—"

The telephone's ring cut him off. He looked at Jessie's plate and shook his head, then went to get the phone. "Yeah." He listened for several seconds. "Yeah? Great! How much more?"

Jessie didn't listen to the rest of the conversation. That would have required a mental effort that was beyond her right now. The evening's events had numbed her emotions and blunted her thinking, and she didn't have the energy to do anything about it.

Coffee seemed to help. It warmed her cold hands and stopped the shivering that seemed to be coming from somewhere deep inside her. She'd finished it by the time Sam hung up and turned to her.

He came back to the table and sat down, and she could see that he was hiding a smile.

"We hit the jackpot. Pavel isn't talking, or that stone-faced Sergei, but your little Ivan is gushing like a broken tap."

"He's talking?"

"Nonstop. He's apparently planning to ask for asylum, and he can't spill the beans fast enough. He told them where Pavel's been staying, in an apartment in Marina del Rey. They searched it, and they found plenty to be interested in. He's been careless, keeping so much stuff in one place. Money, papers, tapes, addresses and phone numbers and a lot of stuff in code. When the cryptographers get done with that, we may have a regular gold mine."

"So you got what you wanted?"

"The bureau got what it wanted. More than we could have anticipated."

"And you Sam? Did *you* get what you wanted?"

Sam shook his head, and grimness flickered across his face. "I didn't want you to have to go through anything like you did tonight. I thought I had all the bases covered, but I screwed that up in a big way. I don't—" He searched for words. "I don't know what to say to you, Jessie."

Jessie shrugged. "It's over now. You don't need to say anything."

"It shouldn't have happened."

"But it's over now—isn't it?"

Sam caught the insecurity in her question and nodded firmly. "It's over."

"Can Kerry come home? Will she be safe?"

"She can come home. She'll be safe."

Jessie nodded slowly and toyed with her coffee cup for a moment. "So," she said at last. "It's finally over. It's kind of hard to believe," she said quietly, her smile rueful.

"You can believe it. You've done the country a great service, Jessie."

She shrugged uncomfortably. "It's nice to know that all this—" she spread her hands, thinking of everything that had happened "—served some purpose." She finished her coffee and got up to take the cup to the sink and rinse it. She dried her hands and turned around, but she didn't meet Sam's eyes. "I guess I'll go pack."

"What?"

"Pack," she repeated patiently.

"Pack? What for?"

"To go home, what else?"

"At this time of night?"

She looked at the window, where dawn was paling the night sky to pearl. "It's not night anymore. The night's over, the operation's over. I can go home now, and sleep in my own bed."

Sam's eyes flickered, and Jessie dropped her gaze to the floor. Poor choice of words. Even if she'd never been near Sam's bed, he had wanted her there, and they both knew it. What he didn't know was how much she wanted to be there, if only he could give her the love she needed.

She darted a glance at Sam and found him watching her. His eyes were the clear, hot blue of a flame, and they were burning into her. She looked away quickly, gripping the edge of the counter until her fingertips whitened, while her heartbeat echoed in her ears. Then, with a jerk, she pushed herself away from the cabinets and hurried out of the kitchen.

Sam sat where he was, listening and thinking. He could hear her moving around the guest room and could imagine what she was doing—taking out her suitcase, opening drawers, taking clothes from the closet. She'd been there only a few days, so why was the thought of her leaving such a bleak one?

He picked up the last bite of his sandwich, then tossed it back on the plate. Why should he care? After all, once she was gone he could get back to his own life, uncluttered and uncomplicated. The way he liked it.

And empty. His mind formed the thought without his conscious cooperation. He was finding that that emptiness didn't appeal to him as it once had. He'd deliberately kept other people out of his life for so long, not only women, but family, friends. He didn't want the family complications, didn't want the demands of a woman's love, didn't want friends who would insinuate themselves into his life and make him need them.

Needing people was the surest way of getting hurt. Needing people, relying on them, was just asking for trouble. You couldn't count on anyone but yourself, and only a fool would leave himself open to that kind of hurt and disappointment. A fool like—

Sam caught his thoughts just in time. He knew better than to let himself become dependent, to let himself need another person. He knew better, and yet—

He walked slowly out of the kitchen and along the hall to the door to the guest room. The door was half-open, and he stood outside, in the shadows, watching her pack.

She worked with rapid, neat movements, taking a garment from the drawer, folding it and placing it in the suitcase. He watched for several minutes as she folded sweaters and slacks and tucked shoes down alongside them.

"Jessie?"

She glanced at him, then turned back to her packing. "Mmm?"

"Don't go."

Her hands faltered for a moment, and a satiny nightgown slithered out of her grasp. She picked it up and began folding it again, a bit more slowly, a bit more carefully. She spoke carefully, without emotion.

"There's no reason to stay."

There was a taut silence behind her. As the seconds ticked past she placed the gown in the suitcase, then picked up a blouse. Behind her Sam shifted his feet, and she heard the small scrape of his shoes on the floor.

"There's every reason!" The words burst harshly out of him. "I don't—" He dropped his voice to a more moderate level. "I don't want you to go."

Jessie hesitated, then packed the blouse with care. She turned around slowly, her eyes shuttered, her voice cold. "I can't imagine why you would want me to stay when you know how I feel about you. You don't want love, Sam. And love is really all I have to offer you. I'm going home."

She turned back, reaching for another blouse, but he caught her arm and spun her around, throwing her off balance. She grabbed for his shoulders to steady herself, but he wrapped his arms around her and pulled her against him, kissing her with a desperate passion.

An answering passion bubbled up in Jessie, a feeling she couldn't control. She locked her arms around his neck, pressed her body into his and kissed him with hunger, with all her love, and with despair, knowing that her love would not be returned.

An eternity passed before she could summon up the strength to twist her face away and push out of his arms. He reached for her again, and she stepped back, shaking her head. Her hair swirled around her face.

"Jessie?"

"No!" She moved a couple of steps away and folded her arms tightly over her chest. "Please, Sam, don't! You told me why you can't love me. Why do you want me to stay?"

"I just—I do, that's all."

"That's not enough. I need more than that, Sam."

His lips tightened, and he shifted his feet, lifting one hand slightly from his side, indicating the door. "Can you leave that for a while? Can we go and sit down? To talk?"

Jessie hesitated for a moment, then nodded. "All right."

She brushed past him and walked quickly to the living room. She bypassed the sofa and sat in a chair with her back to the growing light of day outside, her face in shadow. Sam followed her, more slowly, and took the sofa for himself, a wry twist to his mouth. He leaned forward, his elbows on his knees, his hands dangling between them.

He rubbed his hands together, then planted them on his knees and straightened his arms, sitting up and looking across at her. "I don't know what to say. What do you want me to say?"

"I'm not going to put words in your mouth, Sam. I just want to know why you'd want me to stay. What you feel, right now."

He stared at her for a long moment. "Confused."

"About what?"

He shook his head. "You. Me. What I feel. Why I'm feeling what I feel."

"What are you feeling?"

"I don't want you to go." He spoke quickly, as if he might not get the words out otherwise. "I want you to stay here, with me."

"And you want to make love to me."

The quick flare of heat in his eyes was just as quickly controlled, but when he spoke his voice was husky. "Yes." He ran a hand roughly through his hair. "Yes. But I know what you want, and I don't know if I can give it to you."

"Do you want to?" she asked softly.

Sam looked at her, then lowered his head to study his hands. "Do I want to? I'm not sure. I don't want...to become like my father."

"I see," Jessie said after a long moment of silence.

She got up and walked into the kitchen, where the newly risen sun was streaming through the windows. She started the coffee maker again, and as it began gurgling she went to the window and stood gazing out.

Sam didn't want love. He'd told her why, and she even thought she understood.

His experience had been so different from hers. Deserted by one parent who'd never shown any interest in him, raised by paid nannies and another parent who was a distant workaholic. He'd had only his respect for his father to base his life on, until he'd grown old enough to understand love between men and women and to understand male pride.

And until he'd learned that despite his mother's repeated betrayals his father gave her money, willingly and generously. That had been the last straw, something Sam could in no way understand, something so offensive to him that it had driven him to cut all his ties with his father and move to the opposite side of the country.

And now she knew why he didn't want love. He saw it as a force that weakened and destroyed. He'd never been shown the side of love that ennobled and strengthened.

Understanding brought her no relief. If anything, it made her problem greater. There was no point in arguing the merits of love with Sam. The things he'd seen at a young and impressionable age were bound to be stronger than any argument she could make. She couldn't use words, or any other form of persuasion, to change his viewpoint. The change had to come from within him.

Perhaps he had already changed a little bit. If he hadn't he would be putting her suitcase on the curb and calling a cab, not asking her to stay.

But though he wanted her to stay, he still didn't like the things he was feeling. He wasn't ready to accept those feelings, or to act on them. He wasn't ready to surrender himself to love. And until he was, there was only one thing she could do.

Jessie pushed herself away from the window and walked out of the kitchen. She didn't look into the living room as she passed the doorway, and she was busy packing again before Sam caught up with her.

Chapter 19

What are you doing?"

"It's obvious, isn't it?" She tossed her cosmetic bag on top of her clothes and closed the suitcase. "I'm leaving."

"But I want you to stay. I told you—"

"You told me a great deal, and I'm glad you did, Sam. It helps me understand. But I also understand that you aren't ready for love yet, and that's the kind of relationship I need. I have to go."

She picked up her suitcase and purse and brushed past him, walking steadily toward the door. The door out of his life, Sam thought in sudden panic.

"No!" He caught her in the living room and whirled her around. Her suitcase thudded to the floor and her purse slid off her shoulder as he dragged her roughly into his arms.

"No." He gazed down at her, his face tormented. "No, I can't let you go, Jessie! I can't be without you."

It was the desperation in his tone, as much as his words, that startled her into immobility. That and what she saw in his eyes. She felt suddenly warm, as if a brilliant light had come to life inside her. "Sam—"

Whatever she'd been about to say was smothered by his mouth, coming down on hers in a kiss as desperate as his words. He tightened his arms around her until she could barely breathe. His kiss went on and on, his mouth slanting over hers, probing, tasting, seeking hungrily. Jessie let herself be molded to the hard lines of his body, her back arched like a bow as he pressed her closer and closer, her arms tight around his neck, pulling his lips down to hers.

He released her slowly, reluctantly, and scattered kisses along her cheek and forehead before tucking her head against his chest and resting his face on her hair. His first three shirt buttons were open, and Jessie pressed her lips to the heated skin just below his throat. He gave a low groan of mingled pleasure and strained self-control that turned into something close to a growl when she brushed the tip of her tongue over his skin.

"Oh, God, Jessie, what you do to me..." He tipped her face up to kiss her, then pulled his lips away. His hands, though, moved restlessly over her back, stroking from her shoulders to the first soft curves below her waist. Jessie wriggled a bit, seeking more closeness, and Sam tightened his arm around her waist, stilling her body by pressing it to his.

"Jessie, we have to talk." His voice was a raspy groan.

She touched his face with soft fingers, looking up at him with heavy-lidded eyes. Waiting for him to continue, she drew her fingertips across his mouth. His lips parted, and when she strained upward, reaching for another kiss, he bent his head in spite of his resolve and caught himself in the instant before their mouths touched again.

"We have to talk about you and me," he said in a strained whisper.

"Now?" She reached up to touch his face again, but he caught her fingers. He pressed a kiss to her palm, gripped her hand in his and lowered it to his side.

"Now." He pulled her over to the couch, pushed her down with a plop and sat beside her, very close, an arm around her shoulders, her hand in his. He hesitated, seeking the right words. "I don't want to be unfair to you, Jessie."

She frowned up at him. "How could you be unfair?"

His fingers flexed convulsively on her shoulder. "I told you before that I don't know if I can give you what you want. What you deserve. I know I don't want you to go. Not out of my house, not out of my life. But I don't know any more than that. I know you want love. And you deserve that, Jessie. You deserve a man who can give you all the things you need and want. I—" He drew a shaky breath. "I don't know about love, Jessie. I don't know how to say the words you want to hear. I don't know if I truthfully can say them. I only know I don't want you to go."

"Sam . . ." She stroked his cheek lightly, touched his lips and slid her hand down to rest against his throat. Happiness welled up inside her like a golden, glowing bubble. "Don't you know you already said it?"

"Said what?"

"You said you couldn't let me go. You said you couldn't be without me."

"Yeah." he nodded. "Well, it's true."

She smiled. "Don't you understand what you said?"

"I said I don't want you to go," he repeated, as if that were too obvious to consider. "I understand that."

"You said you love me."

He blinked.

"You said you couldn't be without me," she repeated, smiling gently. "What is that, if it isn't love?"

Sam shook his head. "I don't know. My father says he loves my mother, and he feels nothing but pain. Is that love?"

"Love is caring about someone. Caring for them. Protecting them, the way you protected me in that warehouse. Being there for them and understanding and supporting them, the way you supported me at Edwards, when I couldn't deal with my memories. Love is wanting to please someone, to comfort and cheer and reassure them."

She smiled and ducked her head, then looked up at him again, her cheeks pink, her eyes warm and inviting. "And love is wanting someone with passion—the way you want me."

"Jessie—"

"I love you, Sam. And I believe, whether you know it or not, and whether you are attaching the right words to it or not, that you love me."

"I only know I can't live without you."

She smiled. "That'll do for now."

He began gathering her into his arms, sliding her onto his lap, and unbuttoning his shirt, which she still wore in place of her ruined blouse. Jessie felt the heat start, sliding over her skin, melting into her body. Her head fell back as Sam slid his lips down her throat to the soft valley between her breasts, and she shivered when he nuzzled there, his day's growth of beard rasping gently on her skin. When he lifted his lips, he shifted his hold slightly and stood with her in his arms.

"Sam?" Jessie hooked one arm around his neck and stroked his hair.

"Mmm?" he answered against her.

"If you don't want me to go...I won't go."

Sam's smile was wicked. "I didn't intend to let you."

Jessie's eyes widened. "I see." She looked down at the floor so far below her, and traced her fingertips through the hair on his chest. "Am I a prisoner, then?"

"Depends. Do you want to be?"

"Depends." She looked up at him through her lashes, teasing. "Are you going to have your way with me?"

Sam started to laugh, but the humor faded when he looked into her eyes. "I think," he said, his voice roughened with desire, "that I'm going to love you, Jessamyn. And I think it'll be forever."

That was all Jessie could have wanted.

*   *   *   *   *

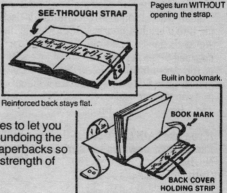

Silhouette Special Edition®

COMING IN APRIL

NAVY BLUES
Debbie Macomber

Between the devil and the deep blue sea...

At Christmastime, Lieutenant Commander Steve Kyle finds his heart anchored by the past, so he vows to give his ex-wife wide berth. But Carol Kyle is quaffing milk and knitting tiny pastel blankets with a vengeance. She's determined to have a baby, and only one man will do as father-to-be—the only man she's ever loved...her own bullheaded ex-husband! Can the wall of bitterness protecting Steve's battered heart possibly withstand the hurricane force of his Navy wife's will?

You met Steve and Carol in NAVY WIFE (Special Edition #494)—you'll cheer for them in NAVY BLUES (Special Edition #518). (And as a bonus for NAVY WIFE fans, newlyweds Rush and Lindy Callaghan reveal a surprise of their own....)

Each book stands alone—together they're Debbie Macomber's most delightful duo to date! Don't miss

NAVY BLUES
Available in April,
only in *Silhouette Special Edition*.
Having the ''blues'' was never
so much fun!

SE518-1

1989
IS THE YEAR
OF THE MAN!

What makes a romance? A special man, of course, and Silhouette Desire celebrates that fact with *twelve* of them! From Mr. January to Mr. December, every month has a tribute to the Silhouette Desire hero—our **MAN OF THE MONTH!**

Sexy, macho, charming, irritating . . . irresistible! Nothing can stop these men from sweeping you away. Created by some of your favorite authors, each man is custom-made for pleasure—*reading* pleasure—so don't miss a single one.

Mr. January is Blake Donavan in RELUCTANT FATHER by Diana Palmer
Mr. February is Hank Branson in THE GENTLEMAN INSISTS by Joan Hohl
Mr. March is Carson Tanner in NIGHT OF THE HUNTER by Jennifer Greene
Mr. April is Slater McCall in A DANGEROUS KIND OF MAN by Naomi Horton
Mr. May is Luke Harmon in VENGEANCE IS MINE by Lucy Gordon
Mr. June is Quinn McNamara in IRRESISTIBLE by Annette Broadrick

And that's only the half of it—
so get out there and find your man!

Silhouette Desire's

MAN OF THE MONTH . . .

MOM-1